SHIP
BREAKER

 LITTLE, BROWN AND COMPANY
New York · Boston

SHIP BREAKER

BY PAOLO BACIGALUPI

Copyright © 2010 by Paolo Bacigalupi

All rights reserved. Except as permitted under the U.S. Copyright Act of 1976,
no part of this publication may be reproduced, distributed, or transmitted
in any form or by any means, or stored in a database or retrieval system,
without the prior written permission of the publisher.

Little, Brown and Company

Hachette Book Group
237 Park Avenue, New York, NY 10017
Visit our website at www.lb-teens.com

Little, Brown and Company is a division of Hachette Book Group, Inc.
The Little, Brown name and logo are trademarks of Hachette Book Group, Inc.

First Edition: May 2010

The characters and events portrayed in this book are fictitious. Any similarity to real
persons, living or dead, is coincidental and not intended by the author.

Library of Congress Cataloging-in-Publication Data
Bacigalupi, Paolo.
Ship breaker : a novel / by Paolo Bacigalupi. —1st ed.   p. cm.
Summary: In a futuristic world, teenaged Nailer scavenges copper wiring from grounded
oil tankers for a living, but when he finds a beached clipper ship with a girl in the wreckage,
he has to decide if he should strip the ship for its wealth or rescue the girl.
ISBN 978-0-316-05621-2
[1. Conduct of life—Fiction. 2. Recycling (Waste)—Fiction. 3. Science fiction.] I. Title.
PZ7.B132185Sh 2010   [Fic]—dc22   2009034424

10 9 8 7 6 5 4 3

RRD-C
Design by David Caplan
Printed in the United States of America

For Arjun

1

NAILER CLAMBERED THROUGH a service duct, tugging at copper wire and yanking it free. Ancient asbestos fibers and mouse grit puffed up around him as the wire tore loose. He scrambled deeper into the duct, jerking more wire from its aluminum staples. The staples pinged about the cramped metal passage like coins offered to the Scavenge God, and Nailer felt after them eagerly, hunting for their dull gleam and collecting them in a leather bag he kept at his waist. He yanked again at the wiring. A meter's worth of precious copper tore loose in his hands and dust clouds enveloped him.

The LED glowpaint smeared on Nailer's forehead gave a dim green phosphorescent view of the service ducts that made up his world. Grime and salt sweat stung his eyes and trickled around the edges of his filter mask. With one scarred hand, he swiped at the salty rivulets, careful to avoid rubbing off the LED paint. The paint itched and drove him crazy, but he didn't relish finding his way back out of the mazelike ducts in blind blackness, so he let his forehead itch and again surveyed his position.

Rusty pipes ran ahead of him, disappearing into darkness. Some iron, some steel—heavy crew would be the ones to deal with that. Nailer only cared about the light stuff—the copper wiring, the aluminum, the nickel, the steel clips that could be sacked and dragged out through the ducts to his light crew waiting outside.

Nailer turned to continue down the service passage, but as he did he banged his head on the duct ceiling. The noise from his collision echoed loud, as if he were sitting inside a Christian church bell. Dust cascaded into his hair. Despite the filter mask, he started coughing as powder leaked in around the poorly sealed edges. He sneezed, then sneezed again, eyes watering. He pulled the mask away and wiped his face, then pressed it back over his mouth and nose, willing the stickum to seal but not holding out much hope.

The mask was a hand-me-down, given to him by his father. It itched and never sealed quite right because it was the wrong size, but it was all Nailer had. On its side, faded words said: DISCARD AFTER 40 HOURS USE. But Nailer didn't have another, and no one else did either. He was lucky to have a mask at all, even if the microfibers were beginning to shred from repeated scrubbings in the ocean.

Sloth, his crewgirl, made fun of him whenever he washed the mask, asking why he even bothered. It just made the hellish duct work hotter and more uncomfortable. There was no point, she said. Sometimes he thought she was right. But Pima's mother told him and Pima to use the masks no matter what, and for sure there was a lot of black grime in the filters when he immersed them in the ocean. That was the black that wasn't in his lungs, Pima's mother said, so he kept on with the mask, even though he felt like he was smothering every time he sucked humid tropic air through the clogged breath-wet fibers.

A voice echoed down into the duct. "You got the wire?"

Sloth. Calling in from where she waited outside.

"Almost done!" Nailer scrambled a little farther into the duct, ripping more staples, hurriedly yanking extra copper loose. The duct's passage went on, but he had enough. He slashed the wire free with the serrated back of his work knife.

"We're good!" he shouted.

Sloth's acknowledging shout echoed back. "Clear!"

The wire whipped away from him, slithering through the crawlspaces, raising dust clouds as it moved. Far down the maze of ducts, Sloth was cranking away at a winding drum, sweat bright on her skin, blond hair pasted slick to her face as she sucked the wire out like a rice noodle from a bowl of Chen's soup ration.

Nailer took his knife and hacked Bapi's light crew code above the place where he had clipped the wire. The symbol matched the swirling tattoos on Nailer's cheeks, the labor marks that gave him a right to work the wrecks under Bapi's supervision. Nailer took out a bit of powdered paint and spit on it, mixing it in his palm, before smearing it over the mark. Now, even from a distance, his scratches gave off an iridescent glow. He used his finger and the remaining paint to write a string of memorized numerals below the symbol: LC57-1844. Bapi's permit code. No one else was competing for this stretch right now, but it was good to mark the territory.

Nailer gathered the rest of the aluminum staples and scuttled back through the ducting on hands and knees, skirting weak points where the metal wasn't well supported, listening to his own echoes and thumps and ringing taps against the steel as he hustled out, all his senses testing for signs that the ducts might break.

His little phosphor LED showed the dust snake slither where the copper cables had gone before him. He crawled over desiccated rat bodies and their nests. Even here, in the belly of an old oil tanker, there were rats, but these ones had died a long time ago. He crawled over more bones, small ones that came from cats and bits of birds. Feathers and fluff floated in the air. This close to the outside world, the access ducts were a graveyard for all sorts of lost creatures.

Ahead, sunlight showed, a glaring brightness. Nailer squinted as he clawed toward the light, thinking that this was what rebirth must be like for the Life Cult, this climbing toward blazing clean sunshine, and then he spilled out of the duct and onto hot steel decking.

He tore off his mask, gasping.

Bright tropic sunlight and ocean salt breezes bathed him. All around, sledgehammers rang against iron as swarms of men and women clambered over the ancient oil tanker, tearing it apart. Heavy crews peeled away iron panels with acetylene torches and sent them wafting off the sides like palm leaves, crashing to the beach sands below, where more crews dragged the scavenge above high tide. Light crews like Nailer's tore at the ship's small fittings, stripping copper, brass, nickel, aluminum, and stainless steel. Others hunted for hidden petrol and ship oil pockets, bucketing out the valuable fluid. An ant's nest of activity, all dedicated to rendering this extinct ship's bones into something usable for a new world.

"Took you long enough," Sloth said.

She hammered at their spool's securing clips, releasing it from the winding spindle. Her pale skin gleamed in the sunlight, her own swirling work tattoos almost black against the flush of her cheeks. Sweat ran down her neck. Her blond hair was chopped short, much like his own, to keep it from catching in the thousands of crevices and whirling bits of machinery that studded their work place.

"We're in deep," Nailer said. "Plenty of service wiring, but it takes a long time to get to it."

"You always got an excuse."

"Quit complaining. We'll make quota."

"We better," Sloth said. "Bapi's saying there's another light crew buying scavenge rights."

Nailer made a face. "Big surprise."

"Yeah. This was too good to last for long. Gimme a hand."

Nailer got on the other side of the spool. They lifted it from its spindle, grunting. Together, they tipped the spool sidewise and let it fall to the rusted deck with a clang. Shoulder to shoulder, they leaned into the weight, legs flexing, teeth gritted.

The spool slowly began to roll. Nailer's bare feet burned against the sun-blasted decking. The cant of the ship made for hard pushing, but under their combined effort, the spool slowly rumbled forward, crunching over blistered preservative paint and loosened metal deck plates.

From the height of the tanker's deck, Bright Sands Beach stretched into the distance, a tarred expanse of sand and puddled seawater, littered with the savaged bodies of other oil tankers and freighters. Some were completely whole, as if crazy sea captains had simply decided to steer the kilometer-long ships onto the sand and then walked away. Others were flayed and stripped, showing rusty iron girder bones. Hulls lay like chunks of cleavered fish: a conning tower here, a crew quarters there, the prow of an oil tanker pointing straight up to the sky.

It was as if the Scavenge God had come amongst the ships, slashing and chopping, dicing the huge iron vessels into pieces, and then left the corpses scattered carelessly behind. And wherever the huge ships lay, scavenge gangs like Nailer's swarmed like flies. Chewing away at iron meat and bones. Dragging the old world's flesh up the beach to the scrap weighing scales and the recycling smelters that burned 24-7 for the profit of Lawson & Carlson, the company that made all the cash from the blood and sweat of the ship breakers.

Nailer and Sloth paused for a moment, breathing hard, leaning against the heavy spool. Nailer wiped the sweat out of his eyes. Far out on the horizon, the oily black of the ocean turned blue, reflecting sky and sun. White caps foamed. The air around Nailer was hazed with the black work of shoreline smelters, but out there, beyond the smoke, he could see sails. The new clipper ships. Replacements for the massive coal- and oil-burning wrecks that he and his crew worked to destroy all day long: gull-white sails, carbon-fiber hulls, and faster than anything except a maglev train.

Nailer's eyes followed a clipper ship as it sliced across the waters, sleek and fast and completely out of reach. It was possible that some of the copper on his spool would eventually sail away on a ship like that, first hauled by train to the Orleans, then transferred to a clipper's cargo hold, where it would be carried across the ocean to whatever people or country could afford the scavenge.

Bapi had a poster of a clipper ship from Libeskind, Brown & Mohanraj. It connected to his reusable wall calendar and showed a clipper with high-altitude parasails extended far above it—sails that Bapi said could reach the jet streams and yank a clipper across smooth ocean at more than fifty-five knots, flying above the waves on hydrofoils, tearing through foam and salt water, slicing across the ocean to Africa and India, to the Europeans and the Nipponese.

Nailer stared at the distant sails hungrily, wondering at the places they went, and whether any of them were better than his own.

"Nailer! Sloth! Where the hell have you been?"

Nailer jerked from his reverie. Pima was waving up at them from the tanker's lower deck, looking annoyed.

"We're waiting for you, crewboy!"

"Boss girl on the prowl," Sloth muttered.

Nailer grimaced. Pima was the oldest of them, and it made her bossy. Even his own long friendship with her didn't shelter him when they were behind quota.

He and Sloth turned their attention back to the spool. With another series of grunts they heaved it over the ship's warped decking and rolled it to where a rudimentary crane had been set up. They hitched the spool to rusted iron hooks, then grabbed the crane cable and jumped aboard the spool as it descended, swaying and spinning to the lower deck.

Pima and the rest of the light crew swarmed around them as they hit bottom. They unclipped the spool and rolled it over to where they'd set up their stripping operation near the oil tanker's prow. Lengths of discarded insulation from the electrical wire lay everywhere, along with the gleaming rolls of copper that they'd collected, stacked in careful lines, and marked with Bapi's light crew claim mark, the same swirled symbol that scarred all their cheeks.

Everyone started unreeling sections of Nailer's new haul,

parting the lengths out amongst themselves. They worked quickly, accustomed to one another and the labor: Pima, their boss girl, taller than the rest and filling out like a woman, black as oil and hard as iron. Sloth, skinny and pale, bones and knots of knees and dirty blond hair, the next candidate for duct-and-scuttle work when Nailer got too big, her pale skin almost permanently sunburned and peeling. Moon Girl, the shade of brown rice, whose nailshed mother had died with the last run of malaria and who worked light crew harder than anyone else because she'd seen the alternative, her ears and lips and nose decorated with scavenged steel wire that she'd driven through her flesh in the hope that no one would ever want her the way they'd wanted her mother. Tick-tock, nearsighted and always squinting at everything around him, almost as black as Pima but nowhere near as smart, fast with his hands as long as you told him what do with them, and he never got bored. Pearly, the Hindu who told them stories about Shiva and Kali and Krishna and who was lucky enough to have both a mother and a father who worked oil scavenge; black hair and dark tropic skin and a hand missing three fingers from an accident with the winding drum.

And then there was Nailer. Some people, like Pearly, knew who they were and where they came from. Pima knew her mother came up from the last of the islands across the Gulf. Pearly told everyone who would listen that he was 100 percent Indian—Hindu Marwari through and through. Even Sloth said that her people were Irish. Nailer was nothing like that. He had no idea what he was. Half of something, a quarter of something else, brown skin and black hair like his dead mother, but with weird pale blue eyes like his father.

Pearly had taken one look at Nailer's pale eyes and claimed he was spawned by demons. But Pearly made things up all the time. He said Pima was Kali reincarnated—which was why her skin was so black, and why she was so damn mean when they were behind quota. Even so, the truth was that Nailer shared his father's eyes and his father's wiry build, and Richard Lopez was a demon for sure. No one could argue that. Sober, the man was scary. Drunk, he was a demon.

Nailer unwound a section of wire and squatted down on the blazing deck. He crimped the wire with his pliers and ripped off a sleeve of insulation, revealing the shining copper core.

Did it again. And again.

Pima squatted beside him with her own length of wire. "Took you long enough to bring out this load."

Nailer shrugged. "Nothing's close in anymore. I had to go a long way to find it."

"That's what you always say."

"You want to go into the hole, you can."

"I'll go in," Sloth volunteered.

Nailer gave her a dirty look. Pearly snorted. "You don't have the sense of a half-man. You'd get lost like Jackson Boy and then we'd get no scavenge at all."

Sloth made a sharp gesture. "Grind it, Pearly. I never get lost."

"Even in the dark? When all the ducts look the same?" Pearly spat toward the edge of the ship. Missed and hit the rail instead. "Crews on *Deep Blue III* heard Jackson Boy calling out for days. Couldn't find him, though. Little lice-biter finally just dried up and died."

"Bad way to go," Tick-tock commented. "Thirsty. In the dark. Alone."

"Shut up, you two," Moon Girl said. "You want the dead to hear you calling?"

Pearly shrugged. "We're just saying Nailer always makes quota."

"Shit." Sloth ran a hand through sweaty blond hair. "I'd get twenty times the scavenge Nailer gets."

Nailer laughed. "Go on in, then. We'll see if you come out alive."

"You already filled the spool."

"Tough grind for you, then."

Pima tapped Nailer's shoulder. "I'm serious about the scavenge. We had downtime waiting for you."

Nailer met Pima's eyes. "I make quota. You don't like my work, then go in yourself."

Pima pursed her lips, annoyed. It was an empty suggestion, and they both knew it. She'd gotten too big, and had the scabs and scars on her spine and elbows and knees to prove it. Light crew needed small bodies. Most kids got bounced off the crew by the time they hit their midteens, even if they starved themselves to keep their size down. If Pima weren't such a good crew boss, she'd already be on the beach, hungry and begging for anything that came her way. Instead, she had another year, maybe, to bulk up enough to compete against hundreds of others for openings in heavy crew. But her time was running out, and everyone knew it.

Pima said, "You wouldn't be so cocky if your dad wasn't such a whip-wire. You'd be in the same position as me."

"Well, that's one thing I can thank him for, then."

If his father was any indication, Nailer would never be huge. Fast, maybe, but never big. Tick-tock's dad claimed that none of them would grow that big anyway, because of the calories they didn't eat. Said that people up in Seascape Boston were still tall, though. Had plenty of money, and plenty of food. Never went hungry. Got fat and tall...

Nailer had felt his belly up against his spine enough times that he wondered what it would be like to have so much food. Wondered how it would feel to never wake in the middle of the night with his teeth chewing on his lips, fooling himself into thinking that he was about to eat meat. But it was a stupid fantasy. Seascape Boston sounded a little too much like Christian Heaven, or the way the Scavenge God promised a life of ease, if you could just find the right offering to burn with your body when you went to his scales.

Either way, you had to die to get there.

The work went on. Nailer stripped more wire, tossing the junk insulation over the ship's side. The sun beat down on everyone. Their skins gleamed. Salt sweat jewels soaked their hair and dripped into their eyes. Their hands turned slick with work, and their crew tattoos shone like intricate knots on their flushed faces. For a little while they talked and joked but gradually fell silent, working the rhythm of scavenge, building piles of copper for whoever was rich enough to afford it.

"Boss man coming!"

The warning call came up from the waters below. Everyone hunkered down, looking busy, waiting to see who would appear at the rail. If it was someone else's boss, they could relax—

Bapi.

Nailer grimaced as their crew boss clambered up over the rail, huffing. His black hair gleamed, and his potbelly made it hard for him to climb, but there was money involved, so the bastard managed.

Bapi leaned against the rail, regaining his breath. Sweat darkened the tank top that he wore for work. Yellow and brown stains of whatever curry or sandwich he'd eaten for lunch dotted the material. It made Nailer hungry just looking at all that food on Bapi's chest, but there was no meal coming until evening, and there was no point looking at food Bapi would never share.

Bapi's quick brown eyes studied them, alert for signs that they'd gone lazy and weren't serious about scavenging for quota. Even though none of them had been idle before, with Bapi watching they all worked faster, trying to demonstrate they were worth keeping. Bapi had been light crew himself once; he knew their ways, knew the tricks of laziness. It made him dangerous.

"What you got?" he asked Pima.

Pima glanced up, squinting into the sun. "Copper. Lots. Nailer found new ducts that Gorgeous's crew missed."

Bapi's teeth flashed white, showing the front gap where a fight had cost him his incisors. "How much?"

Pima jerked her head at Nailer, giving him permission.

"Maybe hundred, hundred and twenty kilos so far," Nailer estimated. "There's more down there."

"Yeah?" Bapi nodded. "Well, hurry and get it out. Don't worry about stripping it. Just make sure you get it all." He looked out toward the horizon. "Lawson & Carlson says a storm's coming. Big one. We're going to be off the wrecks for a couple days. I want enough wire that you can work it on the sand."

Nailer stifled his distaste at the thought of going back down into the blackness, but Bapi must have caught something of his expression.

"Got a problem, Nailer? You think a storm means you get to sit on your ass?" Bapi waved toward the work camps strung along the beach's jungle edge. "You think I can't get a hundred other licebiters to take your place? There's kids down there who'd let me cut out an eye if it would get them up on a wreck."

Pima interceded. "He's got no problem. You want the

wire, we'll get it. No problem." She glared at Nailer. "We're your crew, boss. No problem at all."

They all nodded emphatically. Nailer got to his feet and handed the rest of his wire over to Tick-tock. "No problem, boss," he repeated.

Bapi scowled at Nailer. "You sure you vouch for him, Pima? I can put a knife through this one's crew tats and dump him on the sand."

"He's good scavenge," she said. "We're ahead on quota 'cause of him."

"Yeah?" Bapi relented slightly. "Well, you're boss girl. I don't interfere." He eyed Nailer. "You watch it, boy. I know how your kind thinks. Always imagining you're going to be a Lucky Strike. Pretending you'll find some big old oil pocket and never work another day in your life. Your old man was a lazy bastard like that. Look how he turned out."

Nailer felt a rising anger. "I don't talk about your dad."

Bapi laughed. "What? You gonna fight me, boy? Try and pigstick me from behind the way your old man would?" Bapi touched his knife. "Pima vouches for you, but I'm wondering if you got the sense to know how much of a favor she's doing."

"Let it go, Nailer," Pima urged. "Your dad's not worth it."

Bapi watched, smiling slightly. His hand lingered close to his knife. Bapi had all the cards, and they both knew it. Nailer ducked his head and forced down his anger.

"I'll get your scavenge, boss. No problem."

Bapi gave Nailer a sharp nod. "Smarter than your old man, then." He turned to the rest of the crew. "Listen up, everyone. We don't have a lot of time. If you get the extra scavenge out before the storm, I'll bonus you. There's another light crew coming on soon. We don't want to leave them any easy pickings, right?"

He grinned, feral, and they all nodded back. "No easy pickings," they echoed.

2

NAILER WAS FARTHER into the tanker than he'd ever been. No light crew marks gleamed in the darkness, no evidence of any other duct-and-scuttle workers marred the dust and rat droppings of the passage.

Overhead, three separate lines of copper wire ran ahead of him, a lucky find that meant he might even make Bapi's quota, but Nailer was having a hard time caring. His mask kept clogging, and in the rush to dive back into the hole, he'd forgotten to renew his LED paint patch. Now he regretted it bitterly as darkness closed in.

He ripped down more tangling wire. The passage seemed to be getting narrower, even as the amount of copper increased. He eased forward, and the duct creaked all around, protesting his weight. Petroleum fumes burned in his lungs. He wished he could just quit and crawl out. If he turned around now, he could be back on deck in twenty minutes, breathing clean air.

But what if he didn't have enough scavenge?

Bapi already didn't like him. And Sloth was too damn eager to steal his slot. Her words still lingered in his mind: *"I'll get twenty times the scavenge he does."*

A warning. He had competition now.

It didn't matter that Pima vouched for him. If Nailer failed to pull quota, Bapi would slash out his work tattoos and give Sloth a try. And Pima couldn't do a damn thing about it. No one was worth keeping if they didn't make a profit.

Nailer wriggled onward, driven by Sloth's hungry words. More and more copper came down in his hands. His LED faded to black. He was alone. Nothing but a trail of loosened electrical cable to lead him out. For the first time he feared he might not be able to find his way. The tanker was huge, one of the workhorses of the oil age, almost a floating city in itself. And now he was deep in its guts.

When Jackson Boy died, no one had been able to find him. They'd heard him banging away on the metal, calling out, but no could locate a way into the double hull where he'd trapped himself. A year later, heavy crews cut open a section of iron and the little licebiter's mummified body had popped out like a pill from a blister pack. Dry like leaves, rattling as it hit the deck. Rat-chewed and desiccated.

Don't think about it. You'll just bring his ghost onto the ship.

The duct was tightening, squeezing around his shoulders. Nailer began to imagine himself stuck like a cork in a bottle. Pinned in the darkness, never able to get free. He strained forward and yanked down another length of wire.

Enough. More than enough.

Nailer hacked Bapi's light crew code into the duct's metal with his knife, doing it blind, but at least making a stab at saving the territory for later. He tightened himself into a ball. Knees against chin, elbows and spine scraping the duct walls as he turned himself around. Folding tighter, letting out his breath, fighting off images of corks and bottles and Jackson Boy caught in the darkness, dying alone. Tighter. Turning. Listening to the duct creak as he squeezed against metal.

He came free, gasping relief.

In another year, he'd be too big for this work and Sloth would take his niche for sure. He might be small for his age, but eventually everyone got too big for light crew.

Nailer squirmed back down the duct, rolling the wire ahead of him. The loudest sound was his own rasping breath in the filter mask. He paused and reached ahead for the loosened wire, confirming that it was still there, still leading him out to the light.

Don't panic. You took this wire down yourself. You just need to keep following it—

A scuttling noise echoed behind him.

Nailer froze, skin crawling. A rat, probably. But it sounded big. Unbidden, another image intruded. Jackson

Boy. Nailer could imagine the dead crew boy's ghost in the ducts with him, creeping through the darkness. Stalking him. Reaching for his ankles with dry bone fingers.

Nailer fought down panic. It was just superstition. Paranoia was for Moon Girl, not for him. But the fear was in him now. He started shoving his scavenged wire aside, suddenly desperate for clean air and light. He'd crawl out, renew his LED paint, and then come back when he could see what was what. Screw Sloth and Bapi. He needed air.

Nailer started squeezing around his tangled bundle of copper. The duct creaked dangerously as he squirmed past, protesting the collected weight of himself and the wire. Stupid to gather so much. Should have cut it in sections and let Pima and Sloth spool it out. But he'd been hurrying, and now, of all things, he'd collected too much. Nailer clawed forward, jamming the wire aside. Felt a flush of triumph as he kicked the last tangling wires off his legs.

The duct groaned loudly and shuddered under him.

Nailer froze.

All around, the duct pinged and creaked. It sank slightly, tilting. The whole thing was on the verge of collapse. Nailer's frantic activity and extra weight had weakened it.

Nailer spread out his weight and lay still, heart pounding. Trying to sense the duct's intentions. The metal went quiet. Nailer waited, listening. Finally, he eased forward, delicately shifting his weight.

Metal shrieked. The duct dropped out from under him. Nailer scrabbled for handholds as his world gave way. His fingers seized scavenged wire. For a second it held, suspending him above an infinite pit. Then the wire tore loose. He plummeted.

I don't want to be a Jackson Boy I don't want to be a Jackson Boy I don't—

He hit liquid, warm and viscous. Blackness swallowed him with barely a ripple.

3

SWIM YOU BASTARD swim you bastard swim you bastard…

Swim!

Nailer sank like a stone through warm reeking liquid. It was like trying to swim through thick air instead of water. No matter how hard he fought, the warmth gave way under him, sucking him deeper.

Why can't I swim?

He was a good swimmer. Had never worried about drowning in the ocean, even in heavy surf. But now he kept sinking. His hand tangled in something solid—the copper wire. He grabbed for it, hoping it was still connected to the ducts above.

It slithered through his fingers, slick and slimy.

Oil!

Nailer fought off panic. It was impossible to swim in oil. It just swallowed you like quicksand. He clawed again for the copper and looped the wiring around his hand to counteract its slickness. His sinking stopped. He began hauling himself back up out of the muck. His lungs screamed for air. Hand over hand, he dragged himself higher. He fought the urge to breathe, to give up and fill his lungs with oil. It would be so easy—

He came out of the oil like a whale surfacing, oil sheeting off his face. He opened his mouth to breathe.

Nothing. Just a strange pressure on his face.

The mask!

Nailer tore it off, gasping. Sucked air. Petroleum vapors burned his lungs, but he could breathe. He used the mask's clean interior to scrape at his eyes, clearing oil away. He opened them to an intense stinging and burning. Tears filled his eyes. He blinked rapidly.

Blackness all around. Pitch blackness.

He was in some kind of oil reservoir, maybe a leaked pool, or some secondary storage chamber, or…He had no idea where he was in the ship. If he was really unlucky, he was in one of the main oil reservoirs. He finished wiping his eyes and tossed away the now useless mask. The fumes were dizzying. He forced himself to breathe shallowly as he clung to the wire. His skin burned with its petroleum coating. Hammers rang faintly in the distance—workers banging away at the ship, all unaware of his emergency.

His hands started to slide off the wire. Nailer grabbed

desperately for a better handhold, hooking his arm through the tangles. Overhead, the duct creaked alarmingly. A tingle of fear ran through him. A few strands of wire that stretched to that high overhead duct were all that kept him from drowning. But the safety was temporary. Soon the duct would give way and he'd sink again, his lungs filling with oil, thrashing and gurgling—

Calm down, you idiot.

Nailer considered trying to swim again, but discarded the idea. It was just his mind playing tricks, fantasizing that the liquid all around was actually water. But oil was different. It didn't support a body, no matter how much you wished. It just swallowed you up. Nailer had seen a man on heavy crew drown that way. He'd thrashed briefly in the oil, shouting and panicked, then slipped under, long before anyone could throw him a rope.

Don't panic. Think.

Nailer reached out, fingers straining into the blackness. Reaching for anything: a wall, some bit of floating junk, anything to tell him where he was. His hand found nothing but air and mucky oil. His movements made the duct creak overhead. The wire sank slightly as something gave way. Nailer held his breath, expecting to go under, but the wire stopped sinking.

"Pima!" he shouted.

His voice echoed back fast, bouncing all around.

Nailer clutched the wire, surprised. Judging from the sound, he wasn't in as big a space as he'd thought. There were walls nearby. "Pima!"

Again the fast echo.

This wasn't some giant oil tank. It was much, much smaller. Heartened by the impression of walls, Nailer reached out again. But this time, instead of using a hand, he stretched out into the darkness with this toes.

After two tries, rough metal met his skin. A wall of some sort, and something else... Nailer sucked in a grateful breath. A thin pipe running along its breadth. It was only a centimeter in diameter, but still, it had to be better than a tangle of copper dangling from a failing duct.

Without waiting to reconsider, Nailer lunged for the wall.

As he moved, the ducting overhead shrieked and gave way. Nailer sank, thrashing and scrabbling for the thin pipe. His slick hands touched the wall, slipped off. Caught. He dragged himself up against the wall, clinging by his fingertips. They trembled with the strain. The oil didn't give him any float at all. Already he was tiring. He couldn't support himself for long.

Quickly, Nailer slid along the wall, seeking better handholds. If he was lucky, maybe there was a ladder. He reached a bend in the pipe. It turned sharply downward and disappeared into the oil.

Nailer stifled a sob of frustration. He was going to die.

Don't panic.

If he started crying he was screwed. He needed to think, not bawl like a baby, but already his mind felt drunk and scattered. The fumes were overwhelming. Nailer could see how this would end. He'd hang on for a little longer, inhaling more and more of the poisonous air, clinging like a bug to the wall, but eventually he'd get too tired and high, and he'd slip off.

How could he die in such a stupid way? This wasn't even a storage tank. Just some room full of pooled waste oil. It was a joke, really. Lucky Strike had found an oil pocket on a ship and bought his way free. Nailer had found one and it was going to kill him.

I'm going to drown in goddamn money.

Nailer almost laughed at the thought. No one knew exactly how much oil Lucky Strike had found and smuggled out. The man had done it slow, over time. Sneaking it out bucket by bucket until he had enough to buy out his indenture and burn off his work tattoos. But he'd had enough left over to set himself up as a labor broker selling slots into the very heavy crews that he'd escaped. Just a little oil had done so much for Lucky Strike, and Nailer was up to his neck in the damn stuff.

"Nailer?"

The voice was faint, far away.

"Sloth!" Nailer's voice cracked with relief. "I'm here! Down here! I fell through!" He kicked in his excitement and the oil rippled around him.

A bit of green light illuminated the gloom above. Sloth's scavenge features peered through the duct hole, an LED smear on her forehead.

"Damn. You screwed big-time, Nailer?" she asked.

"Yeah. Big-time screwed." He grinned weakly.

"Pima sent me in for you."

"Tell her I need rope."

26

A long pause. "Bapi won't do it."

"Why?"

Another long silence. "He wants copper. Sent me in for copper. Before the storm comes."

"Just drop me a rope."

"Gotta make quota." Her glow face disappeared. "Pima sent stuff, case I found you. Case you needed help."

Nailer grimaced. "You see a ladder anywhere?"

Another long pause as they both peered at the gloom with her phosphor green paint lighting. Nothing. No ladders. No doors. Just a rusty room filled with black murk.

"What's wrong with you?" Sloth asked. "You broke something?"

Nailer shook his head before remembering she probably couldn't see him well. "I'm swimming in oil. You tell Bapi I'm up to my neck in oil. Thousands of gallons. It's worth his while to get me out. There's a lot of oil for him here."

Another pause.

"Yeah? A lot?"

Nailer realized with a chill that sly Sloth was calculating the advantages.

"Don't think you can do a Lucky Strike," he called up.

"Lucky Strike did it," she responded.

"We're crew," Nailer said, trying to keep his voice from showing fear. "You tell Pima there's oil. You tell her there's a secret stash. If you don't, I'll haunt you like Jackson Boy and come back and gut you while you're sleeping."

Silence: Sloth, thinking.

Nailer felt a sudden wash of hatred for her. The skinny starved girl perched up there had all the power in the world to help or kill, to tell Bapi at least that there was something to be gained from Nailer's survival, and yet there she sat.

He called up. "Sloth?"

"Shut up," she said. "I'm thinking."

"We're crew," he reminded her. "We swore blood oath." But he knew the calculations she was making, her clever mind working the angles, sensing the great pool of wealth, the secret stash that she might pillage later, if Fates and the Rust Saint worked in her favor. He wanted to scream at her, to grab her and drag her down. Teach her what it felt like to die sucking oil.

But he couldn't yell at her. Couldn't piss her off. He needed her. Needed to convince her to help him survive.

"We'll keep it secret," he offered. "We can Lucky Strike together."

Another pause, then she said, "You said yourself you're swimming in it. Soon as anyone sees you, they know you found a pocket."

He grimaced. Too damn smart. That was the problem with girls like Sloth. Too damn smart for his own good. "We're crew," he said again, but he suspected it was pointless. He knew her too well. Knew all of them too well. They'd all starved. They'd all talked about what they'd do if they ever found a Lucky Strike. And here Sloth had been given one. Chances like this didn't just come along. Sloth had to make her gamble. It was her chance.

Please, he prayed. *Please let her be good like Pima. Like Pima and her mom. Let her not be like Dad. Fates, please don't let her be like Dad.*

Sloth interrupted his whispered prayers. "Pima says I'm supposed to hook you up good. If I find you."

"You found me."

"Yeah. That's for sure." A rustling. "Here's food and water."

A shadow fell through the green glow of her forehead phosphor. It hit with a splash. Nailer could just see pale objects floating on the surface, starting to sink. He stretched for them, trying to keep his hand on the wall. Managed to snag a water bottle before it disappeared. Everything else was already gone. The blackness of the room closed in on him again as Sloth disappeared.

"Thanks for nothing!" he shouted after her, but she was already gone.

He had no idea if Sloth would actually report to Pima or if she'd just hurry back, dragging copper, determined to replace him and think of some way to claim the oil prize all to herself. For certain, she wouldn't tell Bapi. Bapi would just call it light crew scavenge and keep it for himself.

That meant they had hours more copper work to prepare for the storm...and that meant he had hours to wait, even if Pima knew where he was and that he needed help.

With one slippery hand and his teeth, Nailer managed to open the plastic bottle and drink while he clung to the wall. He swished the first mouthful and spat it out, trying to clear the oil and gunk from his mouth, and then drank, hard and fast, gulping. Grateful. Unaware until the water was pouring into him how thirsty he'd been. He swallowed the rest greedily, then set the bottle floating in the blackness. If he died this would be the last thing of him on the surface.

A few scrabbling sounds drifted down from above, scraping and tearing.

"Sloth?"

The sound stopped, then started again.

"Come on, Sloth. Help me out."

He didn't know why he bothered. She had made her decision. As far as she was concerned, he was already a corpse. He listened as she busied herself with stripping out the rest of the copper. His fingers weakened. The oil crept up around his chin. Fates, he was tired. He wondered if Jackson Boy had also been betrayed by his crew. If that was why the licebiter hadn't been found until a year later. Maybe someone had let him die on purpose.

You're not going to die.

But he was lying to himself. He was going to drown. Without a ladder. Or a door—

Nailer's heart suddenly beat faster.

If this was some room accidentally filled with oil, then there had to be doors. But they'd all be down below the surface. He'd have to dive down and risk not making it back up. Dangerous.

You'll drown anyway. Sloth's not going to save you.

That was the real truth. He could hang on for a little longer, getting weaker and weaker, but eventually his fingers would fail and he'd slip off.

You're dead already.

It was a curiously liberating thought. He really had nothing to lose.

Nailer slid slowly along the wall, questing down into the murk with his toes, feeling for some bump or ledge that would tell him a door lay below. The first time, he found nothing, but the second, he let himself sink lower, oil lapping up around his jaw. His toes brushed something. He tilted his nose to the sky, letting the oil lap higher, up around his cheeks, closing around his mouth and nose.

A ledge. A rim of metal.

Nailer ran his toe along its width. It could be the top of a doorway, he guessed. It wasn't much more than three feet wide. The ledge itself was a boon. He could almost rest, letting his toes cling to it, taking some of the pressure off his trembling fingers. The ledge felt like a palace.

You can rest now, he thought. *You can wait for Pima. Sloth will tell her you're down here. You can wait it out.*

He killed the hope. Maybe Pima would come save him. Probably, though, Sloth wouldn't say anything about him at all. He was on his own. Nailer balanced on the ledge, on the edge of decision.

Live or die, he thought. *Live or die.*

He dove.

4

IN A WAY, the black muck of the oil was no worse than the blackness above. Nailer let his hands do the work of seeing. He quested down along the rim of the door, sinking deeper, reading its outline.

His hands touched a wheel lock.

Nailer's heart surged with relief. The wheel was the kind used to hold back seawater if a hull breached, a solid airtight door. He tugged at the wheel, trying to remember which way to turn it. It didn't budge. He fought down panic. Yanked on the wheel again. Nothing. It wouldn't move. And he was running out of air.

Nailer kicked for the surface, using the wheel to launch himself upward, praying that he'd make it. He surfaced, flailing. His fingers scrabbled for the thin pipe, miraculously caught hold before he sank again. He wiped frantically at his face, clearing his nose and keeping his eyes shut. He blew air through his lips, pushing oil away from his mouth. Sucked in a fume-laden breath.

With his eyes still closed, he felt again for the doorframe with his toes. He thought he'd lost it for a second, but then he scraped rust and a moment later he was perched again. He smiled tightly. A door with a wheel. A chance. If he could make the damn thing turn.

More scrabbling echoed from above. Sloth at work still.

He called up to her. "Hey, Sloth! I got me a way out. I'm coming for you, crewgirl."

The movement stopped.

"You hear me?" His voice echoed all around. "I'm getting out! And I'm coming for you."

"Yeah?" Sloth responded. "You want me to go get Pima?" Mockery laced her voice. Nailer again wished he could reach up and yank her down into the oil. Instead, Nailer made his voice reasonable.

"If you go get Pima now, I'll forget you were going to let me drown."

A long pause.

Finally Sloth said, "It's too late, right?" She went on. "I know you, Nailer. You'll tell Pima no matter what, and then I'm off crew and someone else buys in." Another pause, then she said, "It's all Fates now. If you got a way out, I'll see you on the outside. You get your revenge then."

Nailer scowled. It had been worth a try. He thought

about the door waiting below him. It might be locked from the far side. Maybe that was why the wheel didn't turn. Maybe...

If it's locked, you die. Same as everything. No use worrying about it.

He took a deep breath and went down again.

This time, with more air, and knowing what he was trying to do, he found the wheel quickly and then took his time working it. He braced his feet on the hatch frame, felt around for the latch handle. First he needed to unseal with the wheel, then he needed to yank the handle. He tried to turn the wheel again. Nothing. He leaned against it, bracing himself sideways and using his legs, fighting to keep a grip.

Nothing.

He hooked his elbow through the wheel. He was running out of air, but he didn't want to give up. He pulled. Pulled again, harder, the wheel digging into the crook of his arm. His lungs were bursting.

The wheel turned.

Nailer redoubled his efforts. Gold and blue and red pulses filled his vision. The wheel turned again, loosening. He was frantic for air, but he stayed down, fighting the urge to kick for the surface, turning the wheel faster and faster until his lungs were heaving. He launched himself upward again, hope running wild as he surfaced.

Eager now, he hyperventilated a final time, huffing high in the blackness.

Dove.

Spinning, spinning, spinning the wheel, his lungs bursting, all or nothing, reckless with the need to get out. Nailer yanked the latch handle. For a second he worried that the door swung inward and that he would never be able to drag the thing open against the pressure of oil holding it closed—

The door blew open.

Nailer was sucked through in a black torrent. He slammed into a wall. Curled into a ball as he tumbled. Oil roared around him. His forehead smashed against metal and he almost took a breath, but forced himself to curl tighter, letting himself be turned and swirled and bounced and slammed through ship corridors like a jellyfish thrown by breakers onto a reef.

He blasted into open air.

Nailer's stomach dropped out of him. Free fall. Involuntarily, his eyes opened. Stinging oil and scalding sun. A mirror bright ocean, almost white with its intensity. Blue waves rushed up to meet him. He had only a second to twist—

He smashed into water. Sea salt swallowed him. The surge and swell of an oily sea. The roll of breakers. Nailer surged upward, kicking for the surface. Broke out into sunlight and waves, gasping. He sucked air, flooding his lungs with shining clean oxygen, starved for all the life he'd been sure he'd lost.

Above him, a tear in the tanker's hull still spewed oil, marking where the ship had vomited him into open air.

Black streams of crude traced down the ship's hide, running in slick rivulets. Fifty feet of fall into shallow water, and he was alive. Nailer started to laugh.

"I'm alive!" he shouted. And then he was screaming, feeling a flood of victory and released terror, drunk on sunshine and waves and the people staring at him from shore.

He swam for the beach, still laughing and drunk on survival. Waves caught him and pushed him into the shore. He realized that he'd been doubly lucky. If the tide hadn't come in, he would have slammed against sand instead of plunging into water.

Nailer crawled out of the breakers and stood. His legs were weak from so long swimming but he was standing on dry land, and he was alive. He laughed madly at Bapi and Li and Rain and the hundreds of other laborers and crew gangs, all of them staring at him dumbstruck.

"I'm alive!" he shouted at them. "I'm alive!"

They all said nothing, simply stared.

Nailer was about to shout again but something in their faces made him look down.

Sea foam lapped around his ankles, rust and bits of wire. Shells and insulation. And intermixed with the ocean froth, his blood. Running down his legs in streams, bright and red and steady, staining the waters with the pounding of his heart.

5

"You're lucky," Pima's mother said. "You should be dead."

Nailer was almost too tired to respond, but he mustered a grin for the occasion. "But I'm not. I'm alive."

Pima's mother picked up a blade of rusted metal and held it in front of his face. "If this was even another inch into you, you would have washed into shore as body scavenge." Sadna regarded him seriously. "You're lucky. The Fates were holding you close today. Should have been another Jackson Boy." She offered him the rusty shiv. "Keep that for a talisman. It wanted you. It was going for your lung."

Nailer reached for the metal that had almost cut him down and winced as his stitches pulled.

"You see?" she said. "You're blessed today. Fates love you."

Nailer shook his head. "I don't believe in Fates." But he said it quietly, low enough that she wouldn't hear. If Fates existed, they'd put him with his dad, and that meant they were bad news. Better to think life was random than to think the world was out to get you. Fates were all right if you were Pima and got lucky with a good mom and a dad who was nice enough to have died before he could start beating you. But the rest of the time? Watch out.

Pima's mother looked up, her dark brown eyes studying him. "Then you get right with whatever gods you worship. I don't care if it's that elephant-headed Ganesha or Jesus Christ, or the Rust Saint or your dead mother, but someone was looking after you. Don't spit on that gift."

Nailer nodded obediently. Pima's mother was the best thing he had going. He didn't want to tick her off. Her shack of plastic tarps and old boards and scavenged palms was the safest place he knew. Here, he could always count on shared crawdads or rice, and even on days when there was nothing to eat, well, there was still the certainty that within these walls—under blue dangling Fates Eyes and a mottled statue of the Rust Saint—no one would try to cut him, or fight him, or steal from him. Here, fear and tension fell away in the presence of Sadna's strength.

Nailer moved gingerly, testing the stitching and cleaning work she'd done. "It feels good, Sadna. Thanks for patching me."

"I hope it does you some good." She didn't look up. She was washing the stainless-steel knives in a bucket of water, and the water had turned red with her work. "You're young, you're not addicted to anything. And say what you like about your father, you've got that Lopez tenacity. You have a chance."

"You think I'll get an infection?"

Pima's mother shrugged, her corded muscles rippling under her tank. Her black skin gleamed in the candlelight of her shack. She'd left her own crew and shift to make sure that he'd been cleaned up. Dropped a quota, thanks to Pima, who had had the sense to run for her when she heard that her missing crewboy was down in the shallows instead of up in the ship.

"I'm not sure, Nailer," she said. "You took a lot of cuts. Skin's supposed to protect you, but water's dirty here, and you were in oil." She shook her head. "I'm not a doctor."

He made a joke of it. "I don't need a doctor. I just need a needle and thread. Patch me up like a sail, I'm good as new."

She didn't smile. "Keep those clean. If you get fever or the skin starts to pus, you find me. We'll put maggots on it and see if that will help."

Nailer made a face, but he nodded at her fierce glare and gingerly sat up. He put his feet down on the floor, watching as Sadna bustled around the single room, carrying his blood water out into the dark, then coming back. He straightened and carefully made his way to the door. He pushed the plastic scavenge door aside so that he could see down the beach.

Even at night, the wrecks glowed with work, people laboring by torchlight as they continued the steady job of disassembly. The ships showed as huge black shadows against the bright star points and the surge of the Milky Way above. The torch lights flickered, bobbing and moving. Sledge noise rang across the water. Comforting sounds of work and activity, the air tanged with the coal reek of smelters and the salt fresh breeze coming off the water. It was beautiful.

Before almost dying, he hadn't known it. But now that he was out, Bright Sands Beach was the best thing he'd ever seen. He couldn't stop looking at it all, couldn't stop smiling at the people walking along the sand, at the cookfires where people roasted tilapia they'd hooked in the shallows, at the jangle of music and the shout of drinking from the nailsheds. It was all beautiful.

Almost as beautiful as the sight of Sloth getting kicked down the beach, her eyes wet with tears for herself, while he was getting stitched up. Bapi had put his knife through her light crew tattoos himself, disowning her completely. She'd never work as a ship breaker again. And probably nowhere else, either. Not after breaking blood oaths. She'd proven that no one could trust her.

Nailer had been surprised that Sloth hadn't protested. He wasn't about to forgive, but he respected that she hadn't begged or tried to apologize when Bapi got out his knife. Everyone knew the score. What was done was done. She'd gambled and lost. Life was like that. There were Lucky Strikes and there were Sloths; there were Jackson Boys and there were lucky bastards like him. Different sides of the same coin. You tossed your luck in the air and it rattled down on the gambling boards and you either lived or died.

"It's the Fates," Pima's mother muttered. "They've taken you now. No telling what they'll do with you." She was staring at him with an expression that almost looked like sadness. He wanted to ask her what she meant, but Pima came in through the door with the rest of the crew.

"Hey, hey!" Pima said. "Look at our crewboy!" She inspected his puckered wounds and stitches. "You'll get some nice scars out of this, Nailer."

"Lucky scars," said Moon Girl. "Even better than a tattoo of the Rust Saint's face." She handed him a bottle.

"What's this?" Nailer asked.

Moon Girl shrugged. "Luck gift. God's got you tight, now. I'm getting close to God."

Nailer smiled and sipped, was surprised at the quality of alcohol that burned his mouth.

Pima laughed. "It's Black Ling." She leaned close. "Ticktock stole it. Crazy licebiter just walked out of Chen's noodle shack with it. He's got no sense, but he's got fast hands." She pulled him toward the shore. "We got a fire going. Let's go get drunk."

"What about work tomorrow?"

"Bapi says that storm's coming for sure." She grinned. "We can strip wire with a hangover, no problem."

The crew gathered around the bonfire, swapping drinks. Pima went away and came back a little while later with a pot of rice and beans and then surprised Nailer again with a stick of grilled pigeon. At his look of surprise, she said, "Other people want to get close to God and the Fates. People saw you come out of the ship. No one gets luck like that."

He didn't question any more but ate greedily, glad to be alive and eating so well.

They drank, passing around the rusty shiv that had nearly killed him. Considered the possibilities of turning it into a talisman, a decoration to hang around his neck. The buzz of alcohol warmed him, made the world seem even better than before. He was alive. His skin sang with life. Even the pain in his back and shoulder where the shiv had driven into him felt good. Being close to death had made everything in his life shine. He rolled his shoulder, savoring the pain.

Pima watched him across the firelight. "You think you can crew tomorrow?"

Nailer made himself nod. "It's just stripping wire."

"Who we getting for scuttle duct?" Moon Girl asked.

Pima grimaced. "I thought it was going to be Sloth. Got to swear in someone new to replace her. Get bloody with someone."

"Lot of good that does," Tick-tock muttered.

"Yeah, well, some people still keep their word."

They all looked down the beach to where Sloth had been dumped. She'd be hungry soon, and needing someone to protect her. Someone to share scavenge with, to cover her back when she couldn't work. The beach was a hard place to survive without crew.

Nailer stared at the bonfires, thinking about the nature of luck. One quick decision by Sloth, and everything about her future was decided. She didn't have many options now, and all of them were ugly. Full of blood and pain and desperation. He took another swig from the bottle, wondering if he pitied her despite what she'd done.

"We could bring Teela on," Pearly suggested. "She's small."

"She's got a club foot," Moon Girl said. "How fast can she move?"

"For light crew, she'd hustle."

"I'll decide later," Pima said. "Maybe Nailer heals quick, and we don't need a scuttle duct replacement."

Nailer smiled sourly. "Or maybe Bapi cuts me out, and sells my slot. Then none of us get to choose."

"Not over my head."

No one said anything. It was too good a night to spoil it with bad speculation. Bapi would do whatever he wanted, but they didn't need to pick that scab tonight.

Pima seemed to sense their doubts. "I talked to Bapi

already," she insisted. "Nailer's got a couple days free. On the boss man's quota. Even Bapi wants to get close to luck like his."

"He's not pissed that I lost that crude to other crews?"

"Well, that too. But the wire came out with you, so he was happy about that. You've got your heal time. Rust Saint's my witness."

It almost sounded good enough to believe. Nailer took another drink. He'd seen enough adult promises turn out to just be wishes that he wasn't going to hold his breath, though. He needed to be crewing tomorrow, and he needed to look useful fast. He carefully worked his shoulder, willing it to get better. A couple days wire-stripping would be a blessing. If anything out of this whole mess was lucky, it was that a storm was coming.

Then again, without the storm, he wouldn't have been back in the hole twice on the same day.

Nailer drank again, enjoying the view of the beach. In the night, you couldn't even see the oil slicks on the water. Just the liquid silver reflections of the moon. Far out on the distant water, a few red and green lights glowed like fairy fire—the running lights of clipper ships crossing the Gulf.

The sailing ships slid silently across the horizon, blown so fast that their lights disappeared over the curve of the earth within minutes. He tried to imagine standing on the deck of one of those ships, leaving the beach and light crew behind. Sailing free and fast.

Pima took the booze bottle from him. "Daydreaming?"

"Nightdreaming." Nailer nodded out at the colored lights. "You ever sail on one?"

"A clipper?" Pima shook her head. "No way. Saw one dock once; they had a whole bunch of half-men for guards. Wouldn't let beach trash paddle close." She grimaced. "The dog-faces put electricity in the water."

Tick-tock laughed. "I remember that. I tried to swim out and started tingling all over."

Pima scowled. "And then we had to drag you back like a dead fish. Almost got us all zapped."

"I would have been fine."

Moon Girl snorted. "The dog-faces would have eaten you alive. That's how they do. Don't even cook their meat. Those monsters always tear in raw. If we left you out there, they'd have been using your ribs for toothpicks."

"Grind that. There's a half-man who muscles for Lucky Strike...what's its name?" Tick-tock halted briefly, stymied. "Anyway, I've seen it. It's got big damn teeth, but it don't eat people."

"How would you know? The ones it eats aren't around to bitch anymore."

"Goats," Pima said suddenly. "The half-man eats goats. When he first showed up on the beach, they paid him goats to work heavy crew. My mom told me he could eat a whole goat in three days." She made a face. "Moon Girl's right. You don't want to tangle with those monsters. You never know when their animal side will try to take your arm off."

Nailer was still watching the lights moving out in the deeps. "You ever wonder what it would be like to ride a clipper? Get out on one of those things?"

"I don't know." Pima shook her head. "Fast, I guess."

"Damn fast," Moon Girl supplied.

"Red-rip fast," Pearly said.

They were all looking out at the water now. Hungry.

"You think they even know we're here?" Moon Girl asked.

Pima spat in the sand. "We're just flies on garbage to people like that."

The lights kept moving. Nailer tried to imagine what it would be like to stand on deck, hurtling across the waves, blasting through spray. He'd spent evenings staring at images of clippers under sail, pictures that he had stolen from magazines that Bapi kept in a drawer in his supervisor's shack, but that was as close as he'd ever gotten. He had spent hours poring over those sleek predatory lines, studying the sails and hydrofoils, the smooth engineered surfaces so different from the rusting wrecks he worked every day. Staring at the beautiful people who smiled and drank on the decks.

The ships whispered promises of speed and salt air and open horizons. Sometimes Nailer wished he could simply step through the pages and escape onto the prow of a clipper. Sailing away in his imagination from the daily mangle of ship-breaking life. Other times, he tore the pictures up and threw them away, hating that they made him hungry for things he hadn't known he'd wanted until he'd seen the sails.

The wind shifted. A black cloud of smelting smoke blew over the beach, enveloping them in haze and ash.

Everyone started coughing and choking, trying to get some clean air. The wind shifted again, but Nailer kept coughing. His time in the oil room had hurt him. His chest and lungs still felt tender and the taste of oil lingered in his mouth.

By the time Nailer looked up from his coughing, the clipper ships were gone. More smelting smoke blew across their campfire.

Nailer smiled bitterly in the acrid wind. That was what thinking about clipper ships got you. A lungful of smoke because you weren't paying attention to what was around. He took another swig from his bottle and passed it to Pcarly.

"Thanks for the luck gift," he said. "I never knew Black Ling was so damn fine."

Moon Girl smiled. "Damn fine drink, for a damn lucky bastard."

"He's lucky, all right," Pima said. "Luckiest bastard I ever saw."

She inspected the other luck offerings that had accumulated over the night. Another stick of pigeon that Nailer offered around to the group, a pack of hand-rolled cigarettes, a bottle of cheap liquor from Jim Thompson's still, a thick silver earring, wide bored. A sea-polished shell. A half-kilo sack of rice.

"Luckier than Lucky Strike?" Nailer teased.

"Not after you lost all that oil," Moon Girl said. "If you were Lucky Strike, you'd have figured out how to sneak it out, instead of wasting it. Be a big rich man now, owning the beach."

The others grunted agreement, but Pima had gone still, her black skin a shadow. "No one's that lucky," she said bitterly. "Everyone daydreaming about being the next Lucky Strike is what made Sloth go bad."

"Yeah, well"—Nailer shrugged—"I still feel lucky today."

Pima made a face. "You weren't just lucky," she said. "You were smart. And Lucky Strike, he was smart, too. Half the crews out here find some cache of oil or copper or whatever and none of them figure out what to do with it. Crew boss grabs it in the end, and they get bumped off the wrecks. Shit." She took another swig from the bottle and wiped her lips on her arm before passing it on to Moon Girl, who drank and coughed. "Luck isn't what you need out here," Pima said. "Smarts is what you need."

"Luck or smarts, I don't care, long as I'm not dead."

"Cheers to that. Still, we get all excited about being like Lucky Strike and we lose our heads. We waste all our money throwing dice, trying to get close to Luck, trying to get the big win. We pray to the Rust Saint to help us find something we can keep for ourselves. Hell, even my mom puts good rice on the Scavenge God's scale for a luck offering, and we just end up like Sloth."

Pima nodded down the beach to where men from the heavy crews had started their bonfires. Nailshed girls were with them, laughing and teasing them, twining slender arms around the men's waists, urging them to drink and spend. "Sloth's down there now. I saw her. Dreaming about a Lucky Strike got her nothing except shame cuts through her crew tattoos, and a whole lot of bad company."

Nailer studied the men's bonfires. "You think she'll come after me?"

"I would," Pima said. "She's got nothing to lose now." She nodded at Nailer's luck gifts. "You better find a good place to stash all that. She'll probably try to steal it. Maybe she finds some sugar daddy down there to take her under his wing, but no one else is going to deal with her. Grub shacks won't take her because the ship breakers won't buy anything from someone with slashed crew tats. Smelter clans definitely won't touch an oath breaker. Liar like that, she's out of options."

Moon Girl said, "She could sell off a kidney. Maybe tap out a couple pints of blood for the Harvesters. They're always buying."

"Sure. She's got those pretty eyes," Pearly said. "Harvesters would take those in a second."

Pima shrugged. "Medical buyers can slice and dice her like a side of pork, but after a while everyone runs out of pieces. Then what?"

"Life Cult," Nailer suggested. "They'd buy her eggs."

"Just what we need." Moon Girl made a face. "Bunch of half-men that look like Sloth."

"Dog DNA would be a step up for her," Pearly said. "At least dogs are loyal."

They all laughed darkly. Started joking about which animals would enhance Sloth's genetic makeup: Roosters at least woke up early, crawdads were good eating, snakes were perfect for duct work, and they didn't have hands, so they couldn't stab you in the back. Every animal they considered was an improvement over the creature who had betrayed them. Ship breaking was too dangerous to not have trust.

"Sloth's about to hit a dead end," Pima said, "but we've got the same problem. Maybe not this year, but soon." She shrugged. "My mom's feeding me extra, trying to get me so I can compete into heavy crew." She hesitated, looked down the beach again to the bonfires and the men. "I don't think I'm going to make it. Too big for light crew, too small for heavy crew, what happens then? How many clans are taking kids who aren't their own?"

"It's bullshit," Pearly said. "You shouldn't have to quit light crew. You do better scavenge than anyone on the ship. You could take Bapi's job in a second, take out slack and double quota." He snapped his fingers. "Just like that. You could take Bapi's job for sure."

Pima smiled. "There's a long line for that job, and it

don't start with us. You've got to buy in big-time, and none of us has that kind of cash."

"It's stupid," Pearly said. "You'd be a better crew boss."

"Yeah." Pima grimaced. "That's where the luck comes in, I guess." She looked around at them seriously. "You should remember that, all of you. If you're just smart or just lucky, it's not worth a copper yard. You got to have both, or you're just like Sloth down at those bonfires, begging for someone to find a use for you." She took another swig from the bottle and handed it back. Stood up.

"I got to get some sleep." She headed down the beach, calling back over her shoulder to Nailer, "See you tomorrow, lucky boy. And be on time. Bapi will cut you for sure if you don't show up and sweat with the rest of us."

Nailer and the rest of the crew watched her go. The last log in the fire crackled, sending sparks. Moon Girl reached into the flame, quickly turning the log deeper into the coals. "There's no way she'll make heavy crew," she said. "No way any of us do."

"You trying to spoil the night?" Pearly asked.

Moon Girl's pierced features glittered in the firelight. "Just saying what we all know. Pima's worth ten of Bapi, but it don't matter. Another year, she's got the same problem as Sloth. It's luck or nothing." She held up a blue glass Fates amulet she kept around her neck. "We kiss the eye and hope things turn out, but we're all just as screwed as Sloth."

"No." Tick-tock shook his head. "The difference is that Sloth deserved it, and Pima doesn't."

"Deserving doesn't have anything to do with it," Moon Girl said. "If people got what they deserved, Nailer's mom would be alive, Pima's mom would own Lawson & Carlson, and I'd be eating six times a day." She spit into the fire. "You don't deserve anything. Maybe Sloth was an oath breaker, but she was smart enough to know you don't deserve things, you gotta take them."

"I don't buy that." Pearly shook his head. "What have you got without your promises? You're nothing. Less than nothing."

Nailer said, "You didn't see that oil, Pearly. It was the biggest Lucky Strike I ever saw. We can all pretend like we aren't like Sloth, but you never saw so much oil for the taking in all your life. It would turn anyone into an oath breaker."

"Not me," Pearly said vehemently.

"Sure. None of us," Nailer said. "But you still weren't there."

"Not Pima," Tick-tock said. "Never her."

And that killed the discussion, because whatever other lies they told themselves, Tick-tock was right. Pima never wavered. She never broke and she always had your back. Even when she was bitching at you to make quota, she always kept you safe. Nailer suddenly wished he could give all his luck to her. If anyone deserved something better, it was her.

Depressed by the turn of conversation, people started gathering the leavings of their meal, dousing the beach wood with sand, and getting ready to return to whatever families or caretakers or safe flops they had.

The wind blew over them and Nailer turned into the freshening breeze. The storm was coming, for sure. He had enough experience on the coast to have the sense of it. It was out there, coming in. A good big blow. It could shut down work for a couple days at least. Maybe give him a chance to rest up and heal.

He inhaled the fresh salty air as it poured over him. Other campfires were dousing out, and there was an increasing scurry of activity as the beach residents started tying down meager belongings in preparation for changing weather.

Out on the horizon, another clipper ship was skating across the Gulf's night waters, running lights glowing blue. He took a deep breath, watching it rush for whatever port would protect it. For once, Nailer was glad to be on shore.

He turned and trudged down the beach toward his own hut. If he was really lucky, his father would be out drinking and he'd be able to slip in unnoticed.

Nailer's home lay at the margin of the jungle surrounded by kudzu vines and cypress, made of palm sheathing and bamboo struts and scavenged sheet tin that his father had tagged with his fist mark to make sure nobody scavenged it while they were away during the day.

Nailer set his luck gifts outside the door. He could

almost remember times when this door hadn't seemed dangerous. Before his mother went feverish. Before his father turned drunk and high. Now, opening the door was always a gamble.

If it weren't for the fact that Nailer was wearing loaned clothes, he wouldn't even risk the return, but still, his other set of clothes lay inside, and if he was lucky, his dad was still out drinking. He scraped open the door and padded through the interior darkness. Opened the jar of glowpaint and smeared a bit on his forehead. The phosphorescence gave dim shadows—

A match flared. Nailer whirled.

His father leaned against the wall behind the door, watching him, a nearly empty bottle of booze gripped in one fist.

"Good to see you, Nailer."

Richard Lopez was a rib-thin conglomeration of ropy muscle and burning energy. Tattooed dragons ran the length of his arms and sent their tails curling up his neck to twine with the faded patterns of his own long-ago light crew tattoos. Fresher, and far more ominous, a whole series of victory scars gleamed on his chest, showing all the men he'd broken when he'd been a ring fighter. Thirteen red and angry slashes there. His very own baker's dozen, he would say, grinning. And then he'd ask Nailer if he was ever going to be as tough as his old man.

Richard lit the storm lamp that hung overhead, setting it

swaying. Nailer held still, trying to guess his father's mood as the man pulled a scavenged chair around and straddled it. The lamp's swinging glare cast shadows across them both, looming and swooping shapes. Richard Lopez was sliding high, burning with amphetamines and liquor. His bloodshot eyes studied Nailer carefully, a snake waiting to strike.

"What the hell happened to you?"

Nailer tried not to show fear. The man didn't have anything in his hands: no knife, no belt, no willow whip. His blue eyes might be crystal bright, but he was still a calm ocean.

"I had an accident on the job," Nailer said.

"An accident? Or you were being stupid?"

"No—"

"Thinking about girls?" his dad pressed. "Thinking about nothing at all? Daydreaming like you do?" He jerked his head toward the torn image of a clipper ship that Nailer had tacked to the wall of their shack. "Thinking about your pretty sailing ships?"

Nailer didn't take the bait. If he protested, it would just make things worse.

His father said, "How you going to pay your way around here, if you're off your crew?"

"I'm not off," Nailer said. "I'm back tomorrow."

"Yeah?" His father's bloodshot eyes narrowed suspiciously. He nodded at the rag sling holding Nailer's shoulder. "With a gimp arm? Bapi doesn't do charity work."

Nailer forced himself not to back down. "I'm still good. Sloth got cut, so I got no competition in the ducts. I'm smaller—"

"Smaller than shit. Yeah. You got that going for you." His father took a swallow from his bottle. "Where's your filter mask?" he asked.

Nailer hesitated.

"Well?"

"I lost it."

Silence stretched between them. "Lost it, huh?" was all his father said, but Nailer could tell that dangerous gears were turning now, fueled by the rattle of drugs and anger and whatever madness caused his father's bouts of frenzied work and brutality. Underneath the man's tattooed features a storm was brewing, full of undertows and crashing surf and water spouts, the deadly weather that buffeted Nailer every day as he tried to navigate the coastline of his father's moods. Richard Lopez was thinking. And now Nailer needed to know what—or he'd never escape the shack without a beating.

Nailer tried an explanation. "I fell through a duct and into an oil pocket. Couldn't get out. The mask couldn't breathe, anyway. It was full of oil. It was done for."

"Don't tell me it was done for," his father snapped. "That's not your say."

"No, sir." Nailer waited, wary.

Richard Lopez tapped his booze bottle idly against the

back of the chair. "I'll bet you'll want another mask now. You were always complaining about the dust with that old one."

"No, sir," Nailer said again.

"No, sir," his father mimicked. "Damn, Nailer, you're a smart one these days. Always saying the right thing." He smiled, showing yellow teeth all splayed out like a hand, but still the bottle tapped against the back of the chair. Nailer wondered if his father was going to try to hit him with it. The bottle tapped again. Richard Lopez's predatory eyes studied Nailer. "You're a smart little bastard these days," he murmured. "I'm almost thinking you're getting too damn smart for your own good. Maybe you're starting to say things you don't mean. Yes, sir. No, sir. *Sir.*"

Nailer could barely breathe. He knew now that his father was mapping out the violence, planning to catch Nailer, to teach him some respect. Nailer's eyes went to the door. Even with his father sliding high, the man had a good chance of catching him, and then everything would be blood and bruises and there was no way he'd get back on to light crew before Bapi cut him.

Nailer cursed that he hadn't just gone straight to the safety of Pima's shack. His eyes went to the door again. If he could just—

Richard caught the flick of Nailer's gaze. The man's features turned cold. He stood and pushed his chair away. "Come here, boy."

"I got a luck gift," Nailer said suddenly. "A good one. For getting out of the oil."

Nailer kept his voice steady, trying to pretend he didn't know his father was planning on beating the hell out of him. Playing innocent. Talking normal, like there wasn't about to be pain and screaming and a chase. "It's right here," he said.

Walk slow. Don't make him think you're running.

"It's just right here," Nailer said again as he opened the door and reached outside. He grabbed Moon Girl's luck gift and offered it to his dad. The bottle gleamed in the lamplight, a talisman.

"Black Ling," Nailer said. "The crew gave it to me. Said I should share it with you. Because I'm lucky for you having me."

Nailer held his breath. His father's cold eyes went to the bottle. Maybe his father would drink. Or maybe he'd take the bottle and hit him with it. Nailer just didn't know. The man had become more unpredictable as he worked less on the crews and worked more in the shadow world of the beaches, as his drugs whittled him down to a burning core of violence and hungers.

"Let me see." His dad took the bottle from Nailer's hand and checked the level of the liquor. "Didn't leave much for your old man," he complained. But he cracked the screw and sniffed the contents. Nailer waited, praying for luck.

His father drank. Made a face of respect. "Good stuff," he said.

The violence seeped out of the room. His father grinned and toasted Nailer with the bottle. "Damn good stuff." He tossed his other bottle into the corner. "Way better than that swill."

Nailer ventured a smile. "Glad you like it."

His father drank again and wiped his mouth. "Get to bed. You've got crew tomorrow. Bapi will cut you for sure if you're late." He waved Nailer toward his blankets. "Lucky boy, you." He grinned again. "Maybe that's what we'll call you from now on. Lucky Boy." The man's yellow horse teeth flashed, suddenly benevolent. "You like the name Lucky Boy?" he asked.

Nailer nodded hesitantly. "Yeah. I like it." He made himself smile wider, willing to say anything to keep his father in this new good mood. "I like it a lot."

"Good." His father nodded, satisfied. "Go to bed, Lucky Boy." His father took another swallow from Nailer's luck gift and settled down to watch the storm as it rolled toward them.

Nailer pulled a dirty sheet over himself. From the far side of the room, his old man muttered, "You did good."

Nailer felt a flush of relief at the compliment. It carried with it the whiff of a father that he remembered from before, when he was small and his mother was still alive. A different time, a different father. In the dim light, Richard

Lopez could almost be the man who had helped Nailer carve the Rust Saint's image into the wall above his mother's sickbed. But that had been a long time ago.

Nailer curled in on himself, glad to feel safe for the night. Tomorrow might be different, but this day had ended well. Tomorrow would handle itself.

6

THE STORM ROLLED onto the coast with all the implacable power of an old-world tank. Towering cloud banks built on the horizon and then swept inward, bearing steady rain. Thunder grumbled over the ocean and lightning lit the underbellies of the clouds, flashing from sea to sky and back again.

The deluge opened.

Nailer woke to the roar of storm on bamboo walls. Wind and water poured in through the open door, lit by explosions of electricity. His father was just a shadow slumped beside him, mouth open, snoring. Wind whirled through the house, scraping Nailer's face with cold fingers, then leaping to the wall and tearing away Nailer's picture of the clipper ship. The paper swirled madly for a moment before being sucked out the window into darkness, disappearing before Nailer could even try to grab it. Rain spattered his skin, coming in cold where palm thatching was already tearing away under the increasing battery of the winds.

Nailer crawled over his father and stumbled to the door. Outside, the beach swarmed with activity, people moving skiffs deeper into the trees, chasing after livestock. The storm looked worse than just a blow, maybe a city killer even, the way the clouds swirled and scattered lightning across the wrecks offshore. Even though the tide should have been out, the waves and breakers were big all across the beach, the storm surge pressing inland.

His father claimed that the storms were worse every year, but Nailer had never seen anything like the monster bearing down on them. He turned back into the shack.

"Dad!" he shouted. "Everyone's moving higher! We need to get out of the surge!"

His father didn't respond. The night crews were pouring off the wrecks. Men and women scrambling down hemp ladders, dangling and dropping like fleas jumping from a dog, plummeting into the increasing surf. Electricity outlined the black hulks against day-bright sky; then everything disappeared into blackness. Rain slashed the beach.

Nailer scrambled around the shack, looking for possessions to salvage. He tugged on his last set of clothes, grabbed the phosphor grease, found the silver earring and the luck bag of rice that he'd been given. The house creaked and heeled as wind gusted. The tin and bamboo wouldn't last long.

The storm was a city killer for sure, what some people called a party wrecker or an Orleans Surge. When Nailer peered back out into the storm's rage, he could see now that everyone was fleeing for heavy shelter. Shadow people clawing out of the darkness, hunched against curtains of wind and water as they dashed for safety. Running for things like the salvage train, with its iron freight cars that might not fly away.

Nailer dragged all their possessions over to his father's inert form. He pulled the sheet off the bed and fumbled one-handed with their belongings. His wounded shoulder burned with pain at the frantic effort. He shoved everything into the sheet and tied it in a bundle. More rain poured through the disintegrating thatch. His father's pale skin gleamed with rain water and yet still he didn't move.

Nailer grabbed a tattooed arm. "Dad!"

No response.

"Dad!" Nailer shook him again. Tried to drive his nails into the man's dragon-decorated flesh. "Wake up!"

The man barely stirred, sunk so deep in amphetamine blowout that nothing affected him.

Nailer rocked back on his heels, suddenly thoughtful.

If they took the full brunt of the city killer, there wouldn't be anything left here. He'd heard that sometimes a surge could move the coastline inland as much as a mile, turning beaches and trees into a murky swamp sea, the new ragged tide line of rising sea levels. A big blow could easily move the hulks of the ships as well. Might shove them right over the house, even if it didn't blow away.

Nailer straightened. He hefted the sheet, groaning at the cumbersome load. When he reached the doorway, the wind blasted him, lashing his face with rain and sand and leaves. More lightning slashed the beach. In the flickering light, a chicken coop tumbled past, all the birds already gone, every one of them lost to the gray roar. Nailer looked back at his father, conflicted emotions warring within him.

The man wasn't moving. The chemicals in his brain were so depleted he wasn't going to come awake even for the storm. Sometimes when the crash was bad, his father could sleep for two days. Nailer normally blessed the peace his father's drug crashes brought. It would be so much simpler...

Nailer set down the sack of possessions. Cursing himself for his own stupidity, he plunged into the storm. The man was a drunk and a bastard, but still, they were blood. They shared the same eyes, the same memories of his mother, the same food, the same liquor... Family, as much as he had.

A maelstrom of sand and copper screws and plastic shards swirled around him, the debris of the ship-breaking business ripping at his skin as he ran barefoot down the beach to Pima's shack. Rust flakes, bits of insulation, a roll of wire. Trash strippings flying like knives.

A gust of wind drove Nailer to his knees and sent him crawling, his shoulder a bright blossom of pain. Sheet metal whipped overhead, flying like a kite—a roof, a bit of ship, it was impossible to tell. It slashed into a coconut palm and the tree toppled, but the blast of the storm was so loud Nailer couldn't hear the collapse.

Crouched on the sand, he squinted through gushing rain. Pima's shack was gone, but the shadows of the girl and her mother were still there, fighting the storm, trailing ropes, struggling to hold onto a blurry shadow.

Nailer had always thought of Pima's mother as big from her work on the heavy crew, but now in the storm, she seemed as small as Sloth. The rain cleared briefly. Sadna and Pima were lashing down a skiff, tying it to a tree trunk as it bent in the wind. Debris scoured them. When he got close he could see that Pima had taken a cut to her face and blood ran freely from her forehead even as she worked with her mother to secure the lines.

"Nailer!" Pima's mother waved him over. "Help Pima hold that side!"

She threw him a line. He twisted it around his good arm and hauled, the two of them handling one end of the skiff, shoulder to shoulder as Pima made the knots fast. As soon as it was knotted, Pima's mother motioned him and shouted, "Get up into the trees! There's a rock hollow higher up! It should give shelter!"

Nailer shook his head. "My dad!" He waved back at his own shack, a shadow still miraculously upright. "He won't wake up!"

Pima's mother stared through the blackness and rain toward the shack. Her lips pursed.

"Hell. All right." She waved at Pima. "You take him up."

The last thing Nailer saw was Sadna's shadow plunging into the wind, running down the beach, surrounded by lightning strikes. And then Pima was dragging him up into the trees, scrambling through the whipping branches and the roar of the storm.

They climbed wildly, desperate to get out of the surge. Nailer looked back again at the beach and saw nothing. Pima's mother was gone. His father's shack. Everything. The beach was scoured clean. Out on the water, fires burned, oils somehow ignited and blazing despite the torrents.

"Come on!" Pima tugged him onward. "It's still a long way!"

They fled deeper into the jungle, scrambling through mud and stumbling over thick cypress roots. Torrents of water rushed down over them, filling the wood-cutting trails of the forest with their own muddy rivers. At last they reached Pima's destination. A small limestone cave, barely big enough to hold them both. They crouched within. Rainwater poured over the brink in a miserable torrent. It pooled around them so that they huddled ankle deep in cold water. Still, it was sheltered from the wind.

Nailer stared out at the storm. A city killer for sure.

"Pima," he started, "I—"

"Shh." She pulled him back from the water, deeper into the hole. "She'll be fine. She's tough. Tougher than any storm."

A tree flew past, flying as if it were a toothpick flung by a child. Nailer bit his lip. He hoped Pima was right. He'd been a fool to ask for help. Pima's mother was worth a hundred of his dad.

They waited, shivering. Pima tugged him closer and they huddled together, sharing heat, waiting for nature's violence to pass.

7

THE STORM RAGED for two nights, trashing the coastline, tearing away anything that wasn't tied down. Pima and Nailer huddled through it, watching the roar and rain and holding close as their lips turned purple and their skins pimpled with cold.

On the third day, in the morning, the skies suddenly cleared. Nailer and Pima forced their stiff limbs to move and stumbled down to the beach, joining a ragged assemblage of other survivors who were streaming toward the sands.

They broke through the last of the trees and Nailer stopped, dumbstruck.

The beach was empty. Not a sign of human habitation. Out in the blue water, the shadows of the tankers still loomed, randomly scattered like toys, but nothing else remained. The soot was gone, the oil in the waters, everything shone brightly under the blaze of morning tropic sun.

"It's so blue," Pima murmured. "I don't think I've ever seen the water so blue."

Nailer couldn't speak. The beach was cleaner than he'd ever seen in his life.

"You're alive, huh?"

Moon Girl, grinning at them. Covered with mud from whatever bolt-hole she'd found, but alive nonetheless. Behind her, Pearly and his parents were coming onto the beach, shocked expressions on their faces as they tried to register the changes.

"All in one piece." Pima searched down the beach. "You see my mom?"

Moon Girl shook her head, her piercings glinting in the sun. "She might be over there." She waved vaguely toward the train yard. "Lucky Strike's giving out food to anyone who wants it. Credit for everyone until the ship breaking starts again."

"He saved food?"

"Couple rail cars full."

Pima tugged Nailer. "Come on."

A crowd of people were gathered around the scavenge train, all of them waiting for Lucky Strike to dole out supplies. Pima and Nailer scanned the faces, but there was no sign of Sadna.

Lucky Strike was laughing and saying, "No worries! We

got enough for everyone! No one's starving while we wait for old Lawson & Carlson to come back from MissMet. The rust buyers might be hiding from hurricanes, but Lucky Strike's taking care of everyone."

Lucky Strike was grinning, his long black dreadlocks tied back, but Nailer knew he was also telling people there wouldn't be any rioting for food. And if there was anyone people would obey, it was Lucky Strike.

Lucky Strike had been collecting real power ever since his first bit of luck freed him from heavy crew. Now he smuggled everything from antibiotics to crystal slide into Bright Sands Beach. He had deals worked with the boss men to do whatever he liked. His hand was in the gambling dens and the nailsheds and a dozen other businesses, and the money just rolled in, turning into gold nuggets that he hung glittering from the tips of his dreadlocks or else drove through his ears in thick gleaming rings. The man dripped wealth.

"Keep back!" Lucky Strike shouted. "Keep on back!" He was smiling and looked confident, but he had a line of hired goons standing behind him to back up his authority.

Nailer scanned the arrayed thugs, recognizing some of the killers that his father ran with. It seemed like Lucky Strike had collected the best of the worst for his protection. Even the half-man was there. The monster's huge muscled form loomed over the rest of the thugs, its doglike muzzle snarling and showing its teeth to scare back the hungry people.

Pima caught the direction of Nailer's gaze. "That's the

one my mom's heavy crew used to pull sheet iron. Said he could lift four times what a man could."

"What's it doing up there?"

"Must have figured out that working muscle for Lucky Strike pays better than heavy crew."

The half-man bared its fangs again and rumbled a warning. The crowds that had been closing in on the train cars backed off.

Lucky Strike laughed. "Well, at least you all listen to my killer dog, huh? That's right. Everybody step back. Or my friend Tool here will teach you a lesson in manners. I mean it, everyone, give us some space. If Tool doesn't like you, he'll eat you raw."

The crowd mumbled discontent, but they gave way under Tool's gaze.

"Pima!"

Nailer and Pima turned at the shout. It was Sadna, hurrying toward them, Nailer's father in tow. Sadna swept up to hug Pima.

Nailer's father halted a step behind. He inclined his head. "Guess you saved my ass, Lucky Boy."

Nailer nodded carefully. "Guess so."

Suddenly his father laughed and grabbed him. "Damn, boy! You're not going to hug your old man?" It hurt Nailer's stitches and Nailer winced in the man's grip, but he didn't fight the embrace. His dad said, "I woke up in the middle of that damn storm and had no idea what the hell was going on. Almost killed Sadna before she explained things."

Nailer glanced worriedly at Pima's mother, but Sadna just shrugged. "We worked it out."

"Damn right." His dad grinned and touched his jaw. "She hits like sledgehammer."

For a moment Nailer worried that his father was carrying a grudge, but for once the man wasn't sliding high. He seemed almost rational. As clean as the beach. Already, he was craning his neck to see how food was being distributed.

"Tool's up there?" He laughed and clapped Nailer on the shoulder. "If Lucky Strike'll hire that dog, damn sure he'll take me. We'll eat good tonight." He began shoving through the crowd toward Lucky Strike's guard detail. He didn't look back at Sadna or Nailer or Pima at all.

Nailer breathed a sigh of relief. No hard feelings, then.

The inventory of the beach and the ship breakers continued. Rumor had it that they'd missed the heart of the storm. It had passed to their east, up Orleans Alley, roaring through the old city ruins and then tearing farther north into the sea wreckage of Orleans II. Damage all the way up through the guts of the place, people said.

Which meant that they'd been lucky at Bright Sands, and missed being flattened.

Even with a glancing blow from the storm, the damage to Bright Sands Beach was immense. They found bodies everywhere, tangled in kudzu vines of the jungle, stuck in the trees high up, floating out in the surf. Lucky Strike organized scavenge parties to take care of the dead, burning them or burying them according to their rituals, and making the place safe from disease. Names rolled in.

Bapi had gone missing, either torn apart in the storm or drowned, but gone nonetheless. No one knew if Sloth was alive or dead. Tick-tock and his entire family were found, no sign of damage on them, but all of them dead anyway.

All the scrap and rust buyers who contracted with Lawson & Carlson had fled inland to wait out the storm. With no companies like GE buying scrap for their manufacturing operations, or shipping companies like Patel Global Transit looking to buy scavenge to sell overseas, the ship-breaking yards were idle. The accountants and assayers and corporate guards who weighed and purchased the raw materials that came off the wrecks had left, and with no one around to buy their product, the ship breakers used their days cutting and renewing their shacks, scavenging the jungle, and fishing for food in the ocean. Until things got organized, people were on their own.

Pima and Nailer went scavenging for food, collecting green coconuts that had fallen, before turning to the pools and tides. Out in the distance, the outcrop point of an island was visible.

"There's crabs out that way," Pima said.

"Yeah? Should we go that far?"

Pima shrugged. "Better scavenge without competition, right?" She indicated the silent ships. "It's not like anyone's going to miss us."

They took a hemp sack and a bucket and went seeking,

working their way across the sand, out along the spit that led to the island. All around, the ocean was a glittering mirror. Breakers rolled up to the shore, white as a baby's teeth. The black hulks of the broken ships stood out in the sun, looming monuments to a world that had fallen apart.

Far out on the horizon, a clipper ship skated the ocean, its high sail unfurled. Nailer paused in his collections and watched as it carved across the blue water. So close, and yet so far.

"You going to keep daydreaming there?" Pima asked.

"Sorry." Nailer bent and ran his hand through another tide pool, wincing a little at the movement but still feeling better than he had in days. His bruises were almost all faded, even if his arm was still in a sling and even if there was an annoying burn of soreness in his shoulder. They continued out along the promontory. In places they could look down through clear waters and see where old houses had been built, their concrete foundations showing in the deeps.

"Check it out," Pima said, pointing. "That one must have been a huge house."

"If they were so rich," Nailer asked, "why did they build where they were going to get drowned?"

"Hell if I know. Even rich people are stupid, I guess." Pima pointed out, deeper into the bay. "Not as stupid as the ones who made the Teeth, though."

The waters over the Teeth were calm, a light breeze rippling across them. A few black struts and chunks of construction protruded up through the waves. Beneath the surface, tall brick and steel buildings lurked, their crumbling structures hidden by the water. The people who had built the Teeth had misjudged the sea rise quite a lot. The only time any of their buildings showed was at low tide. The rest of the time, the city ruins were entirely hidden.

"You ever wonder if there's any good scavenge down there?" Nailer asked.

"Not really. People had plenty of time to strip the easy stuff."

"Yeah, but still, there must be some iron and steel we could recover. Stuff that wasn't so scarce when they gave up."

"No one's going after rusty steel when we've got all these ships to gut."

"Yeah, I guess so." Still, it galled him to think of what wealth might lie beneath the waves.

They waded around the rich people's ruins and continued across the spit, aiming for the green tuft of the island. The last bit of distance was a wide sand plain, revealed in low tide, and made easy walking.

They reached the island and climbed up through trees and kudzu vines and bushes, making good time, even with Nailer's bad shoulder. They crested the island. The wide blue ocean came into view. It was almost as if they were out in the middle of the ocean now, so far off shore. With the wind coming off the water, Nailer could pretend he was actually on a deep-sea vessel, speeding toward the horizon. He stared out to the curve of the earth, to the far side of the world.

"Wish you were here," Pima murmured.

"Yeah."

This was as close as he would ever come to the deep ocean. If he thought about it too much, it hurt. Some people were born lucky and sailed on clipper ships.

And then there were beach rats like him and Pima.

Nailer tore his eyes from the horizon and scanned the bay. In the deep water, the shadows of the Teeth undulated. Sometimes ships caught on the Teeth if they weren't familiar with the local coast. He'd seen a fisher hang up and sink on the old struts when it had run itself into the whole mass of towers and then been unable to win free. Some of the ship breakers had gone down, swimming for the scavenge. Depending on tide levels, the Teeth had real bite.

"Come on," Pima said. "We don't want to get caught out here by the tide."

Nailer followed, working his way downslope, letting Pima help him over the rough sections.

"Your dad get drunk yet?" Pima asked suddenly.

Nailer thought back on the morning and his father's good mood. The man sharp-eyed and laughing and ready for the day—but also jittery, the way he was when he didn't have his crystal slide or a handful of red rippers.

"He should be good for a while yet. Lucky Strike won't let him crack heads unless he's clean. Probably won't start until tonight."

"I don't know why you saved his ass," Pima said. "All he does is hit you."

Nailer shrugged. The island's undergrowth was surprisingly thick, and he had to push it aside to keep it from whipping him in the face as he forced through. "He didn't used to. He used to be different. Before all the drugs and before my mom died."

"He wasn't that great before. He's just worse now."

Nailer grimaced. "Yeah, well..." He shrugged, stymied by conflicted emotions. "I probably wouldn't have made it out of the oil room if it weren't for him. He's the one who taught me to swim. You think I don't owe him something for that?"

"Depends how many times a day he cracks your head." Pima made a face. "You give him enough chances, he's going to kill you."

Nailer didn't respond. If he thought about it too much, he didn't know why he'd saved his father, either. It wasn't like Richard Lopez made his life any easier. Probably it was because people said family was important. Pearly said it. Pima's mom said it. Everyone said it. And Richard Lopez, whatever else he was, was the only family Nailer had left.

Still, Nailer couldn't help wishing that he'd ended up with Sadna and Pima, and not Richard Lopez. He wondered what it would be like to live in their shack all the time, and not just when his father was sliding high. To know that he wouldn't have to leave after a day or two and return to his father's place. To live with people you could count on to protect your back.

The undergrowth opened. They stepped out amongst the

tide pools and jagged rocks of the island's tip. Granite intrusions poked above the water and formed a sort of breakwater that defended the island from some of the worst of the new storms. Pima started scooping up storm-stunned croakers and small redfish, throwing them into her bucket. "There's a lot of fish. More than I thought."

Nailer didn't answer. He stared at the rocks beyond. Between them, something reflected like glass, glinting and white.

"Hey, Pima." He tugged her shoulder. "Look at that."

Pima straightened. "What the hell?"

"That's a clipper ship, isn't it?" He swallowed, took a step forward. Stopped. Was it a mirage? He kept expecting it to evaporate. The white boards and fluttering silk and canvas remained. "It is. It has to be. It's a clipper."

Pima laughed softly behind him. "No. You're wrong, Nailer. That's not a clipper ship at all." Suddenly she dashed past him, sprinting for the ship. "That's scavenge!"

Her laughter floated back to him on the wind, teasing him. Nailer shook himself from his stupor and dashed after her. A whoop of joy escaped his lips as he ran across the sand.

Ahead, the gull-white hull of the wreck gleamed in the sunlight, beckoning.

8

THE SHIP LAY on its side, swamped and broken, its back snapped. Even destroyed, it was a beautiful thing, utterly unlike the rusting iron and steel hulks they tore apart every day.

The clipper was big, a ship used for fast transit and freight on the Pole Run, over the top of the world to Russia and Nippon. Or else across the rough Atlantic to Africa and Europe. Its hydrofoils were retracted, but with the carbon-polymer hull shattered, Nailer could see into its workings: the huge gears that extended the foils, the complex hydraulics and precision electronic systems.

The ship's deck was tilted toward them, showing a Buckell cannon and the high-speed reels for the parasails. Once, when Bapi was in a good mood, the man had told Nailer that the big cannon could send a sail thousands of feet into the air to catch high winds that would then yank the ship up onto its hydrofoils and take it skimming across the waves at speeds faster than fifty knots.

Nailer and Pima stopped short, staring at the looming wreckage. "Fates, it's beautiful," Pima breathed.

Even dead it looked like a regal hawk, cracked and shattered, but with a beauty still inherent thanks to the feral grace of its lines. It had the sleek, aerodynamic design of a hunter, every angle purpose-built to reduce drag to the merest fraction. Nailer's eyes swept over the broken clipper's upper decks, the pontoons and stabilizers and the cracked remains of the fixed-wing sails, all of it white, almost blazingly white in the sun. Not a bit of soot or rust anywhere. There wasn't a drop of oil leaking, despite the shattered hull.

Back at the ship-breaking yards, the old tankers and freighters were nothing in comparison, just rusting dinosaurs. Useless without the precious oil that had once fueled them. Now they were nothing but great wallowing brutes leaking their grime and toxins into the water. Reeking and destructive when they'd been created in the Accelerated Age and still destructive even after they were dead.

The clipper was something else entirely, a machine angels had built. The name on the prow was unreadable to either of them, but Pima recognized one of the words below.

"It's from Boston," she said.

"How do you know?" Nailer asked.

"One of my light crews worked on a Boston Freight ship, and it had the same word. I saw it on every single door in the whole damn wreck while we were taking it apart."

"I don't remember that."

"It was before you got on crew." She paused. "The first letter's B, and it's got the S—the one like a snake—so it's the same."

"Wonder what happened?"

"Had to be the storm."

"They should have known better, though. They have satellite talkies for those ships. Big eyes down on the clouds. They should never get hit."

It was Pima's turn to look at Nailer. "How would you know?"

"You remember Old Miles?"

"Didn't he die?"

"Yeah. Some kind of infection got into his lungs. He used to work galley on a clipper ship, though, before he got thrown off. He knew all kinds of stuff about how clippers work. Told me they've got hulls made of special fiber, so they slide through the water like oil, and they use computers to keep level. Measure water speed and wind. He definitely told me they talk to the weather satellites, just like Lawson & Carlson do for when a storm's coming."

"Maybe they thought they could outrun the storm," Pima guessed.

Both of them stared at the wreckage. "That's a lot of scavenge," Nailer said.

"Yeah." Pima paused. "You remember what I said a couple nights ago? About needing to be lucky *and* smart?"

"Yeah."

"How long you think we can keep this a secret?" She jerked her head back to the beach and the ship-breaking yards. "From all them."

"Maybe a day or two," Nailer guessed. "If we're really lucky. Then someone comes out. Fishing boat or a trader will spot it, even if the beach rats don't."

Pima's lips compressed. "We got to claim this for us."

"Fat chance." Nailer studied the broken ship. "No way we can defend a claim like this. Patrols will be looking for it. Corporate goons. Lawson & Carlson will want a piece, if it's full salvage—"

"It's salvage all right," Pima interrupted. "Look at it. It's never going to move again."

Nailer shook his head stubbornly. "I still don't see how we can keep it to ourselves."

"My mom," Pima suggested. "She could help."

"She's got heavy crew. If she disappears to come down and work on it, people will notice." Nailer glanced back toward the beach. "If we aren't back for light crew tomorrow, people are going to wonder where we are, too." He massaged his aching shoulder. "We need goons. And even if we got thug muscle, as soon as they knew about the ship, they'd take it for themselves, too."

Pima chewed her lip, thoughtful. "I don't even know how to register scavenge."

"Trust me, no one's going to let us register this."

"What about Lucky Strike? He's got contacts with the bosses. Maybe he could do it. Keep Lawson & Carlson off us."

"And he'd take it away from us, too. Just like everyone else."

"He's giving out food right now," Pima pointed out. "No one else is doing that. Advances for anyone who can bring two friends to vouch they're good for it once work gears up again."

"We're just licebiters to him. He doesn't need rust from us. Food's one thing..." Nailer stared at the wreck in frustration. So much wealth, if only they could lock it down. "This is stupid. We're just weighing copper in the ducts. We have no idea what's on board. Let's go in and see what we're talking about."

"Yeah." Pima shook her head. "You're right. Maybe there's something good and light we can hide. Then we'll decide about the rest."

"Yeah. Maybe there'll be a reward for the ship, if we report it."

"A reward?"

Nailer shrugged. "I heard about it on a radio play once, at Chen's noodle shack. You get bounty for helping someone out."

"Why don't you just call it bounty, then?"

Nailer made a face. "'Cause they called it a reward." He spat. "Come on. Let's check it out."

They made their way over the last rocks to the ship. At low tide, the hull was surrounded by ankle-deep water. A few fish sat in pools, others lay beached on the sand, rotting with streamers of seaweed. Up close the ship got bigger. Not like the rusting monoliths of the Accelerated Age, but still, it loomed over them. Pima clambered up the shattered edge of the clipper and slipped inside, her hands fast and accomplished from years on wrecking crews. Nailer followed more slowly, hoisting himself aboard with his one good hand.

The ship was on its side, so crawling through its passages was a bit like being in the ducts, an unexpected familiarity to something that should have been so different. Nailer scanned the wreckage. Glints of metal, bits of people's clothes strewn around, all kinds of junk, the stink of rotting fish.

"Swank stuff," he said. He fingered a gown that looked like it was silk. "Look at this clothing."

Pima made a face of dismissal. "Who needs clothes like that?" She clambered out of the hole and up onto the cant of the upper deck, scrabbling along until she found hatch access. A minute later she called, "I found the galley!" Then whistled. "Come look at all this!"

Nailer struggled up to join her. The galley was trashed, all fallen out, but many of the bins of food were still locked in place: rice and flour in sealed containers. Pima started unlatching drawers. Bottles spilled out in a rain of broken glass and the puff of spices. She wrinkled her nose and coughed.

Nailer sneezed. "Slow down, crewgirl."

"Sorry." She coughed again. Opened a locker. Meat spilled out, spoiled already in the heat, big floppy steaks better than anything they could get anywhere on the beaches. They both put their hands over their mouths, breathing shallowly as stink enveloped them.

"I think they had electric cooling in here," Nailer said. "It's the only way they could have kept all that meat."

"Damn. They had it good, huh?"

"Yeah. No wonder Old Miles was so sad he got kicked off."

"What'd he do?"

"He said he was drunk, but I think he was selling red rippers."

Pima peered inside the locker, looking to see if anything was worth saving. Pulled her head out gagging. The reek of the spoiled meat was too strong. They kept going through the ship.

They found the first body in one of the cabins, a shirtless man, his eyes still wide, crabs lurking in his guts. Pima turned away, gagging at the smell of death in the closed room, then peered in again. Fish flopped in a shallow pool beside the man's head. It was hard to tell if the man had drowned or if the ugly gash on his forehead had done him in, but he was dead.

"Well, he won't care if we scavenge," Pima muttered.

"You going to scavenge him?" Nailer asked.

"He's got pockets."

Nailer shook his head. "I'm not touching him."

"Don't be a licebiter." Pima took a breath and crept close to the dead man. Flies exploded in a cloud, buzzing in the warmth of the room. Pima tugged at the man's pants and ran her fingers through his pockets. She was acting tough, but Nailer could tell she was unnerved. They'd both heard stories of fresh scavenge. Bodies came with the territory, but it was still scary to look into a man's dead eyes and think that he'd been walking the decks only a little while earlier, before the storm took it all away and gave it to a couple kids on the shoreline.

Nailer scanned the rest of the cabin. It was big. A cracked photo on the floor showed the man wearing a white jacket with stripes on his sleeves. Nailer picked up the picture and studied it. "I think this was his ship."

"Yeah?"

Nailer scanned the walls. There was an old-style spyglass secured with brackets. Pieces of paper with all sorts of writing on it, seals and official-looking stamps. And then this picture of the man with the braid on his shoulder and him standing in front of a clipper ship, smiling. Nailer couldn't tell if it was the same ship as the wreck or not, but it was obvious the man was full of pride. Nailer glanced over at the bloated torn-open corpse and blew out his breath, thoughtful.

As if sensing his thoughts, Pima looked up from her work. "It's all luck, Nailer. Just luck and the Fates. It's all we got." She flashed scavenged coins at him meaningfully.

It was enough money to feed them for a week. Copper coins and a damp wad of Chinese red paper cash. "Today we're the lucky ones."

"Yeah." Nailer nodded. "And tomorrow maybe we're not."

The captain hadn't been lucky. And now Nailer and Pima were flush because of it. Weird to think about that. The captain lay bloated, his face puffed and purpled, the sun baking and ruining his flesh. Flies buzzed easily around his face: his lips and eyes, the blood on his head, the tear in his stomach. Whole clouds settled back on him as soon as Pima stepped away.

Nailer studied the cabin again, thoughtful. Brass on the walls, all kinds of scavenge. It was a swank boat, for sure. The captain's cabin was rich, and even though the ship was as large as a cargo ship, it didn't look like a working vessel. Everything seemed too nice, all silk and carpeted corridors and brass and copper and little glass lanterns. He and Pima kept going through cabins. They found carved furniture, sitting rooms, lounges, a bar with shattered liquor bottles, staterooms, art on the walls mangled and torn, oil paintings tossed about and punctured.

Down below, in the engineering rooms, where mechanical systems controlled the ship, they found more bodies.

"Half-men," Pima whispered.

A trio of them, bloated and drowned. Their bestial faces looked weirdly hungry with their long tongues hanging out of their sharp-toothed mouths. Yellow dog eyes stared dead at Pima and Nailer, gleaming dully in the tropical sunbeams that penetrated the torn room.

"These people must have been damn swank if they could afford all these half-men."

"That one looks like you," Nailer commented. "You sure you haven't been selling eggs?"

Pima snorted laughter and jabbed an elbow into his ribs, but even she didn't suggest scavenging them. There was something just too creepy about the genetically designed creatures to consider getting close to them.

Nailer and Pima split up and continued to explore the ship. Pima found another dead half-man in the upper decks, strapped to the wheel and drowned. *So much death,* Nailer thought. The people must have been complete idiots to get caught in a city killer. He shoved open another door and whistled, low and surprised.

A table, tilted on its side, crammed against the wall, dark black wood as deep as night. Shattered glass everywhere, goblets thrown about…

"Pima! Check this out!"

She came running. The room was loaded with silver: silver candlesticks, silver tableware, silver platters, silver bowls…a huge Lucky Strike, all for the taking.

"That's a lot of scavenge," Pima gasped.

"That's enough to pay off all our work debts. With that much cash you could set up scavenge on your own. Even buy Bapi's light crew slot."

"Come on!" Pima said. "Let's clear it out before anyone

else shows up. We're rich, Lucky Boy!" She grabbed him and kissed him right, left, and full on the lips, laughing at his surprised expression. "Ohhh, Lucky Boy! We're rich! We're gonna be bigger than Lucky Strike!"

Infected by her spirit Nailer started to laugh, too. They gathered the silver to them, mounding it around, piling it high. They picked through shattered china, broken goblets, and the half-moons of delicate-stemmed glassware, unearthing more and more wealth.

Pima went to find something to hold it all. She returned with hemp sacking that they would have called scavenge just a few minutes ago, could have sold off for a couple copper lengths, and would have called it a good day—and now it was just something to hold the real treasure: all that silver. Serving trays and forks and knives went into the sack. Forks so small that they disappeared in Nailer's hand, spoons so big and deep they could have been used as ladles at Chen's grub shack where he served a hundred head at a time.

Nailer straightened. "I'm gonna see what else there is. There might be more like this."

Pima grunted acknowledgment. Nailer clambered back into the main passage and made his way past a sitting room full of fallen paintings and shattered statuary. Even with a full light crew it would take them several days to strip the clipper of all the brass and copper and wiring. Once he and Pima took the first scavenge off, they'd have to come up with a plan. There had to be some way to get a share of the rest.

Lucky and smart. They needed to be lucky and smart.

The problem was, this Lucky Strike was almost too big to be smart about.

He found another cabin door and kicked it open. An odd room, full of dolls and waterlogged stuffed bears. Gleaming wooden trains built like little maglevs. A torn painting hung on one wall: a clipper ship, maybe even this one, painted from high up, looking down on the deck. All the faces below were looking up, staring into the heights. The artist was pretty good, the painting almost like a photograph. Looking into it gave Nailer a spooky feeling, as if he were about to fall into the painting and onto the deck of that ship. Land on all those people with their swank clothes and cool eyes staring up at him. It was dizzying. He turned away from the image and scanned the cabin again. On the far side of the room there was another door. He crawled along the wall that was now a floor and hefted the door open.

A bedroom: coverlets everywhere and a huge shattered bed. And a beautiful girl, dead in a mangle, staring at him with wide black eyes.

Nailer sucked in his breath.

Even bruised and dead, she was pretty, pinned under the pile of her bed and the weight of all the stuff that had crushed her. Her black hair strung across her face like a wet net. Wide dark eyes stared. Her blouse was torn and soaked, the fabric a complex weave of color and silvery threads. She was young. Not like the captain and the half-men. Maybe Pima's age. A rich girl, with a diamond-pierced nose.

He would have envied her if she wasn't so dead.

He called out to Pima. "Found another deader!"

"Another half-man?" Pima called back. Nailer didn't answer. Didn't take his eyes off the dead girl. Scrambling sounds came from behind, and then Pima appeared.

"Damn," she said. "Too bad."

"Pretty, huh?"

Pima laughed. "Didn't know you liked corpses."

Nailer made a face of disgust. "If I want a girl, there's plenty of live ones, thanks."

Pima grinned. "Yeah, but this one won't slap you like Moon Girl did when you tried to kiss her. Lips look a little cold, though. Kiss that one and she'd take you down to the Scavenge God's scales for sure."

"Ugh." Nailer made a face. Pima spent too much time around heavy crews. It gave her a hard-edged sense of humor.

"She's got gold on her," Pima said.

Nailer had been looking at the girl's black eyes, but Pima was right. Gold around her slender brown throat, gold on her fingers. If it was real, it was a fortune, worth more than anything they'd found so far.

As one, he and Pima crawled across the wreckage to the broken body. The girl's corpse was buried under furniture. None of it had even been secured, as if the rich swanks thought a storm wouldn't dare rearrange their furniture. As if they were gods, and didn't just predict the weather with their instruments and satellites, but also told it what to do.

Nailer shivered at the sight of the broken rich girl. There were lessons there, as powerful as the ones Pima's mother taught when she explained how they were to survive into adulthood. Pride and death came just as fast whether you were Bapi thinking you were the boss of the light crew forever, or whether you were this shattered girl with her fine toys and fine clothes and pretty gold and jewels.

They crouched beside the body. "At least there's no crabs," Pima muttered. She took the girl's necklace and yanked. The girl's head jerked back like a marionette's and the chain parted. The golden pendant swung before them, mesmerizing wealth in Pima's fist. One quick grab and they were richer than anyone except maybe Lucky Strike. They both started working on the dead girl's rings, tugging them from the cool flesh, trying to get them off.

"Damn," Nailer muttered, tugging harder. "Her fingers got all stiff."

"Yours stuck too?" Pima asked.

"They're all fat and waterlogged. None of the rings come off."

Pima drew her work knife. "Here."

Nailer made a face of disgust. "You just going to chop her fingers off?"

"No worse than cutting the head off a chicken. And at least she's not gonna squawk and flap around." Pima set the knife against the girl's finger. "Do it with me?"

"Where do I cut?"

"On the joint," Pima indicated. "You can't cut through the bone. This way, they pop right off."

Nailer shrugged and got out his own knife. He set it against the joint where it would part easily. He pressed his blade into the girl's flesh. Blood welled up as he cut.

The girl's black eyes blinked.

9

"Blood and rust!" Nailer leaped back. "She's not a deader! She's alive!"

"*What?*" Pima scrambled away from the girl.

"Her eyes moved! I saw them!" Nailer's heart hammered in his chest. He fought the urge to bolt from the cabin. The girl lay still now, but his skin was crawling. "I cut her and she moved."

"I didn't see—" Pima stopped midsentence.

The drowned girl's dark eyes focused on her. They went from Pima to Nailer, and back to Pima.

"Fates," Nailer whispered. Cold fingers ran up his spine, raising hackles. It was like their knives had summoned her ghost back into her body. The dead girl's lips started to move. No words came out. Just a barely audible hiss.

"That's some creepy shit," Pima murmured.

The girl continued whispering, a steady stream of sibilants, a chant, a plea, all so low they could barely make out the words. Against his better judgment, Nailer crept forward, drawn by her eyes and desperation. The girl's gold-decorated fingers twitched, reached for him.

Pima came up behind. The girl strained toward them, but they both stayed out of her grasp. More whispered words: prayer sounds, begging, an exhalation of storm and salt terror. Her eyes searched the cabin, widened in fear, terrified by something only she could see. Her gaze locked on Nailer again, desperate, pleading. Still she whispered. He leaned closer, straining to understand her words. The girl's hands fluttered weakly against his arms, reached up to touch his face, a movement light as butterflies as she tried to pull him close. He leaned in, letting the drowned girl's fingers clutch at him.

Her whispering lips brushed his ear.

She was praying. Soft begging words to Ganesha and the Buddha, to Kali-Mary Mercy and the Christian God...she was praying to anything at all, begging the Fates to let her walk from the shadow of death. Pleas spilled from her lips, a desperate trickle. She was broken, soon to die, but still the words slipped out in a steady whisper. *Tum karuna ke saagar Tum palankarta hail Mary full of grace Ajahn Chan Bodhisattva, release me from suffering...*

He drew away. Her fingers slipped from his cheek like orchid petals falling.

"She's dying," Pima said.

The girl's eyes had become unfocused. Her lips still moved but she seemed to be losing energy now, losing her will to pray. The words were a quiet punctuation to the larger sounds of the ocean and coast outside: gulls calling, the surf, the creak and shift of the wrecked ship.

Gradually the words stopped. Her body stilled.

Pima and Nailer exchanged glances.

The gold on the girl's fingers glittered.

Pima lifted her knife. "Fates, that's creepy. Let's get the gold and get the hell out of here."

"You gonna cut her fingers off while she's still breathing?"

"She's not breathing for long." Pima pointed at the bed and sea chests and debris piled on top of her. "She's a goner. If I slit her throat, I'm doing her a favor." She crept close and prodded the girl's hand. The drowned girl didn't respond. "She's dead now, anyway." Pima pressed the knife to the girl's finger again.

The girl's eyes snapped open.

"Please," she whispered.

Pima pressed her lips together, ignoring the words. The girl's free hand brushed at Pima's face and Pima swatted it away. Pima leaned on the knife and blood welled up. The girl didn't flinch. Didn't pull away, just watched, black eyes begging as the knife cut into her brown skin.

"Please," she said again.

Nailer's skin crawled. "Don't do it, Pima."

Pima glanced up at him. "You going to get squeamish on me? You think you're going to save her? Be her white knight like in Mom's kiddie stories? You're just a beach rat and she's a swank. She gets out of here, this ship's hers and we lose everything."

"We don't know that."

"Don't be stupid. This is only scavenge if she's not standing on it saying it's hers. All that silver we found? All this gold on her fingers? You know this boat's hers. You know it. Look at the room she's in." Pima waved a hand at the wreckage around them. "She's no servant, that's for sure. She's a damn swank. We let her out, we lose everything."

She looked at the girl. "Sorry, swank. You're worth more dead than alive." She glanced at Nailer. "If it makes you feel better, I'll put her down first." She moved the knife to the girl's smooth brown throat.

The girl's eyes went to him, starving for salvation, but she didn't speak again. Only stared.

"Don't cut her," Nailer said. "We can't make a Lucky Strike like this...It would be like Sloth was with me."

"It's not the same at all. Sloth was crew. She swore blood oath with you. She didn't have morals. But this swank?" Pima tapped the drowned girl with her knife. "She's not crew. She's just a boss girl with a lot of gold." She made a face. "If we pigstick her, we're rich. No more crew for life, right?"

The gold glittered on the girl's fingers. Nailer struggled with his conflicting emotions. It was more wealth than he had ever seen. More wealth than most of the crews collected in years off the ships, and yet it decorated this girl's fingers as casually as Moon Girl pierced her lip with steel.

Pima pressed her case. "This is once in a lifetime, Nailer. We play it smart, or we're screwed for life." She was shaking and a glitter of tears showed in her eyes. "I don't like it either." She looked down at the girl. "It's not personal. It's just her or us."

"Maybe she'll give us a reward for saving her," he said.

"We both know that's not the way it works." Pima looked at him sadly. "That's for fairy tales and Pearly's mom's stories about the rajah who falls in love with his servant girl. We either get rich, or we die on heavy crew—if we're lucky. Maybe we walk oil scavenge until our legs get sores and your dad beats your head in. What else? The Harvesters? The nailsheds? We can always run red rippers and crystal slide out to the wrecks until Lawson & Carlson string us up. That's what we get. And swanky here? She goes right back to her rich girl life."

Pima paused. "Or we get out. With this gold, we get out for good."

Nailer stared at the girl. A few days ago, he would have cut her. He would have apologized to those desperate eyes, and put the knife in her neck. He would have made it a fast kill so she wouldn't suffer—he wouldn't hurt her the way his dad liked to hurt people—but still he would have cut her dead, and then he would have stripped that gold off her waterlogged corpse and walked away. He would have felt sorry, sure, would even have put an offering on the Scavenge God's scale to help her get on to whatever afterlife she believed in. But she would have been dead and he would have called himself lucky.

Now, though, the dark reek of the oil room filled his mind—the memory of being up to his neck in warm death staring up at Sloth high above him, her little LED paint mark glowing—salvation if only he could convince her, if only he could reach out and touch that part of her that cared for something other than herself, knowing that there was a lever inside her somewhere, and if only he could pull it, she would go for help and he would be saved and everything would be fine.

He'd been so desperate to get Sloth to care.

But he hadn't been able to find the lever. Or maybe the lever hadn't been there after all. Some people couldn't see any farther than themselves. People like Sloth.

People like his dad.

Richard Lopez wouldn't hesitate. He'd slash the rich girl's throat and take the rings and shake the blood off them and laugh. A week ago, Nailer knew for a fact that he could have done the same. This swank girl wasn't crew. He didn't owe her anything. But now, after his time in the oil room, all he could think of was how much he'd wanted Sloth to believe that his life was just as important as hers.

The gold on the drowned girl's fingers glittered.

What was wrong with him? Nailer wanted to punch a wall. Why couldn't he just be smart? Why couldn't he just crew up and cut the girl and take the scavenge? Nailer could almost hear his father laughing at him. Mocking him for his stupidity. But as Nailer stared into the drowned girl's pleading eyes, they might as well have been his own.

"I'm sorry, Pima," he said. "I can't do it. We got to help her."

Pima slumped. "You sure?"

"Yeah."

"Hell." Pima wiped her eyes. "I should pigstick her anyway. You'd thank me later."

"Don't. Please. We both know it's not right."

"Right? What's right? Look at all that gold."

"Don't cut her throat."

Pima grimaced, but she withdrew her knife. "Maybe she'll let us keep the silverware."

"Yeah. Maybe."

Already he was regretting the choice, watching his hopes for a different future fall away. Tomorrow he and Pima would be ship breaking again, and this girl would either live and walk away, or she'd alert the rest of the Bright Sands ship breakers to the scavenge, and either way, he was out of luck. He'd been lucky, and now he was throwing it away.

"I'm sorry," he said again, and he wasn't sure if it was Pima he was sorry for, or himself, or the girl who blinked at him with wide black eyes, and who, if he was very lucky indeed, might not make it through the night. "I'm sorry."

"Tide's coming in," Pima said. "If you're going to be a hero rescuer, you'd better do it quick."

The girl was stuck under all sorts of junk, a wealth of sea chests and the big four-poster bed. It took them almost an hour to pull all the stuff free. The girl didn't say anything more as they worked. Once she gasped as they shifted a chest off her, and Nailer worried that they'd perhaps crushed her in the shifting wreckage, but when they finally pulled her body free, soaked and shivering in the failing light, she seemed whole. Her skin was bloody and her clothes were torn and sopping, but she was alive.

Pima inspected her body. "Damn, Nailer, she's almost as lucky as you." And then she made a face of disgust when she realized that with Nailer's bad arm, Pima was going to be the rescuer after all.

"She's not going to kiss you for a thank-you if you don't crew up." She smirked.

"Shut up," Nailer muttered, but he was suddenly aware of the girl's slim form under her wet clothes, the curve of her body, the flash of thigh and throat that showed in the torn fabric of her skirt and blouse.

Pima just laughed. She levered the drowned girl out of the cabin and down through the canted corridors of the ship until they spilled out the hole in the hull. The girl was heavy, barely able to walk or help in any way. She might as well have been a corpse, Pima commented as she grunted and dragged the girl out. It took both of them to lower her over the side and into the lapping waters of the tide, Nailer awkwardly holding her and lowering her down into Pima's upstretched arms, and then both of them staggering and stumbling in the increasing surf.

"Get the damn silver," Pima grunted. "At least get that sack off. If anyone else finds the ship, we want that hidden."

Nailer clambered back through the ship, collecting. When he stood again at the edge of the hull's cracked hollow, Pima was standing alone in the water, foam up to her thighs. For a moment he thought she'd drowned the girl, but then he saw a flash of pale clothing on the rocks at the base of the island.

Pima grinned. "You thought I pigstuck her, didn't you?"

"No."

Pima just laughed. Waves sloshed around her, splashing up her dark legs, soaking her shorts. The ship creaked in the roll of the waves. "Tide's coming," Pima said. "Let's get going."

Nailer looked across the bay to where the ship-breaking yards shone in the fading sun. "We're never going to get her back over the sand in time."

"You want me to run for a boat?" Pima asked.

"No. I'm beat. Let's hold here on the island and cross in the morning. Maybe we can think of some way to deal with the rest of the scavenge by then."

Pima glanced back at the girl where she lay balled up and shivering. "Yeah, okay. She won't care, one way or the other." She pointed back into the ship. "But if we're staying, let's find what we can in there. There's food. Plenty of other stuff. We'll camp on the island and bring her over tomorrow."

Nailer gave her a mock salute. "Good idea."

He headed back to the pantry, hunting. He found muffins waterlogged with salt. Bruised mangoes and bananas and pomegranates, all scattered through the galley. Saltbeef that was still good and seemed to have barely been touched. A cured ham. There was so much meat he couldn't believe it. Against his will, he was already salivating.

He dragged everything back to where the hull was cracked. He climbed down carefully, cradling everything in a net bag he found in the galley. The water was getting deeper, all right. It tugged and drew at him as he slogged out of the surf, keeping the food high. After ferrying everything from the ship, he noticed their rescued girl shivering and went back to the ship again. It was almost dark inside now. He found blankets of rich wool, damp but still warm, and dragged them out with the rest of the scavenge.

He crossed with waves at his waist, yanked about by frothing surf, holding the blankets over his head. He stumbled up on shore and dumped his load of blankets. He glanced at where the girl was shivering. "You still didn't kill her, huh?"

"I told you I wouldn't." Pima jerked her head toward the shivering girl. "You got stuff for a fire?"

Nailer shrugged. "Nah."

"Come on, Nailer!" Pima made a face of exasperation. "She'll need a fire if you want her to live." She headed back into the wreck, slogging through the rush of the darkening waves.

"See if there's fresh water in there, too!" Nailer called after her.

He picked up the load of blankets and started hauling them to higher ground, hunting for something on the hillside that had a semblance of being flat. Eventually he found an area beside the roots of a cypress tree that wasn't so bad. He started clearing space amongst the rocks and kudzu vines.

By the time he clambered back down to the shore, Pima had returned with a load of the clipper's cracked furniture. She had also found a store of kerosene and a sparker in the mix of trash in the galley. After a few more times shuttling loads of food and fuel up to their camp, they finally hauled up the drowned girl. Nailer's right shoulder and upper back burned with all the activity, and he was glad he hadn't been forced onto light crew today. It was bad enough just doing this little bit of work.

Soon they got the furniture burning merrily, and Nailer cut slices of ham for them to gnaw on. "Good eating, huh?" he said, when Pima held out her hand for more.

"Yeah. Swanks live pretty damn good."

"We're pretty swank ourselves," Nailer pointed out. He

waved at the scavenged wealth around them. "We're eating better than Lucky Strike tonight."

As soon as he said it, he thought it could be true. The fire flickered before him, casting light on Pima and the drowned girl. Illuminating the bags of food, the sack of silver and tableware, the thick wool blankets of the North, the gold glittering on the drowned girl's fingers, shining like stars in the crackle of the campfire. It was more than anyone in the ship-breaking yards had. And all of it was just wreckage for the drowned girl. Her wealth was huge. A ship full of food and luxury, her neck and fingers and wrists draped in gold and jewels, and a face more beautiful than anything he had ever seen. Not even Bapi's magazine girls had been so pretty.

"She's damn rich," he muttered. "Look at everything she's got. It's more than even the magazines have." In fact, he was realizing that the magazine pictures were pretending to reach this level of wealth, and yet somehow had no idea how to attain it. "You think she's got a house of her own?" he asked.

Pima made a face. "Of course she has a house. All rich people have houses."

"You think it's as big as her ship?"

Pima hesitated, working over the thought. "I guess it could be."

Nailer chewed his lip, considering their own rough shelters on the beach: squats made of branches and scavenged planks and palm leaves that blew away like trash whenever storms came.

The fire warmed and dried them and they were silent for a long time, watching as the furniture of the ship crackled and burned.

"Check it out," Pima said suddenly.

The girl's eyes, closed for a long time, were now open, watching the fire. Pima and Nailer studied the girl. The girl studied them in turn.

"You're awake, huh?" Nailer said.

The girl didn't respond. Her eyes watched them, silent as a child. Her lips didn't move. She didn't pray; she didn't say anything. She blinked, staring at him, but still she said nothing.

Pima knelt down beside her. "You want some water? You thirsty?"

The girl's eyes went to her, but she remained silent.

"You think she's gone crazy?" Nailer asked.

Pima shook her head. "Hell if I know." She took a small silver cup and poured water into it. She held it before the girl, watching. "You thirsty? Huh? You want some water?"

The girl made a weak motion and strained toward the cup. Pima brought the water to her lips and she sipped awkwardly. The girl's eyes were more focused, watching both of them. Pima tried to give her more water, but she turned her face away and made to sit up instead. When she had pushed herself completely upright, she drew her limbs inward, curling her arms around her legs. The firelight flickered orange and bright on her face. Pima offered the water again, and this time the girl drank fully, finishing it and eyeing the jug wistfully.

"Give her more," Nailer said, and again the girl drank, this time taking the cup in her own shaking hand. Water spilled down her chin as she drank greedily.

"Hey!" Pima grabbed the cup back. "Watch it! That's all the water we've got tonight."

She gave the girl a look of annoyance, then turned and rifled through the sack of fruit that Nailer had gathered. She came up with an orange that she sliced into wedges and offered to the girl. The girl took a wedge and ate greedily, then accepted another. She was almost feral in her fascination as she watched Pima slice chunks from the orange. But after another few bites, she lay down again, seeming to fold onto the ground with exhaustion.

She smiled weakly and murmured, "Thank you," and then her eyes closed and she went silent.

Pima pursed her lips. She got up and pulled the blanket more fully over the girl's still form. "Guess you've got a live one, Nailer."

"Guess so." Nailer didn't know if he was relieved or saddened by the girl's survival. She lay peaceful now, eyes closed, breathing deeply, asleep it seemed. If she had died, or been crazy, it would have been so much easier.

"I sure hope you know what you're doing," Pima muttered.

10

IF HE WAS HONEST with himself, Nailer could admit he had no idea what he was doing. He was making it up as he went along, some new version of a future, and all he really knew was that this strange swank girl needed to be part of it. This rich girl with her diamond nose jewel and her gold rings and fingers all intact, with her dark glittering eyes alive instead of dead.

He sat on the far side of their furniture fire, arms wrapped around his knees as he watched Pima give her the rest of the orange. Two girls, two different lives. Pima dark, strong, and scarred, tattooed with light crew information and lucky symbols; crop-haired, hard-muscled, and sharply alive. This other one, a far lighter brown, untouched by sun, with long black flowing hair, and movements all smooth and soft, polished and precise, her face and bare arms unmarred by abuse or stray wiring or chemical burns.

Two girls, two different lives, two different bits of luck.

Nailer tugged at his wide-bored earrings. He and Pima both had their share of marks, everything from the tattoos that let them work the crews, to their own carefully worked ink skin scars, showing blessings of the Rust Saint and the Fates. But this girl wasn't marked at all. No decorative tattoos, no work marks, no light gang tats. Nothing. A blank. He was a little shorter than her, but he knew he could kill her if he had to. He couldn't beat Pima in a fight, but this one, she was soft.

"Why didn't you kill me?"

Nailer startled. The girl's eyes were open again, watching him across the fire, reflecting the blaze of shattered ship furniture and picture frames. "Why didn't you kill me when you had the chance?" she whispered.

Her words were cultured, exquisite in her mouth, clipped and close and precise. As if she were one of the boss men who came down to watch the work and paid out cash bonus for good salvage. Perfectly formed words, with not a break in them, not a hard edge. She accepted the last of the orange slices from Pima and ate them, taking her time and seeming to savor them. Slowly, she pushed herself upright again.

Her eyes went from Nailer to Pima. "You could have just let me die." She wiped the corner of her mouth with the palm of her hand, licking at the last of the orange's juice. "I couldn't get out. You could have been rich with my gold. Why?"

"Ask Lucky Boy," Pima said, disgusted. "It wasn't my idea."

The girl looked at him. "You're called Lucky Boy?"

Nailer couldn't tell if it was an honest question or if she was making fun of him. He stifled his unease. "Found your wreck, didn't I?"

Her lips quirked. "I guess that makes me a Lucky Girl then, doesn't it?" Her eyes twinkled.

Pima laughed. She squatted beside her. "Yeah. Sure. Lucky Girl. Damn lucky." For a moment her eyes lingered hungrily on Lucky Girl's hands, on the gold glittering against her brown skin. "Damn lucky."

"So why not take my gold and walk away?" She held up her hand where the thin slivers of their blades had cut. "You could have had my fingers for Fate amulets, right? Could have had my gold and my finger bones, too."

Her smooth features had hardened. She was clever, Nailer realized. Soft, but not stupid. Nailer couldn't help thinking that he'd made a mistake letting her live. It was hard to tell when you were being smart, and when you were being too smart for your own good. And this girl...she already seemed to be taking over the space around the fire. Owning it. Asking the questions instead of answering them.

Lucky Strike always said there was a fine line between clever and stupid and laughed his head off every time he said it. Watching this girl across the fire taunt and tease him, Nailer suddenly had the feeling that he understood.

"I think one of my fingers would have made a nice amulet for you," she said to him. "Would have made you exquisitely lucky."

Pima laughed again. Nailer scowled. Dozens of futures extended ahead of him, depending on his luck and the will of the Fates…and the variable that this girl presented. He could see those roads spinning away from him in different directions. He was standing at their hub, looking down each of them in turn, but he could see only so far, one or two steps ahead at best.

And now, as he stared at the sharp eyes of this perfectly unblemished swank, he realized that he had missed a factor. He didn't know anything about the girl. He knew about gold, though. Gold bought security, salvation from the ships and the breaking and light crew. Lucky Strike had gone down that road. Nailer would have been smarter to simply let Pima pigstick the girl and be done with it.

But what if there were other roads? What if there was a reward for this rich girl? What if she could be useful in some other way?

"You got crew who'll come looking for you?" he asked.

"Crew?"

"Someone want you to come home?"

Her eyes never left his. "Of course," she said. "My father will be hunting for me."

"He rich?" Pima asked. "Swank like you?"

Nailer shot her an annoyed glance. Amusement flickered across Lucky Girl's face. "He'll pay, if that's what you're asking." She held up her fingers. "And he'll pay you more than just my jewelry." She pulled a ring off and tossed it to Pima. Pima caught it, surprised. "More than that. More than all the wealth I've got on my ship." She looked at them seriously. "Alive, I'm more valuable than gold."

Nailer exchanged glances with Pima. This girl knew what they wanted, knew them inside and out. It was as if she were a beach witch, and could throw bones and see right into his soul, to all his hunger and greed. It pissed him off that he and Pima were so obvious. Made him feel like a little kid, stupid and obvious, the way the urchins looked when they were hanging out behind Chen's grub shack, hoping he'd toss out bones for them to pick over. She just knew.

"How do we know you're not lying?" Pima asked. "Maybe you've got nothing else to give. Maybe you're just talking."

The girl shrugged, unconcerned. She touched her remaining rings. "I have houses where fifty servants wait for me to ring a bell and bring me whatever I want. I have two clippers and a dirigible. My servants wear uniforms of silver and jade and I gift them with gold and diamonds. And you can have it, too... if you help me reach my father."

"Maybe," Nailer said. "But maybe all you've got is some gold on your fingers and you're better off dead."

The girl leaned forward, her face lit by the fire, her features suddenly cold. "If you hurt me, my father will come here and wipe you and yours off the face of the earth and feed your guts to dogs." She sat back. "It's your choice: Get rich helping me, or die poor."

"Screw it," Pima said. "Let's just drown her and be done."

A flash of uncertainty crossed the girl's face, so quick Nailer might have missed it if he hadn't been watching closely, but he caught the slight widening of her eyes.

"You should watch yourself," he said. "You're alone. No one knows where you are or what happened to you. You could be drowned in the ocean for all anyone knows. Maybe you just disappear and the wind and waves don't remember you even existed." He grinned. "You're a long way from your swank servants."

"No." The girl drew her blankets around her like a cloak and looked out at the moonlit ocean and the far waves. "The GPS and distress systems in the ship will tell them where to look. It's only a matter of time now." She smiled. "My 'crew' will be coming very soon."

"But right now, you've only got me and Pima," Nailer said. "And you definitely ain't our crew." He leaned forward. "Maybe your people really will hurt us bad—yank out our guts, cut off our fingers—but that doesn't scare us, Lucky Girl." He drew out the words of the nickname, mocking. He waved back toward the ship-breaking yards. "We die here every day. Die all the time. Maybe I'm dead tomorrow. Maybe I was dead two days ago." He spat. "My life isn't worth a copper yard." He looked at her. "So the only way your life is worth more than that gold on your fingers is if it gets us out of this place. Otherwise, you're just as good dead."

As soon as the words were out of his mouth, he realized it was true. He was in Hell. The ship-breaking yards were Hell. And wherever this girl came from, whatever she was, it had to be better than anything else he knew. Even Lucky Strike, who everyone thought lived like a king, was nothing in comparison to this spoiled sleek girl. Fifty people answering to her. Lucky Strike could muster Raymond and Blue Eyes and Sammy Hu, and that was enough for most of his leg-breaking jobs, but it was nothing outside. And even Lucky Strike smiled and scraped when the big bosses from Lawson & Carlson rolled in on their special train to inspect the breaking, before it rolled out again to wherever swanks lived. This girl was from a whole different planet.

And she was going back to it.

"If you want to stay alive," he said, "you take us with you when you go."

She nodded slowly. "That's fair."

"She's lying," Pima said. "Buying time, that's all. She's not our crew. As soon as her people show, she's gone and we're back in the yards." She glanced back to where the invisible hulks of the wrecked ocean vessels lay along the beach. "If we're lucky."

"That true?" Nailer studied the swank carefully, trying

to divine if she was a liar. "You going to ditch us? Dump us back with the rest of the ship breakers while you go back to being swank?"

"I don't lie," the girl said. She didn't look away from his gaze. She held, hard as obsidian.

Nailer took out his knife. "Let's see, then."

He came around the fire to her. She flinched away, but he grabbed her by the wrist, and even though she struggled, he was stronger. He held the knife in front of her eyes. Pima grabbed her by the shoulders, steadying her.

"Just a little blood, Lucky Girl. Just a little," she said. "Just to make sure, right?" The girl didn't stand a chance against Pima's strength.

Nailer dragged her hand toward him. She fought all the way, jerking and twisting, but it was nothing, and soon he had her hand outstretched before him. He pressed the blade to her palm and looked up at her, smiling. "You still swear now?" he asked, looking into her eyes. "We going with you when you go?"

The girl was breathing fast, scared and panicky, her eyes going from the blade to him and back again. "I swear," she whispered. "I swear."

Still, he studied her face, hunting for signs that she'd betray them, that she'd pull a Sloth and stab them in the back. He glanced at Pima. She nodded a go-ahead.

"Guess she wants it."

"Guess so."

Nailer slashed her palm. Blood welled and the girl's hand

spasmed, fingers trembling at the gash. He was surprised she didn't scream. Nailer slashed his own hand and made a fist with hers.

"Crew up, Lucky Girl," he said. "I got your back, you got mine." He held her eyes with his own.

Pima jostled the girl. "Say it."

Lucky Girl stuttered, but she said the words. "I got your back, you got mine."

Nailer nodded, satisfied. "Good."

He pried open her bleeding hand and drove his thumb into the slash of her open wound. She gasped at this new pain and then he pressed his thumb to her forehead. She flinched as he applied the bloody tattoo between her eyes, a third-eye mark of shared destiny. She trembled and closed her eyes as he marked her.

"Now you mark him," Pima said. "Blood with blood, Lucky Girl. That's how we do it. Blood with blood."

Lucky Girl did as she was told, her face frozen as she drove her own thumb into his palm and marked him well.

"Good." Pima leaned close. "Now me."

When it was done, they went down to the black water and rinsed the blood from their hands before hiking back up into the vegetation. The sea was all around, leaving the three of them alone in the darkness as they slowly climbed up to their beacon fire. Nailer's shoulder was tender and inflamed from all the activity and it made climbing difficult. Lucky Girl scrambled ahead of them, loud in the vegetation, unused to climbing, breathing heavily, her clothes torn. Nailer watched her slim legs and smooth form under her skirt.

Pima smacked him. "What? You think you're getting with her after you stuck a knife in her hand?"

He grinned and made a shrug of embarrassment. "She's damn pretty."

"Probably cleans up nice," Pima agreed; then she lowered her voice. "What do you think? Is she really crew?"

Nailer paused in the climb, rotating his shoulder carefully, feeling the sear of his wound across his back. "Being crew wasn't worth a scrap of rust with Sloth. Crew don't mean anything except that we're all sweating together on the same ship." He shrugged and winced at the pain again. "Still, it's worth a gamble, right?"

"You serious about leaving here?"

Nailer nodded. "Yeah. That's the smart thing, right? The *real* smart thing. Nothing here for us. We need to get out, or we die here same as everyone else. Even Lucky Strike got trashed in the storm. Being light crew boss didn't do Bapi any good at all. Just got him killed."

"Lucky Strike did a lot better than us."

"Sure." Nailer spat. "That's what the pig in the pen says when his brother gets knifed for dinner." He shrugged. "You're still in the pen. Still gonna die."

11

NAILER WOKE TO SUN pouring over him, and the luxury of knowing that he still had another couple of hours before the tide would be far enough out for them to make their way back to shore. By this time on any regular day, he would have been on light crew, deep in a duct with LED glowpaint smeared on his forehead like a luck mark, sucking dust and mouse droppings and sweating in the darkness.

The sun shone down through the rustling of ferns and stunted cypress of the island in dapples of light and shadow. Voices interrupted his thoughts.

"No, don't put all the damn wood on at once. Do it slow."

Pima's voice. Lucky Girl said something in return that Nailer couldn't make out but sounded like she wasn't much interested in Pima telling her what to do.

He sat up and gasped with pain. His whole shoulder was on fire, a brutal pain that dug deep and burned like acid. He'd worked it too much yesterday for sure. Too much effort hunting scavenge and getting Lucky Girl out, and now he'd screwed it up again. He moved his arm gingerly, trying to get it to loosen up. The pain was intense.

"You awake?

He looked up. Lucky Girl, peering through the ferns. In the daylight, she was still pretty. Her light brown skin was smooth and clean, freshly scrubbed. She'd pulled her long black hair back and tied it in a knot so that it was out of her way, showing the delicate structure of her face. She grinned at him. "Pima wants to know if you're up."

"Yeah, I'm up."

"Get over your beauty sleep, Nailer," Pima called. "It's breakfast time."

"Yeah?" Nailer pushed himself upright and forced through the ferns to where the girls crouched around a newly built fire. Down on the water, the ship was still there, shifted by the tide, but so tangled in the rocks that it hadn't fled down the coast. Luck was holding, he supposed, especially if they wanted Lucky Girl's people to find her quickly.

He looked around for whatever they were eating. He didn't see anything prepared. "What's for breakfast?" he asked, puzzled.

"Whatever you make," Pima said, and she and Lucky Girl laughed.

"Ha ha." Nailer made a face. "Seriously, what you got?"

"Don't look at me." Pima leaned back on the sandy ground. "I made the fire."

Nailer gave her another dirty look. "We're not on light crew here. You're not the boss of me."

Pima laughed. "Guess you're going to be damn hungry, then."

Nailer shook his head. He started rifling through the sacks of food they'd pulled off the ship the night before. "Don't be surprised when you find snot in yours."

Pima sat up. "You spit in my food, I'll spit in your mouth."

"Yeah?" Nailer turned around. "You wanna try?"

Pima just laughed. "You know I'd kick your ass, Lucky Boy. Just make breakfast and be glad we let you sleep."

Lucky Girl interceded. "I'll help."

Nailer shook his head. "Don't worry about it. Pima doesn't cook because she'd screw it up. All muscle, no brains." He started pulling fruit from a sack, digging through the rest of the food. "Check it out." He pulled out a pound sack of grain.

"What is it?" Pima sat up, interested.

"Wheat berries."

"They good?"

"Pretty good. They chew better than rice." He paused, thoughtful. "You swanks have sugar?" he asked Lucky Girl.

"Down on the ship," she answered.

"Really?" Nailer looked down to the water. He didn't want to have to climb all the way down and come back up. "Can you get some sugar and some fresh water?"

Lucky Girl nodded, surprisingly eager. "Sure."

Nailer kept rifling through the food as Lucky Girl disappeared down the hillside. "Man, I can't believe how much food they have."

"Regular feast every day," Pima said.

"Remember that pigeon Moon Girl brought me for a luck gift?"

"Good eating."

Nailer jerked his head toward Lucky Girl, scrambling into the ship. "Bet she wouldn't think so."

"Is that why you want to leave with her?"

Nailer shrugged. "Never really thought about it until last night..." He trailed off, trying to explain what was in his mind. "You saw her cabin, right? All the scavenge? It's nothing to her. And look at all her rings. Take that diamond out of her nose and you or me, we're rich. But she doesn't even notice."

"Yeah, she's rich all right. But she's not crew. No matter what you say. And I don't trust her. I asked her about her family, who they were..." Pima shook her head. "She ducked and dodged like Pearly when you ask him why he thinks he's Krishna. She's hiding stuff. Don't be fooled just because she looks so sweet."

"Yeah. She's smart."

"More than smart. Sly. You know all that gold on her fingers? Some of it's missing today. Don't know where she hid it, but it's gone now. She's saying all kinds of things about us being crew, but she's running her own game, too."

"Like we aren't?"

"Don't blow me off, Nailer. You know what I mean."

Nailer looked up at the tone in Pima's voice. "I hear you, Boss Girl. We'll watch her close. Now lemme cook." He found a sack of some kind of small dried red fruits and tasted one. They were tart and sweet in a mix. Pretty damn good. He tossed one to Pima. "You know what this is?"

She tasted. "Never had it." She held out her hand. "Gimme some more."

He grinned. "No way. I'm using them. You'll just have to wait."

He set the sack out beside the wheat berries and stared at all the food, so casually kept in the ship. "I never really thought about how bad it is here. Not until yesterday. Not until her." He paused. "But you got to think, if she's that rich, there's other swanks out there. There's money out there. And it ain't here. Even Lucky Strike's a joke, in comparison to what she's got."

"So you think you can just go live with her or something? Happily ever after?"

"Don't make fun of me. Even the people on her crew are richer than Lucky Strike."

"If she's telling the truth."

"You know she is. And you know if we stay here, we never get anything."

Pima hesitated. "You think we can take my mom?" she asked.

"Is that what you're worrying about?" Nailer smiled. "We saved the swank's life. She owes us big-time blood debt. 'Course we can take her."

"What about Moon Girl? Pearly? Rest of light crew?"

Nailer paused. "Lucky Strike didn't share," he pointed out finally. "He worked his own deal."

"Yeah..." Pima didn't sound convinced, but her next words were interrupted by Lucky Girl scrambling back up out of the greenery and vines.

"Got it!" she panted, smiling.

"Nice." He grinned at Pima. "She'd be good on light crew when work starts up again, huh?"

Pima didn't smile. "She'd sell pretty good to the nailsheds, too." She turned away.

Lucky Girl frowned. "What's wrong with her?"

"Nothing," Nailer said. "She just gets moody when she's hungry."

As he took the jar of water that Lucky Girl had carried up, he gasped. His shoulder was on fire. He almost dropped the water.

Pima looked up. "What's wrong with you?"

"My back," Nailer said through gritted teeth. "It hurts like a snake bite."

"That means it's infected," Pima said. She hurried over.

"No." He shook his head. "We cleaned it."

"Lemme see." She pulled off the bandaging and sucked in her breath. Lucky Girl took one look and gasped.

"What the hell did you do to yourself?"

Nailer craned his neck around, but he couldn't see. "How bad is it?"

Lucky Girl said, "It's really infected. There's pus everywhere." She came closer, businesslike. "Let me take a look. I'm trained in first aid. From my school."

"Swanky," Nailer muttered, but Lucky Girl didn't respond. Her fingers probed and pressed against the wound. He flinched at the searing fire.

"You need antibiotics," she said. "This smells awful."

Pima shook her head. "We don't have those here."

"What do you do when you're sick?"

Nailer grinned weakly. "Let the Fates decide."

"You're insane." Lucky Girl stared at his wound again. "I should have something on the *Wind Witch*," she said. "There's a whole medical closet. There ought to be some kind of 'cillin."

Nailer shook her off. "Let's eat first."

"Are you crazy?" Lucky Girl looked from him to Pima. "You don't wait on something like this. You take care of it now."

Nailer shrugged. "Now or later, what's the difference?"

"Because it just gets worse and worse." Her face hardened. "And then you die from it. This looks like you've got a superbacteria. We need to do something fast, or you're not going to make it."

Without warning, Lucky Girl shoved her thumb into his back, into the heart of the wound. Nailer screamed and scrambled away. He clutched at his shoulder, gasping. The pain was so bad he thought he'd black out.

When he had himself under control he yelled, "What'd you do that for?"

"Crew up, Nailer." Lucky Girl made a face. "You can't collect a reward for saving me if you're dead. Let's get your ass down to my ship and get you fixed up."

"Crew up." Pima laughed and hit Lucky Girl on the shoulder. "Swank's starting to talk like us." She grinned again, then gave Nailer a serious look. "She's got a point. Your mom would have been damn glad to have money for some 'cillin. You want to go out like she did?"

Sweating and sobbing. Skin like fire. Her neck swollen with infection. Eyes red and pus-filled.

Nailer shivered. "Okay, you want to play doctor, go for it." He snagged an orange as he started down the hillside. "I'm not going out like she did, though. Won't happen."

Despite his words, it was hard to get down to the water, and it was worrying. His arm and shoulder and back were all on fire. Lucky Girl and Pima guided him down, going slowly, both of them helping, reaching out to support him like he was an old lady made of sticks.

As he made his way farther down the hill, Lucky Girl's words lingered, unwelcome. A reward wouldn't do him any good if he was dead. He forced down his rising fear, but still it tickled at the back of his mind.

He'd seen other people's wounds turn nasty, sick with rot and gangrene; seen their stumps crawling with maggots where they'd gone bad after having an amputation. Despite his bravado, a trickle of fear ran strong in him. His mom had prayed to Kali-Mary Mercy and she'd died in a haze of flies and fever pain. A superstitious part of Nailer wondered if the Scavenge God was balancing the scales of his Lucky Strike with a sickness that would kill him before he got to reap the rewards. Sadna was right. He should have made more offerings to the Scavenge God and the Fates after he got out of the oil room. Instead, he'd just spit on that luck.

They reached the ocean. The ship had rolled during the night, turning itself nearly upright; it made it harder for them to climb aboard. Pima finally hauled Nailer up, groaning, her muscles flexing as she dragged him up like a dead pig, then left him lying on the carbon-fiber decking while she and Lucky Girl went below.

When they finally came back, they were both shaking their heads.

"It's all broken open," Lucky Girl said. "The ocean must have gotten it." She surveyed the wreckage of the ship. "I don't see anything in the water." She shook her head again. "It's all lost now."

Nailer shrugged, making a show of nonchalance. "When your people get here, they can give me medicine." But even as he said it, he wondered how much time he had. He was shaking now, and even though he sat in hot sun, he felt chilled.

"With your satellites it won't be long, right?"

"Yeah. Sure." Lucky Girl sounded uncertain.

Pima nodded at the girl's jewelry. "With your gold we could buy medicine from Lucky Strike, no problem."

Lucky Girl looked up from her study of Nailer. "This Lucky Strike has medicine?"

"Sure," Pima said. "He's crewed up with the boss men. Gets them to bring things on the train."

"No." Nailer shook his head. "We can't let anyone know about the wreck. They'll pull the scavenge." He shivered. "We need to keep low until Lucky Girl's people show up. Then we can do whatever we want. We let people know now, and they'll come after our scavenge with everything they got."

"It's not your scavenge," Lucky Girl said fiercely. "It's the *Wind Witch,* and it's my ship."

Pima shook her head. "Just a wreck now. And you're only alive because Nailer's nicer than most of our people. Had himself some kind of religious experience out there. Got the fever eye, now, for sure."

Nailer shook his head. "I don't have fever eye."

Pima shot him a glance. "You don't think you're paying the price for all your luck?"

"What's fever eye?" Lucky Girl asked.

Pima stared at her. "You don't know fever eye?"

127

She shook her head. "Never heard of it."

"When dying people look into the future? Last look before the Fates take them?"

"I don't have fever eye." Nailer felt tired. He sat heavily on the canted deck, perched in the sun. "Maybe if I wash it, it will make it better."

"Don't be stupid." Pima spat. "Nothing's going to make that better except medicine."

Nailer put his head on his arms. "How long? Till your people come?"

Lucky Girl shrugged. "The GPS tracker will bring them. Soon, I think."

"You're that important?"

She seemed embarrassed. "Pretty much."

"Who're your people?" he asked. "You're cagey about it."

She hesitated.

"We're crew," Pima reminded her.

"My name's Chaudhury. Nita Chaudhury."

They shrugged. "Never heard the name."

"I have my mother's name, until I inherit." She hesitated. "My father's name is Patel." She waited expectantly.

There was a pause; then Pima said, "Patel? Like Patel Global Transit?" Pima and Nailer exchanged glances as shock rolled over them. "You're a boss girl?" Nailer asked. Pima's face turned furious. She lunged at Nita and shook her. "You're one of the damn blood buyers?"

"No!"

"Patel Global buys all kinds of scavenge down here," Pima said. "We see their logo all the time. Them and General Electric and FluidDesign and Kuok LG. Everyone's always talking about keeping quota so the blood buyers won't find another supply. Go across to Bangladesh or Ireland. Lawson & Carlson won't even supply filter masks because they say they've got to keep costs low."

"I don't know." Nita looked embarrassed. "It's a corporate priority...to source from recycled materials vendors." She hesitated. "Ship breaking would be one possible trade source for raw components." She looked away. "I've never really followed that side of the company."

"You goddamn swank." Pima's face had turned harsh. "You're lucky we didn't know who you were when you were still lying under your bedroom furniture."

"Leave her alone, Pima." He was feeling worse, feeling tired and nauseous. "We got bigger problems." He pointed to the horizon. "Check it out."

Pima and Nita turned. All three of them stared across the sand flats to where the last of the tide was trickling away. From the direction of the ship-breaking yards, a crew of people was headed toward them—eight or ten, all in a knot.

"That your crew coming for you?" Pima asked. "Maybe your blood buyer people?"

Nita ignored the jibe and craned her neck to stare across the waters. "I can't tell." She scrambled into the ship and came back with a spyglass. She trained it on the distant walking forms. "I'm seeing a lot of scars and tattoos. Your people?"

Pima took the glass and peered through.

"Well?" Nita pressed. "Is it one of your scavenge crews?"

Pima shook her head. "Worse than that." She handed the spyglass to Nailer.

"What do you mean worse?" Nita asked.

Nailer cradled the spyglass in his good hand and peered at the distant beach. The view slid over reflecting sand and salt water pools until he found the figures hurrying across. He focused on the faces, found the leader. "Blood and rust," he cursed softly.

"What's wrong?" Nita asked again. "Who is it?"

Pima sighed. "His dad."

12

RICHARD LOPEZ WAS FAST, coming across the sand flats where the water had run out. He had a surprisingly big crew with him as well, all his hungry ones, the ones who did rough work, kept the yards in line when it suited them, did nothing the rest of the time. They glinted with scavenge jewels, with steel necklaces and copper twists on their biceps. Crew tattoos snaked over their skin. Men and women who had done heavy crew work and then slipped out of the yards and into the twilight life of the beach with its nailsheds and gambling dens and opium holes.

Nailer watched them, forcing down the creeping fear he felt at the sight of his father's grinning features in the spyglass. He recognized a couple of the others. A hard-faced stringy woman who everyone called Blue Eyes and who scared Nailer maybe even more than his father scared him. He startled at the sight of another, a full foot taller than any of the others and massively muscled. Tool, the half-man, who Nailer had seen last at Lucky Strike's side. He recognized another, Steel Liu, a skull cracker from the Red Python gang. All of them bad news, no matter how you cut it.

The dragons on his father's shoulders rippled. His father was leading the whole band, striding ahead, grinning, showing his tangled yellow teeth. Through the scope, he was so big it felt as though the man had already arrived.

Nailer shivered and it wasn't just the creeping infection in his back that chilled him. "We need to hide."

"You think they already know we're here?" Pima asked.

"We better hope not." Nailer tried to get to his feet, but it was too tiring to stand. He motioned for Pima's help.

"What's wrong with his dad?" Nita asked.

Nailer made a face as Pima hauled him upright. It was too difficult to describe all the things that Richard Lopez was. Talking about his dad was like talking about city killers. You thought you understood them, and then they were on you and they were so much worse than you remembered. "He's bad," he muttered.

Pima got herself under his arm, supporting him, and started helping him down the slope of the deck. "I saw him kill a man in the ring," Pima said. "Beat him down and killed him, even after everyone said he'd already won. Beat him bloody, left him with his head cracked open."

Nailer's face felt like it was carved from wood. He looked again across shimmering water to his father's progress across the sands. He and his crew were coming fast. This time of day they were probably already sliding high.

"If they get hold of Lucky Girl, she's dead," Pima said. "Your dad won't want her getting in the way of scavenge."

Nailer looked over at Nita. "This would be a good time for your people to show up."

Nita shook her head. "Too soon, I think." She didn't even look to the horizon. "What else can we do?"

Nailer and Pima exchanged glances. "Let's get out of here," Pima said. "Let them search the ship. There's plenty of good scavenge. Maybe it'll keep them busy and we can sneak back to the beach later. Tonight or something."

Nailer stared at the antlike forms. "He'll still be looking for me, even when we go back."

"We don't know that. He's so damn high, he probably doesn't even remember he has a son."

Nailer remembered the time when his father, high and angry, had taken a man twice his size, blurringly fast, a broken bottle and blood on the ground. He blew air out through his lips. "Yeah, let's get out of here."

"You're sure we can hide?" Nita asked.

"You better hope so," Nailer said through gritted teeth

as they helped him slide clumsily over the side. "If they catch us..." He shook his head.

"But aren't you family?"

"Doesn't mean anything if the man's sliding," Pima answered. "Even Nailer's afraid of his dad when he's high."

"Sliding? That's a drug?"

Nailer and Pima exchanged glances. "Crystal slide. You don't know it?"

She looked puzzled.

"Red ripper?" Pima tried.

"Bloodrock," Nailer said. "Steely breeze? Hornytoads? Bliss bleeders?"

She sucked in her breath. "Bleeder?"

They both shrugged. "Could be."

She looked at them both, horrified. "That's what surge rats use. Combat squads. Half-men. It's for animals." She caught herself. "I mean..."

"Animals, huh?" Nailer exchanged a tired smile with Pima. "That's about right. Just a bunch of animals here, making money for you big bosses."

Nita had the grace to look embarrassed. Nailer stumbled out of the surf and stared up at the island's foliage above. Dizziness washed over him. He held out a hand to the rich girl. "Help me. I don't think I can climb."

The haul back up into the island undergrowth was a nightmare of pain and struggle. Finally they huddled again at their makeshift camp. Nailer curled on the ground, panting and dizzy. Two hundred feet below, the white hull of the clipper was visible through the greenery. Shouts of pleasure echoed up to them. Cheers from the men and women as they swarmed onto the scavenge. They were laughing and whooping. Nailer tried to prop himself up, to see what was happening below, but he was feeling worse and worse. Chills swept over him in steady surges even though the sun was pouring down on him.

"I need blankets," he whispered. The girls wrapped him, but still he couldn't stand the sweeping chills and the ice that filled him. He shivered uncontrollably. Sweat dripped in his eyes. His teeth chattered, waves of fever surging through.

Below, his father and his cronies clambered over the wreck with the feral grace of tiger monkeys.

"We are so screwed," Pima muttered.

Nailer could barely speak through his chattering teeth. He wanted to tell Pima to check the far side of the island, to make sure they weren't going to be surprised, to tell swanky Nita Chaudhury that she needed to keep her damn head lower, that the adults below weren't smart but they were plenty sly, and they'd look around sometime. At some point, they'd get tired of hooting about all the wealth, and start making sure they had the scavenge protected for themselves.

He wished they'd fled before the tide had come. It was stupid not to assume that someone would be coming. The ship was too big not to attract notice. Little scavengers only had so much time to profit before the lions rolled in and took the vast share of the meat. And now they were hiding and watching and stuck, while the lions stalked through the ship's carcass and laughed and cracked open liquor they'd found in the galley. They tossed plates of silver onto the deck and shattered fine china against the rocks with shouts of pleasure, china that even he and Pima had guessed might be more valuable than the silver it sat beside. Then again, if you couldn't smelt it, it wasn't worth a copper yard on a ship-breaking beach, so maybe they were right to destroy it all, maybe they should light the damn ship on fire, turn the sky black...

Nailer shivered. He was going crazy. He needed to lie still. He was so tired. Needed to lie down and rest.

"We need to get you back to the yards," Pima whispered.

Nailer shook his head. "No. They'll get Lucky Girl."

"I don't care. Let her hide or be found. You need medicine now."

He could barely force the words through his chattering teeth, but he stared at her as hard as he could, trying to make Pima understand. "She's crew, yeah? Bloodmarked just like me and you."

Pima looked away. Nailer knew what she was thinking. There was crew, proved over years of scavenging together and sharing the take, sharing the risks of thefts, putting aloe on belt marks after a bad night with Richard Lopez, fighting to get onto light crew and then sweating hard to keep the quota coming through...

And then there was day-old crew.

"Pima." He clutched at her. "If you think I've got the fever eye then you better believe we need to keep our Lucky Girl safe, even if she's a blood buyer. We need her."

Pima didn't answer.

Nita crouched beside him, studying him with concern. "He needs a doctor."

"Don't tell me what he needs," Pima snapped. "I know damn well what he needs." She peered through the ferns at the men below. "No way we can get him across the flats without them catching sight of us, and then they'll want to know what we found." She shook her head. "We're trapped."

"I could go down," Nita offered. "It would distract them."

Nailer shook his head violently. Pima stilled, studying her. She looked to the men again, grimacing. "If you actually knew what you were offering, I'd let you do it." She shook her head. "No way." She glanced at Nailer. "You're crew, anyway." She almost said it like she meant it.

"Well, well," a familiar voice interrupted. "What we got here?"

The sunburned face of Nailer's father peered through kudzu vines, grinning. "I thought we saw something moving—" His eyes widened with surprise. "Nailer?" His eyes flicked back and forth, skitter quick, high and fast, looking all of them over. "What are you kids up to? Scavenging ahead of us?"

His gaze fell on Lucky Girl. "And who's this pretty little thing?" His eyes scanned her, wide and fascinated; then he grinned again. "Soft girl like you could only come off a big boss boat." He smiled at Nailer. "Didn't know you were crewing with swanks, boy." His wide blue eyes swept over her body, lingered. "Pretty."

"She's our crew," Nailer said through his shivering.

"Yeah?" A knife flickered into Richard's hand. "Come on down, then. All of you together. Let's get a good look at what the light crew's got for us." He turned and shouted, "Up here!"

A moment later, Blue Eyes and the half-man Tool and a couple others surrounded them and goaded them out of their camp. They scrambled clumsily back down through the weeds and ferns, with Nailer's dad's friends all making comments. They whistled at Pima and Nita, slapped and pinched them. Laughed harder when Pima tried to fight.

When they were out and collected on the clipper ship, the men and women gathered around.

"You have scavenge for us?" the huge half-man asked. He lifted Nita up as though she weighed nothing at all, bringing her face close to his own blunt, doglike features. He studied her jeweled nose ring with his yellow eyes.

"It's a diamond," he announced. Everyone laughed. One huge finger touched the jewel. "Do you want to give it to me? Or should I rip it off your pretty face?"

Nita's eyes widened. She reached up and unclasped her jewelry.

"Damn," Richard said. "Look at all that gold."

While the half-man held her, he and Blue Eyes ripped the rest of the rings off Nita's fingers. Nita cried out, but Nailer's father held his knife to her neck and she held still as Blue Eyes ripped the gold off, leaving bloody streaks. They all whistled at the amount of blinding metal. More than a year's profit in one of the rings, let alone all of them. The adults were rich, and they were drunk on it.

Nailer crouched, shivering on the deck, watching as they tore away Nita's wealth. Even with the sun burning down from overhead, he was freezing. And now he was almost uncontrollably thirsty as well. The last of the rain and storm water had evaporated and if there was more water in the bowels of the ship, he couldn't stand to find it, and none of his father's crew was likely to let Pima or Nita go look. All of the adults hunkered on the vessel, calculating their scavenge and scheming how to ensure their claim.

"We'll have to cut Lucky Strike in," his father announced finally. "We get half, but we don't end up bloody, and he can move the scavenge out on the train."

The rest of the crew nodded. Blue Eyes glanced over at Nailer and Pima and Nita. "What about the swank?"

"Our little girlie?" His father looked over at Nita. "You going to fight us for scavenge, sweetheart?"

"No." Nita shook her head. "It's all yours."

Nailer's father laughed. "Maybe you say so now, and maybe you change your mind later." His knife flashed in his hand. He came over and crouched beside her, the big knife gleaming over his knuckles, ready to slit her open the way he gutted fish. No big thing to dump her intestines on the ground. Just a way to get food. Not even personal.

"I won't stop you," Nita whispered, her eyes dilating in terror.

"No." Nailer's father shook his head. "You're right about that. Because your guts are going to be feeding the sharks and no one's going to care what you say, yes or no. Maybe in your big boss house people care what happens to you." He shrugged. "Here, you're nothing at all."

Through his delirium, Nailer could see his father's building willingness to do violence. He recognized the signs from when his father would strike, quick as a cobra, and slap Nailer upside the head or yank him close to sink a fist into his stomach.

The gutting knife gleamed bright in the high sun. His father dragged Nita close. Nailer tried to speak, tried to say something that would save her, but he couldn't get the words out. The chills were coming so fast now.

Out of nowhere Pima lunged, her knife flashing.

Nailer tried to cry out, to warn her, but his father beat him to it. He slammed Pima aside. She sprawled on the decking. Her knife skittered across the carbon fiber and disappeared over the side. Pima was bigger than most of the light crew, but she was nothing against his father's crystallized speed. The man grappled with her for a moment, then twisted her into a choke hold. His crew rushed over, shouting. Tool got to her first and yanked her upright, lifting her from the deck entirely. He pinned Pima's arms behind her, leaving her writhing and struggling fruitlessly.

A necklace of blood beads glinted ruby on his father's neck.

"Damn girl, you nicked me." He grinned and ran his fingers down the wound. Held up his hand slicked with blood. Nailer was amazed that Pima had come so close. She'd been so fast. His father inspected the red smear thoughtfully, then showed it to her. "Close." He laughed. "You should fight in the ring, sweetheart."

Pima struggled against the restraining hands. Nailer's father slipped close. "You almost got lucky, girl." He gripped Pima's face with his bloody fingers. "So damn close." He held up his knife in front of her eyes.

"My turn now, right?"

"Cut her," someone in the gang whispered. "Open her wide," Blue Eyes urged. "We'll scavenge her blood for an offering."

Pima shuddered in Tool's grip, but she didn't flinch as Richard touched her cheek with his blade. She'd gone away already, Nailer guessed. She knew she was dead. He could recognize it, her acceptance of the Fates.

"Dad." Nailer coughed. "She's Sadna's girl. She saved you in the storm."

His father hesitated, holding the knife to Pima's face. He traced it across the girl's jaw.

"She tried to kill me."

Nailer tried again. "Even up with Sadna. Life for life. Balance the scales."

His father scowled. "You always were the smart boy, weren't you? Always trying to tell your dad what to do. Always full of yourself." He let his knife slide down between Pima's breasts to her stomach. He looked over at Nailer. "You trying to tell me what to do now? You telling me I can't put her guts on the ground? Think I can't open her if I want?"

Nailer shook his head violently. "You want to gut her, that's your right. She d-drew b-b-blood." His teeth chattered. It was a fight just to stay conscious. Pima and Nita were staring at him. Nailer continued. "Y-y-you want her b-blood, it's yours. It's your r-r-r-right." He was feeling worse, feeling more and more dizzy. He took a breath, trying to remember even what he wanted to say. Forced the words out, carefully enunciating. "Pima's mom helped me pull you out when the storm came. No one else would have helped me. No one else could have." He shrugged helplessly. "We owe Sadna."

"Damn, boy." Richard cocked his head. "It still sounds to me like you're trying to tell me what to do."

Tool's voice rumbled. "Perhaps a lesson for the girl, instead of a death. A gift of wisdom to the young."

Nailer looked up at the half-man, surprised, and tried to press his advantage. "I'm just saying we owe her mom a blood quota, and everyone knows it. It's bad karma if people think we don't pay back."

"Bad karma." Nailer's father scowled at him. "You think I care?"

"Balancing a blood quota shows no weakness," Tool rumbled.

Richard looked from Nailer to Tool. "Well, look at this. I guess everyone wants the girl alive." He smirked, then lifted his knife and drove it for her gut.

Pima cried out, but Richard stopped short of spilling blood. He grinned as he withdrew the blade's point from where it dented her skin. "Looks like you get a free one, girlie."

He took one of her hands in his and looked into her eyes. "We're balancing the scale, 'cause of your mom," he said. "But if you put a knife on me again I'll strangle you with your guts. Got it?"

Pima nodded slowly, not blinking, eye to eye. "Got it."

"Good." Richard smiled and pried open her hand.

Pima gasped as he grabbed her pinky. Bone crackled. Nailer flinched at the sound. Pima screamed and then choked off her pain, whimpering. Richard took her ring finger. Pima's breath came in ragged gasps. He smiled, getting his head down so they were eye to eye again. "Now you know better, don't you?"

Pima nodded frantically, but still he wrenched her finger. Another bone snapped and she cried out.

"Learn your lesson yet?" he asked.

Pima was shaking, but she managed to nod.

Nailer's father grinned, showing his yellow teeth. "Glad

to know you won't forget." He examined her broken fingers, then got into her face again, his voice low with promise. "I was nice to you. I could have taken every finger you got and no one would have said I was wrong, even with a blood debt." His eyes were cold. "Remember that I didn't take as much as I could have."

He stepped away and nodded at the half-man. "Let her go, Tool."

Pima collapsed to the deck, whimpering and cradling her hand. Nailer forced himself not to go to her, not to try to comfort her. He wanted to curl up in a ball on the hot deck and close his eyes, but he couldn't; he wasn't done yet. "Y-y-you going to gut the swank now?" The shivering was uncontrollable.

His father glanced over at the bound girl. "You got something to say about that, too?"

"She's damn r-r-rich," Nailer stuttered. "If her people are looking for her, she's worth something." A wave of shivering overtook him. "M-m-maybe worth a lot. Maybe more than the sh-ship."

His father evaluated the girl, considering. "You worth a reward?" he asked.

Nita nodded. "My father will be looking for me. He'll pay to keep me safe."

"That right? A lot?"

"This was my personal clipper. What do you think?"

"I think you've got an attitude." Nailer's father smiled, feral and pleased. "But you just bought your guts back, girlie." He showed her his knife. "And if your dad won't pay enough, we'll pig-open you and see how you squeal."

He turned to his crew. "All right, boys and girls. Let's get the scavenge off. I don't want to share too much with Lucky Strike. Everything light and valuable, off the ship."

He turned and looked out at the sea. "And hurry. Tides and the Scavenge God don't wait for anyone." He laughed.

Nailer let himself lie back on the deck. The sun blazed overhead. He was freezing. His father crouched beside him. When he touched Nailer's shoulder, Nailer cried out. Richard shook his head.

"Damn, Lucky Boy, looks like you're going to need some medicine." He looked out across the bay to the ship-breaking yards. "As soon as we get some of this scavenge off, we'll go make a deal with Lucky Strike. He should have a 'cillin. Maybe even a suppressor cocktail."

"I n-n-n-eed it s-s-soon," Nailer whispered.

His father nodded. "I know, son. I know that. But when we show up, we're going to have to explain how we can pay for your meds, and then there'll be questions about how your old man got so much silver and gold." One of Nita's rings flashed in his hand. "Look at this here." He held it up to the light. "Diamonds. Rubies probably. You found a swanky girl, all right." He shoved the ring into his pocket. "But we can't sell until we've got the muscle in place. Otherwise they'll try and pull it all out from under us."

He looked at Nailer seriously. "This was a lucky find, boy. We got to play it smart though, or we'll lose it all."

"Yeah," Nailer said, but he was losing interest in the conversation. He was tired. Cold and tired. Another wave of shaking swept over him. His father yelled at his men to bring some blankets.

"I'll be back," he said. "Soon as we have the score secure, we'll get your meds." He stroked Nailer on the cheek; his pale eyes looked as bright and crazed as Nailer felt his own must be.

"I won't let you die, son. Don't you worry. We'll get you taken care of. You're my blood and I'll take good care of you."

And then he was gone and Nailer sank into fever.

13

"SO THAT'S YOUR DAD, huh?"

Nailer opened his eyes to find Nita kneeling beside him. He was lying on solid ground, the sound of the ocean far distant. A rough blanket covered him. It was nighttime. A small fire crackled beside them. He tried to sit up, but his shoulder hurt and he lay back again. Felt bandages, new ones, different from the ones Sadna had given him a lifetime before.

"Where's Pima?"

Nita shrugged. "They've got her fetching food."

"Who?"

She nodded over at two shadows who sat not far away, smoking cigarettes and passing a bottle of booze back and forth, their gang piercings twinkling in the darkness, rings running along the ridges of their eyebrows and studding down the bridges of their noses. One, Moby, pale as a ghost, stringy and angular from sliding crystal. The other, that huge loom of shadow and muscle, the half-man Tool. They smiled at Nailer as he moved.

"Hey, hey, looks like Nailer's gonna live." Moby waved his liquor bottle at Nailer in a sort of toast. "Your dad said you were a tough little rat. Didn't think you were going to make it, though."

"How long have I been down?"

Nita studied him. "I'm not sure you're really up."

"I'm up."

"Three days, then, so far."

Nailer tried to open his memories, seeking any recollection of the last three days. There were dreams, nightmares, but nothing solid, periods of heat and cold and shaking images of his father peering into his eyes...

Nita glanced back at the two men. "They were betting on whether you'd live."

"Yeah?" Nailer grimaced and tried to sit up. "What were the stakes?"

"Fifty Red Chinese."

Nailer looked at her, surprised. Those were big stakes. More than a month's wages on heavy crew. The scavenging of her ship must have been successful. "Who bet on me living?"

"The skinny one. The half-man was sure you were dead." She helped him sit up. He didn't feel like he had a fever anymore. Nita pointed at a bottle of pills, swank pills by the lettering on the side. "We've been grinding those up and putting them in water. The other guy"—she paused, hunting for a name—"Lucky Strike. He sent a doctor."

"Yeah?"

"You're supposed to keep taking the pills, four a day for another ten days."

Nailer eyed the pills without enthusiasm. Three days unconscious. "Your people haven't showed up yet?" he asked. It seemed obvious that they hadn't.

Nita glanced over at the men, suddenly nervous, then shrugged. "Not yet. Soon I think."

"Better hope so."

She gave him a dirty look. As she turned away from him, he spied the manacle that connected her ankle to one of the big cypress trees. She caught the direction of his gaze. "They're not taking any chances."

Nailer nodded. A minute later Pima appeared, chaperoned by a third adult. Blue Eyes. The woman had scars carved into her arms and legs, bits of scrap steel embedded in her face and necklaces of scavenge twined around her throat. A long zipper of scar tissue in her side showed where she had made a devotional sacrifice to the Harvesters and the Life Cult. She shoved Pima forward.

Moby glanced over. "Hey, careful with the kid. She's got my dinner."

Blue Eyes ignored him, instead looked at Nailer. "He's alive?"

"What's it look like?" Moby answered. "'Course he's alive. Unless he's a zombie, walking dead. Wooooooooo." He laughed at his own joke.

Pima distributed metal tins to the adults, rice and red beans and ground sausage spiced. Nailer watched the food as it was passed around, entranced. It was astonishingly good eating. He didn't remember the last time he'd seen so much meat passed around so casually. As the food was handed to Moby and Tool, Nailer found himself salivating. Moby started to eat even as Blue Eyes watched him. "You tell Lopez his kid is alive?" she asked.

Moby shook his head between mouthfuls of rice and beans that he shoveled in with his hand.

"What the hell does he pay you for?" Blue Eyes asked.

"He just woke up," Moby protested. "Two minutes back in the world of the living, if that." He elbowed Tool. "Back me up. The little rat just woke up."

Tool shrugged, scooped up a handful of rice and meat chunks. "Moby isn't lying this time," he rumbled. "As he says, the little rat just woke up." He smiled, showing sharp canine teeth. "Just woke up in time for dinner." He popped the mass of food into his mouth.

Blue Eyes made a face. She took Moby's tin away and handed it to Nailer. "Go get your own feed, then. Boss man's kid eats first. And tell the boss he's awake."

Moby scowled at her, but he didn't protest. Just got up

and headed out. Pima crouched beside Nailer, spoke in a low voice. "How you doing?"

Nailer made himself smile even though he was already feeling tired again. "Not dead yet."

"Must be a good day, then."

"Yeah." He dug into the food.

Pima jerked her head at Nita. "We need to talk. Lucky Girl's people haven't showed up yet." Her voice dropped to a whisper. "Your dad's starting to get jittery."

Nailer glanced at the guards. "Jittery how?"

"He's got his eye on her. Maybe like he wants to hand her over to Blue Eyes and the Life Cult. Keeps talking about how much copper he could make off her pretty eyes."

"She know what he's planning?"

"She's not stupid. Even a swank like her can figure it out."

Blue Eyes interrupted their conversation, squatting down beside them. "Having a nice chat?"

Nailer shook his head. "She's just checking on me."

"Good." Blue Eyes smiled, hard and cold. "Then shut up and finish your food."

Tool showed his teeth from where he sat on his stump. "Good advice," he rumbled.

Pima nodded and slipped away without protest.

That was more telling than anything else. She was afraid. Nailer glanced at her hand, saw that her broken fingers were splinted on a bit of driftwood. Nailer wondered if it was their breaking or something else that had happened in the last three days that made Pima so wary.

Nita finished her food, said to no one in particular, "I'm getting pretty good at eating with my hands."

Nailer glanced over. "What else would you eat with?"

"Knife, fork, spoon?" She almost smiled and then shook her head. "Never mind."

"What?" Nailer pressed. "You making fun of us, Lucky Girl?"

Nita's face turned careful, almost fearful, and he was glad about that. He scowled at her. "Don't go looking down on us 'cause we don't have your swank ways. We could have cut your fingers off and your damn knife and fork and spoon wouldn't have been much good then, would they?"

"I'm sorry."

"Yeah, sorry after you already said it."

"Shut up, Nailer," Pima said. "She's sorry."

Tool stared at Nita with his dead yellow eyes. "Maybe not as sorry as she could be. Right, boy?" He leaned forward. "Do you want me to teach your swank a lesson in manners?"

Nita suddenly looked very frightened indeed. Nailer shook his head. "No. Never mind. She gets it now."

Tool nodded. "Everyone does eventually."

Nailer shivered at the half-man's flat words, the disinterest in his voice. This was the first time he'd been this close to the creature. There were plenty of stories about him, though. About where he got the vast webwork of scars that decorated his face and torso. About how he waded through the swamps, hunting for alligators and pythons. People said he wasn't afraid of anything. That he'd been engineered so he couldn't feel pain or fear. He was the only thing Nailer had ever seen his father talk about with careful respect rather than abusive authority. The half-man was damn scary, and watching the way Tool looked at the girl, he thought he knew why.

"Never mind," Nailer said again. "She's fine."

Tool shrugged and went back to his food. They all sat in silence. Beyond the ring of their firelight, there was nothing except animal sounds and insects, the black wildness of the jungles and swamps, the swelter of the interior. From the distant sound of the surf, Nailer guessed they were at least a mile from shore. He lay back on the ground watching the flames flicker. The food had been good, but he was tired again. He let his mind drift, wondering what his father was planning, and why Pima looked so worried, and what was going on behind Lucky Girl's swank eyes. He drifted off.

"Damn, boy, you're awake, I hear."

Nailer opened his eyes. His father crouched over him, smiling, his tattooed dragons and bright crystal slide amphetamine eyes on him.

"I knew you'd make it," his dad said. "You're tough like your old man. Tougher than nails, right? Just like I named you. Just like your old man." He laughed and punched

Nailer's shoulder and didn't seem to notice Nailer flinch at the pain. "You look a lot better than a few days ago." Richard Lopez's skin was pale and sweating in the firelight and his grin was wide and feral. "Wasn't sure if we'd be putting you down with the worms."

Nailer made himself smile, trying to gauge his father's crystal-bright mood. "Not yet, I guess."

"Yeah, you're a survivor." He glanced over at Nita. "Not like the rich girl. She'd have been dead a long time ago, if it wasn't for me saving her swank ass." He smiled at her. "I'm almost hoping your dad doesn't show up, girl."

Nailer sat up and folded his legs under himself. "Her crew hasn't showed?"

"Not yet."

His father took a swig of whiskey and offered the bottle to Nailer. Pima spoke up from across the circle. "Doctor said he's not supposed to drink."

Nailer's dad scowled at her. "You trying to tell me what to do?"

Pima hesitated. "Not me. Lucky Strike's doctor said it."

Nailer wanted to tell her to shut up, but it was already too late; his father's mood had shifted, a storm gathering where there had only been clear skies before.

"You think you're the only one who heard that damn pill man?" Richard asked. "I'm the one that brought that pill man out. I paid him and I got him to put my boy back together." He went over to Pima, the whiskey bottle swinging loose in his hand. "And now you're telling me what he said?" He leaned close. "You want to tell me again? Just in case I didn't hear you?"

Pima had enough sense to shut up and duck down. Nailer's dad examined her. "Yeah. Smart girl. I thought you wanted to shut the hell up. No sense, kids these days."

He grinned at his goons. Blue Eyes and Moby grinned back. Tool just studied Pima with his dog eyes. "You want me to teach her a lesson?" he rumbled. "Remind her?"

Richard asked, "What do you think, girl? You need a little lesson from Tool here? Maybe see if he teaches any better than me?"

Pima shook her head. "No, sir."

"Look at that." Richard smiled. "Polite now, ain't she?"

Nailer tried to intervene. "How come the swank's still here? Where's her people?"

Richard's attention swung back to Nailer. "Wish we knew, don't we? Girl *says* there's people looking for her. *Says* someone gives a damn. But nobody's come looking. No ships. No people in on the train, looking on the coast. Not a single swank showing up, asking questions." He licked his lips as he studied Nita. "It's starting to look like no one gives a damn about one little rich girl. Maybe she's not even worth her kidney weight. Be tragic if we ended up scavenging our rich girl for spare parts, wouldn't it?"

"Should we try to reach out to her people?" Nailer asked. "Find a way to tell them where she is?"

"Wish we knew where they were. From over in Houston, she says. The Uppadaya Combine. Some kind of shipping clan. Lucky Strike's got some people trying to track them down."

Nailer startled. "Uppadaya?" He broke off as Pima flashed a warning signal. Nailer glanced at her, puzzled. Why had Nita lied about her name? If she was really with Patel Global, there should have been ways to contact her people, right here on the beach. "What's your plan?" he asked instead.

"Hard to say. I've been thinking she must be worth a lot, seeing as how swank she is, but I'm also thinking that she's a bit of trouble for us. Maybe these Uppadaya have big connections, boss connections, the kind that bring their skull-crackers in and make trouble for hard-working people like us." Nailer's father paused, thoughtful. "Maybe I'm thinking she's too damn dangerous and we're better off if she's feeding the pigs. We already have her ship, and sure as hell she knows too damn much about us now." He said it again, quieter. "Too damn much."

"But she's got to be worth something."

Richard shrugged. "Maybe she's worth a whole hell of a lot, and maybe that's even worse than if she's worth nothing." He looked up. "You're a smart kid, Nailer, but you should pay attention to your dad. I've got some years on my skin, and I'll tell you, a swank like her always means trouble for people like us. They don't give a copper yard about us, but they sure like their own. Maybe they pay us for her and then maybe they come back with guns and clear us out like a snake nest, instead of saying thank you."

Nita protested. "We wouldn't—"

"Shut up, swank." Richard's voice was flat, disinterested. He turned his cold eyes on her. "Maybe you're worth something. Maybe not. But I know for damn sure that your flapping mouth annoys the hell out of me." He pulled out his knife. "I hear much more out of you and I think I'll take those pretty lips off. Make you smile even when you're sad, little swank." He stared at her. "You think your crew would want you back without your lips?"

She fell silent. He nodded, satisfied. He sat down with Nailer, put his head low, close, almost touching. Nailer could smell the sweat and whiskey of him, see the redness of his eyes.

"You had the idea, boy." Richard glanced at the girl. "But the more I think about it, the worse it sounds. We got a big score off the ship. Everything's going to be different now. We're damn rich, all set up with Lucky Strike. That clipper's down to the ribs now. Got real crews stripping it. Another couple days, it'll be like that ship never existed." He grinned. "Not like breaking one of those old tankers. These little ships come apart easy." He glanced over at Lucky Girl. "This girl doesn't do us any good, though. Maybe she makes big bosses pay attention to us. Maybe she makes us targets. Maybe gets people asking questions about scavenge and where it came from and who owns it and who gets rich from it."

"No one would say anything to the swanks."

"Don't kid yourself," Richard muttered. "They'd sell their mothers for a chance to pull a Lucky Strike."

"Give it time," Nailer whispered. "Give it a little time and we'll be even richer."

All he could think of was how badly he wanted to get away from his father with his twitchy eyes and fast, high smile, the face of a man deep in his slide.

Richard's eyes went to the girl again. "If she wasn't so pretty, I would have bled her out already. She draws too much attention." He shook his head. "I don't like it."

Nailer said, "Maybe we can get her people to pay for her without knowing who sold her. She's still secret, right?"

Nailer's dad grinned. "Just my crew." He studied Blue Eyes and Moby and Tool. "Maybe too many, though. Secrets don't keep when someone's throwing cash around." He glanced at the girl. "Keep an eye on her for another day; we'll see what turns up." He stood and Nailer struggled to his feet as well, but his father pressed him back. "You stay here. Rest. Sadna's asking questions about where you and Pima went. I'm playing dumb, you know? Don't want anyone else knowing what's going on. Make sure they don't make any trouble."

"Sadna's looking for us?" Nailer tried to keep the hope from his voice.

"She heard a rumor maybe we found Pima." He shrugged. "She's got no cash, though. And no one talks without Red Chinese in their hands." He turned and nodded to Tool and Blue Eyes and Moby. "Keep 'em tight."

The three of them nodded, Blue Eyes smiling, Moby

swigging from his bottle, Tool impassive. Richard disappeared into the vines and night screech of the jungle, a pale skeleton of a man fading into the blackness.

When Richard was gone, Moby grinned and took another swig from his bottle. "You're running out of time, girlie," he said. "Your people don't show up quick, maybe I'll take you for my own. You look like you'd make a nice little pet."

"Shut up," Tool rumbled.

Moby glared at him but closed his mouth. Tool glanced at Blue Eyes. "You watching first?" Blue Eyes nodded. Tool pushed Moby a little ways away, both of them bedding down in the nearby bushes. Soon a snore marked where Tool lay, and Moby's voice, complaining still, was barely audible through the ferns. Mosquitoes swarmed around them. Nita slapped miserably at the bloodsuckers. Everyone else ignored them.

Blue Eyes came over and put a chain cuff around Pima's wrist, then turned to Nailer.

"You going to give me trouble?"

"What?" Nailer gave her a look of incredulity. "You going to tell my dad you put a cuff on me? I'm the one who came up with this Lucky Strike."

Blue Eyes hesitated. She seemed tempted to chain him as well, but also uncertain, not entirely sure if he was a captive or an ally. He stared back at her, challenging. Nailer knew what she was seeing, a skinny ribbed boy just out of a fever and crazy Richard Lopez behind him. It wasn't worth it.

Sure enough, Blue Eyes gave up on the idea. She sat down on a rock and picked up a machete, started sharpening it. Pima and Lucky Girl stared at him, their eyes full of meaning. The fire burned lower. He didn't like his father's hints. The man was on the verge of decision and anything could tip him.

Nailer stretched out on the ground beside Pima. "How's your fingers?"

She smiled and held up her hand. "Pretty good. Glad he didn't decide to teach me five lessons."

"Hurt much now?"

"Not as much as the money we lost." Her voice was brave, but he thought the fingers must hurt awfully. The splint looked ragged. She followed the direction of his gaze. "Maybe we can break 'em again and get 'em to grow straight."

"Yeah." He looked over at Lucky Girl. "How you doing? Anything broke on you?"

"Shut up!" Moby yelled from the bushes. "I'm trying to sleep."

Nailer lowered his voice. "Your people coming soon?"

Lucky Girl hesitated. Her eyes flicked fearfully from him to Pima and then to Blue Eyes a little ways away. "Yeah. They're coming."

Pima looked at her. "Yeah? That right? *Patel?*" She drew out the name. "They really coming, or you just full of lies? Someone from your crew could be down on the beach right now, some blood buyer from your clan, if you're really a Patel, but you're not saying anything. What's with that?"

Again the skitter eyes of fear. Lucky Girl pushed her black hair off her face and stared at Pima defiantly. "What if they aren't coming?" she whispered fiercely. "What you gonna do then?"

Her voice had taken on some of the hard edge of Pima and Nailer's own inflections. Nailer would have laughed if she hadn't seemed so fearful. She was lying. He'd seen enough liars in his life to know. Everyone was always lying to him. Lying about how much they'd worked, about how much quota they'd filled, about whether they were afraid, about whether they were living fat or starving. Lucky Girl was lying.

"They aren't coming." He stated it as fact. "You've got no one looking for you. I don't think you're even a Patel."

Lucky Girl glanced at him fearfully. Her gaze went again to Blue Eyes, obsessively sharpening her machete. Pima tugged her earrings thoughtfully, cocking her head. "That right, girl? You're worth nothing?"

Nailer was surprised to see that Lucky Girl was on the verge of tears. Even Sloth hadn't cried when she'd been kicked down the beach with knife slashes through her crew tattoos, but here this soft girl was on the verge of crying because she'd been caught in a lie. "Where are your people?" he asked.

She hesitated. "North. Above the Drowned Cities. And I *am* Patel. But they won't know where to look for me." She paused. "I'm not supposed to be here at all. We threw away our GPS beacons weeks ago, trying to get away."

"From who?"

She hesitated, then finally said, "My own people."

Nailer and Pima exchanged puzzled looks.

Nita explained quietly. "My father has enemies within our company. When we got caught in the storm, they were pursuing us. Everywhere we went, they anticipated us. If they catch me they will use me as leverage."

"So no one's coming looking for you?"

"No one you would want to meet." She shook her head. "When our ship wrecked, two other ships were pursuing us, but they turned back from the storm."

"So that's why you were sailing into a city killer? You were running?"

"It was either that or surrender." She shook her head. "It wasn't a choice we could make."

"So no one's coming for you." Nailer couldn't help repeating it, trying to get his head around this new fact. "You jerked us around this whole time."

"I didn't want you to take my fingers."

Pima let out her breath in a slow hiss. "You should have given yourself up to whoever was chasing you. Nailer's dad is worse than anything they could do to you."

Lucky Girl shook her head. "No. Your people...they have an excuse. The ones who hunted me..." She shook her head again. "They are worse."

"So you wrecked a whole ship and tried to drown yourself just so they couldn't catch you?" Nailer asked. "Killed your whole crew so you could stay free?"

She glanced over. "They were..." She shook her head. "Pyce's people would have killed them all anyway. He wouldn't have wanted witnesses."

Pima grinned. "Damn, the swanks and the rust rats are all the same at the end of the day. Everyone's looking to get a little blood on their hands."

"Yes." Nita nodded seriously. "Just the same."

Nailer considered the situation. Without someone to buy Nita back, she was worth nothing. Without strong friends or allies on the beach, she was just meat. No one would even blink if she went under the knives of the Harvesters. Blue Eyes could hand her over to her cult, and no one would think twice about protecting her.

Pima looked Nita over. "Hard life here, for a swank like you. You won't survive unless you get yourself a protector, and there's not much percentage in sheltering something like you."

"I can work. I can—"

"You can't do anything unless we say so," Pima said brutally. "No one cares about a swank like you one way or the other. You got no crew. No family. You don't got your goons and money to make them respect you, either. You're worse off than Sloth. At least she knew the rules. Knew how to play the game."

"You really don't have any people, then?" Nailer asked. "No one who might help you?"

"We have ships..." Nita hesitated. "Our clan has ships

and some of the captains are still loyal to my father. They come to the Orleans for the Mississippi trade. If I could get there, I could reward you—"

"No more reward talk, Lucky Girl." Pima shook her head. "You've run out of that."

"Yeah." Nailer glanced over at Blue Eyes, who was sharpening a new machete. "How 'bout we quit the lying?" He nodded at Nita's scarred palm. "We shared blood and you're still lying to us."

Nita gave him a dirty look. "You would have cut my throat if you didn't think I was valuable."

Nailer grinned. "Guess we'll never know. But we got you now and you're not worth a copper yard." He fell silent.

Pima watched him. "It's a damn long way to the Orleans," she said. "Gators and panthers and pythons. Lots of good ways to die."

Nailer considered. "Don't only have to go overland."

"Can't sail it. Your old man would know a skiff was missing and be after you in no time."

"I'm not thinking about a skiff."

Pima stared at him. "Blood and rust." She shook her head. "No way. You remember Reni? You remember what he looked like afterward? There wasn't anything left of him. Just meat pieces."

"He was drunk. We won't be."

Pima shook her head. "It's crazy. You just got your shoulder pulled back together and you want to wreck it again?"

"What are you talking about?" Nita asked.

164

Nailer didn't answer her directly. It was possible. It was just possible. "You a good runner, Lucky Girl?" He looked her over. "You got soft skin, but you got any muscles under your skirts? You fast?"

"She's too soft," Pima said.

Nita looked at him fiercely. "I can run. I took first in the hundred meter at Saint Andrew's."

Nailer smiled at Pima. "Well, then, if Saint Andrew says she can run, then she must be pretty fast."

Pima shook her head and made a small prayer to the Fates. "Swanks run on funny little tracks against other swanks. They don't run for their life. They don't know how."

"She says she can run." Nailer shrugged. "I say we let Fates judge."

Pima glanced at the girl. "You better be as fast as you say, 'cause you only get one chance."

Nita didn't blink. "I ran out of chances a long time ago. It's all Fates now."

"Yeah, well, welcome to the club, Lucky Girl." Pima grinned and shook her head. "Welcome to the damn club."

14

RUNNING OR NOT, they needed to get away from their captors. In whispered conference they made a plan and settled in to wait. It was a fight for Nailer to stay awake. Even though he'd been out for three days, he was still having a hard time keeping his eyes open. The breezes in the trees and the warmth of the night made him sleepy. He put his head down, telling himself he would keep watch. Instead, he slept, woke, and slept again.

Blue Eyes, alert and wide-awake, switched to Tool, who simply sat and stared. Every time Nailer peeked between slitted lids there was Tool, staring back at him with his yellow dog's eyes, patient as a statue. Finally, Tool stood down to Moby. The skinny bald man settled himself comfortably against a stump and started drinking. He was half reclined and it wasn't long before he had drunk himself back into his deep slumber, trusting in the shackles and the sleeping forms of young people for his sense of security.

Nailer lay awake, waiting. Glad to still be unrestrained. Even if he wasn't one of this adult crew, he was one of his father's and so he had some trust. Between association with his father and their own memories of him as a feverish invalid, he had some wiggle room. He wasn't a risk in their minds, just a skinny light crew kid recovering from sickness. That was all to the good.

The problem was that Blue Eyes had the keys to the girls' shackles, and she scared the hell out of him. Nobody who got in with the Life Cult was good news. Novices were always looking for new recruits. And they were always hungry for sacrifices.

As soon as Moby was snoring, Nailer began easing toward where he had seen Blue Eyes bed down. He went slowly, as slowly as any child who has learned to steal at an early age, whose best chance of survival is in silence and remaining unnoticed.

He gripped his duct knife with sweaty fingers, his hand slick with fear. There was no way to search Blue Eyes and find the keys without waking her. The knife felt small and useless in his palm, a toy. This was a necessary thing, but he didn't have to like it. It wasn't as if he felt guilty. He didn't. Blue Eyes had done worse in her time and would do worse in the future. He had seen her torture people who held back on quota, or who fell behind on loans. He had seen her take off a man's hand for stealing from Lucky Strike, and then watched the man bleed out under her cool blue gaze. And who knew how many beach rats she'd drugged and collected into the mysteries of her church? She was hard and deadly and Nailer had no doubt that if his father asked her to do it, she would kill him and Pima and Lucky Girl, and sleep well afterward.

He didn't feel guilty.

And yet still, as he stole close, his heart pounded in his chest and the blood thudded in his ears like beach drums. It was the sort of killing that his father would accomplish with quick efficiency. Richard Lopez understood the qualities of kill or be killed intimately, the zero-sum calculations that said it was better to be alive than dead, and he would not have hesitated to take advantage of a sleeping opponent.

Quick and fast, Nailer told himself. *Across the throat and be done.*

A few years before, his father had made him kill a goat, to show him the method of the knife, to show how a blade pierced flesh and snagged on tendons. Nailer remembered his dad crouching over him, wrapping his fist around Nailer's own. The goat had lain on its side, legs bound, its sides heaving up and down like a bellows, breath whistling through its nostrils as it sucked its last air. His dad had guided Nailer's hand, setting the knife against the goat's jugular.

"Press hard," he'd said.

And Nailer did as he was told.

Nailer parted the ferns. Blue Eyes lay before him, her breathing gentle. In sleep, her features were smooth, unbitten by the smolder of violence that lurked there otherwise. Her mouth was open. She lay on her belly, arms tucked under her and held close against the relative cool of the night. Nailer said a prayer to the Fates. Her neck wasn't as exposed as he had hoped. He needed to strike fast. She needed to die immediately.

He slipped close and steeled himself. Readied the knife and leaned in, holding his breath.

Her eyes opened.

Panicked, Nailer rammed the knife into her throat, but Blue Eyes moved too fast. She rolled away, bouncing to her feet. She swept up her machete. She didn't say anything. Didn't shout or beg or yell in anger. Her shadow blurred. Nailer leaped back as her machete whistled past his face. She lunged after him again. Nailer raised his knife, but instead of coming at him again with her blade, Blue Eyes simply swept a leg under him. Nailer crashed to the ground. Blue Eyes landed on top of him, driving the air from his lungs. She slapped his knife away, leaving his fingers numb and stinging.

He lay panting, pinned under her weight. Blue Eyes pressed the machete to his neck.

"You poor dumb kid," she muttered.

Nailer's breath rasped out of him. He was shaking with fear. Blue Eyes smiled and hefted her machete. She gently touched his right eye with the blade. "I grew up with men sneaking up on me in the middle of the night." The blade moved and tapped lightly on his left eye. "Little licebiter like you doesn't stand a chance." She grinned and moved the machete back to his right eye.

"Pick," she said.

Nailer was too frightened to understand. "W-what?"

Blue Eyes touched each of his eyes significantly with her blade.

"Pick," she said again. "Right or left?"

"My dad—"

"Lopez would take both." She smiled. "And I will too, if you don't choose." Again the blade caressed his eyeballs. "Right or left?"

Nailer steeled himself. "Left."

Blue Eyes grinned. "Right it is."

She flipped the machete and drove it toward his eye.

A whirl of shadow crashed into Blue Eyes. The machete stabbed past his head, leaving a burn on his cheek, and Blue Eyes's weight came off him. She rolled, locked in struggle with another form. Shouts rose all around in the darkness. Steel clashed, accompanied by the screams and whimpers and grunts of people fighting. There were people all around.

Blue Eyes and her opponent rolled, tangled limbs flashing, a furious scuffle. In the moonlight, Nailer could make out his savior: Pima's mother, grappling with Blue Eyes for the machete. Sadna slammed a fist into Blue Eyes's face. Bone crunched. Blue Eyes bucked and tore free of Sadna's grasp. She rolled and came up with her machete. The two women circled.

"Break off, Blue Eyes," Sadna said. "It's not your fight."

Blue Eyes shook her head. "Boy owes me, Sadna. Thought he could take my blood. Can't let that go."

And then she swept forward, faking high with the machete before slashing low. Sadna leaped back over a mossy log and scrambled for footing. Blue Eyes plunged after her, seeking an opening. The blade whirled. Blood sprayed from Sadna's hands where she tried to ward off a blow. Sadna cried out but didn't falter, dodged out from under Blue Eyes's follow-up cut.

Blue Eyes lunged again, testing. "Run, Sadna," she said. "Run." Blood ran from her nose where Sadna had crushed it, but she didn't seem to care. When she smiled, her teeth were black with it.

Nailer scrambled to find his knife. All around, other bodies grunted and fought, a tangle of forms that had to be Sadna's heavy crew. He fumbled through the grasses, seeking the gleam of his blade.

Sadna slipped behind a tree, using it for a shield. Blue Eyes circled, chasing her, then stopped and smiled. "I'm not playing chase," she muttered. "You want the boy alive or not?" She turned and lunged for Nailer. He scrambled away, but it was enough to bring Sadna out from behind the tree. Blue Eyes reversed from her feint and surged toward Sadna in a flash of steel.

"No!" Nailer shouted.

The world seemed to slow. Blue Eyes's machete carved for Sadna's throat. Nailer watched, horrified, expecting a flare of blood from Sadna's neck. But Sadna wasn't there. She ducked and tumbled on the dirt, crashing into Blue Eyes's legs and knocking the other woman off her feet.

Again they rolled, entangled, a whirl of limbs and the machete's blade. Nailer cast about for his knife, saw it lying in the leaves. He grabbed it as Blue Eyes came up on top of Sadna, her machete pressed against Sadna's throat. Sadna's own fists gripped the machete as well, fighting to keep the edge from pressing home. Her breath rasped raggedly under the blade. Blue Eyes increased the pressure.

Nailer slipped toward Blue Eyes, his knife slick in his hands. Sadna's eyes widened as he came up behind. Blue Eyes, warned of the threat, started to turn.

Nailer leaped onto her back and rammed the knife into her neck. Hot blood poured over his hand. Blue Eyes screamed as his blade tore at the corded muscle of her neck. *Just like killing a goat*, Nailer thought inanely.

But Blue Eyes didn't die. Instead she reared up, carrying him clinging on her back. He tried to yank out the knife and stab her again, but the blade was stuck. Blue Eyes flailed for him, trying to reach around and get hold of him, then bent forward sharply and tumbled him over her back. He clung desperately, but she hammered him off with the hilt of her machete. Light exploded in his head. He hit the ground.

Blue Eyes stood over him, one hand pressed against her

gushing wound and the knife still embedded in her neck. She swung her machete at Nailer, a clumsy swing that nonetheless whistled through the air. Her gaze followed him, devil bright, determined to take him with her to whatever afterlife her cult promised. Curses bubbled out of her mouth and blood with it, thick. She lunged again for Nailer.

Nailer dodged, trying not pin himself up against a tree or allow himself to trip. Why didn't she die? Why wouldn't she just die? Superstitious fear shot through Nailer. Maybe she was actually a spirit, a zombie creature that could not be killed. Maybe the Life Cult had done something to her, made her immortal.

Blue Eyes slashed again, but as she lunged forward to follow up, she tripped and sprawled on the ground. Still she reached for him. Nailer stood frozen before her. Her hand touched his feet, clutched for his ankle. Her blood was black in the moonlight, a deep pool spreading. Nailer yanked his foot away from her twitching fingers. Blue Eyes stared up at him. Her lips moved, promising death, but no words came out.

Sadna pulled him away from the dying woman. "Come on. Let her go."

Blue Eyes's blood was all over him. The dying woman's eyes followed him, hungry. Her fingers twitched.

Nailer shuddered. "Why won't she die?"

Sadna glanced at the shuddering woman. "She's dead enough." She ran her hands over him. "Are you okay?"

Nailer nodded weakly. He couldn't take his eyes off Blue Eyes. "Why won't she die?" he whispered again.

Sadna pursed her lips. "Sometimes people have more will to live. Or you don't hit them right and they don't lose their blood fast enough. Sometimes they just don't stop the way you want them to." She glanced over at the woman. "Look, she's gone now. Let her go."

"She's not."

Sadna jerked his face around to look into her dark eyes. "Yes, she is. She's gone. And you're not. And I'm glad you were there when I needed you. You did good."

Nailer nodded. He was shaking with adrenaline. Pima and Lucky Girl were freed and they ran over to where Sadna and Nailer squatted.

"Damn," Pima said. "You're as fast as your dad. Even with that bad arm of yours."

Nailer glanced at her. A shiver of fear washed over him. He'd killed things before. Chickens. That goat. But this was different. He threw up. Pima and Lucky Girl backed off, exchanging glances.

"What's his problem?" Pima asked.

Sadna shook her head. "Killing isn't free. It takes something out of you every time you do it. You get their life; they get a piece of your soul. It's always a trade."

"No wonder his dad's such a devil."

Sadna shot her daughter a hard look and Pima fell silent. Other people from Sadna's heavy crew were all around, cleaning up from the attack. It turned out that Richard had had more sentries posted than Nailer had guessed. Perimeter guards that he had never even seen. He felt doubly lucky that Sadna and her crew had arrived. He and Pima and Lucky Girl would never have gotten out on their own.

Suddenly Tool's doglike face rose from the shadows.

"Watch out!" Nailer screamed.

Sadna spun, then relaxed at the sight of the half-man. She turned back to Nailer and patted his arm. "He's fine. He's the one who told us where to look for you. We've got good history, don't we, Tool?"

Tool came over and stared down at the body of Blue Eyes, his expression flat. For a long time, he didn't say anything. Finally he turned his dog gaze on Nailer. "A good kill," he said. "As fast as your father."

"I'm not my father."

"Not as skilled." Tool shrugged. "But the potential is there." He nodded at the black puddle around Blue Eyes and smiled, showing his needle teeth. "Blood tells. You have good potential."

Nailer shuddered at the thought of mirroring his father. "I'm not like him," he said again.

Tool's smile disappeared. "Don't be too sorry for Blue Eyes," the half-man rumbled. "It's human nature to tear one another apart. Be glad you come from such a successful line of killers."

"Leave him alone," Pima said.

"Where's Lucky Girl?" Nailer asked.

"The rich girl?" Sadna pointed. "She's gone down to the beach. Her people are here, looking for her. A whole clipper ship of them showed up an hour ago." She looked over at

Tool. "Richard was trying to meet with them, looking to broker a deal."

"Her people are here?" Nailer glanced at Pima, puzzled. "She told us no one knew where she was..." He trailed off, wondering if he'd been lied to again.

Nita burst back into the clearing. "It's them!"

"Your people?" he asked skeptically.

She shook her head, gasping. "The ones who were chasing me. Pyce's people. And he's got half-men."

Sadna studied her. "The ones on the beach...they're your enemies?"

Nita could barely get a breath. "They want me, for leverage against my father."

"Well, they know you're here," Sadna said. "Richard as much as claimed it when they came ashore."

Lucky Girl's face took on a shade of panic. "I can't let them catch me. I need to hide."

Sadna and Tool exchanged glances. "If you go into the jungle—"

Tool shook his head. "Lopez will know to hunt for her. How will you supply her with food? Who will stand for her if he catches her? Better for her to flee."

Nailer spoke up. "We were planning on catching the salvage train to the Orleans. She says she's got crew there who would protect her."

Sadna frowned. "You can't go into the loading yards. No one gets in there without Lucky Strike knowing. And Richard and Lucky Strike are tight now."

176

"We can catch the train outside, once it's moving."

"Dangerous."

"Not as dangerous as waiting around to see what kind of deal my dad cuts with the swanks."

Tool looked thoughtful. "It could be done. If they are quick."

"She says she's fast," Nailer said.

"If she isn't, she could die."

"No worse than she ends up otherwise."

"What about you, Nailer? Is that a risk you want to take?"

Nailer started to answer, then stopped. Was it? Did he really want to tie himself to this girl? He shook his head, irritated. The fact was, he had already set himself in conflict with his father. There was no hope of resolution now, no matter how much he might have wanted it. Richard Lopez would never leave an insult like the killing of his crew unanswered.

"It's not safe for me here," Nailer said. "Not now. He'll come after me with everything he's got. He can't afford to lose this much face. Too many people would be laughing."

Sadna shook her head. "I can't do this thing. I can't leave my crew. No one will be with you."

"With me and Pima—"

Pima shook her head. "No. I'm not doing it."

"You're not?"

"I'm not leaving my mom."

"But we talked about getting out. Getting away from

177

here." Nailer tried to keep the desperation from his voice. For some reason he had assumed they were crew and that they were together.

"You talked about it. Not me."

Nailer stared at her. Pieces clicked into place. Pima had family. Something to cling to. Something solid. Of course she wouldn't risk the run. He should have seen it. Nailer forced himself to nod. "Still, we can catch the train and make it to the Orleans in two days. It can't be that hard."

Pima held up her hand, showing him her splinted fingers. "You think? Reni had both hands for the jump, and he still ended up looking like ground pork."

Sadna looked down toward the beach. "We can broker a truce with your dad, Nailer. I can protect you."

"If you think so, then you really don't know my dad." Nailer shook his head. "Anyway, I don't want that. I want out. Lucky Girl says she'll get me out if I help her."

Sadna glanced at the girl. "And you believe her?"

"I'm telling the truth—" Nita started hotly.

Sadna waved her to silence. "Really?" She looked at Nailer. "You're sure she's worth it?"

"No one ever is," Tool rumbled.

"My father can pay," Nita said. "He can reward—"

"Shut up!" Pima said. She turned to Nailer. "Nailer decides. He's the one to take you. He's the one to take the risk." She grabbed Nailer and pulled him aside. She lowered her voice. "You're sure about this?" She glanced back at Nita. "The girl's sly. Every time she tells us something, it turns out it's only half true."

"I believe her."

"Don't. Swanks don't think like us. She'll have an angle. You sure you're watching yourself?"

"There's no risk. I've got nothing here. There's no way I can keep clear of my dad if I stay." Nailer shrugged, pulled away from Pima's grip. "My dad will never forget this. No matter what anyone says, he'll never forget." He looked at Nita and spoke loudly to the group. "We'll go. I'll take her."

A flurry of activity down below startled them all. Pima scrambled up on a boulder, peering through the foliage. "Get up here, Lucky Girl," she said.

Nita climbed up beside Pima, and Nailer joined them. Out on the dark water, a pale ship was anchored, lights glowing like the day, bright LED spots sweeping the water, catching the shapes of boats rowing toward shore. Nita shook her head. "They're coming for me."

"They'll pay a reward, too," Pima's mother said to Nailer.

"Mom." Pima shook her head.

"We're crew," Nailer said stubbornly. "I'm not selling her."

Pima's mother studied Nailer. "You run and Richard Lopez will hunt you forever. You can never come back." She looked down. "You can still make a peace. Broker a deal and sell the girl to those people down there, and Richard *will* forget. You don't think so, but money will make him forget plenty. Moby and Blue Eyes and the rest are nothing in comparison to the amount of money we're talking about."

Nita watched fearfully. If he sold her, they'd be rich, for certain. He could buy peace from his father.

Lucky and smart. I need to be lucky and smart.

The smart thing was to give Nita up, to buy the safety he couldn't beg for. But just handing her over to her enemies made him feel nauseous. The smart thing was to turtle down and let the girl go and make a profit in the bargain. Her fight wasn't his. He looked to Pima. She just shrugged.

"I told you what I thought."

"Blood and rust," he muttered. "We can't just give her to them. It'd be like giving Pima to my dad."

"But a lot safer for you," Tool suggested.

Nailer shook his head stubbornly. "No. I'll take her to the Orleans. I know how to hop the trains."

"This isn't light crew and a short quota," Tool said. "You won't get second chances. You make a mistake now and you die."

"You ever jumped the train?" Sadna asked.

"Reni told me how."

"Before he went under the wheels," Sadna said.

"We all die," Tool rumbled. "It's only choosing how."

"I'm going," Nailer said. He looked at Nita. "We're going."

180

Something in the way he said it got it through this time. No one tried to protest. They just accepted it and nodded, and suddenly Nailer felt as if he'd made the wrong decision. He realized that a part of him had wanted them to talk him out of it. To find a way to convince him not to run.

"You'd best be going, then," Tool rumbled. "Richard will be coming to sell the girl soon."

"Good luck," Pima's mother said. She dug into her pocket and offered Nailer a handful of bright linen Red Chinese cash. "Run hard. Don't come back."

Nailer took the money, surprised at the amount, feeling suddenly alone. "Thanks."

Pima ran back to the camp, and returned with a small pack that had been Blue Eyes's. She handed it to Nailer. "Your scavenge."

Nailer took the pack, feeling water sloshing in it. He looked at Nita. "Ready?"

Nita nodded eagerly. "Let's get out of here."

"Yeah." He pointed through the jungle. "The tracks are that way."

They started out of the clearing, but Tool called after them, "Wait." Nailer and Nita turned back. Tool studied them with his yellow killer's eyes. "I will go as well, I think."

Nailer felt a shiver of fear. "We're fine," he said at the same moment as Pima's mother smiled brilliantly and said, "Thank you."

Tool smiled slightly at Nailer's hesitation. "Don't be so quick to turn down help, boy."

Nailer had a dozen retorts, but all of them were based in his distrust of the half-man's motives. The creature frightened him. Even if Pima's mother trusted him, Nailer didn't. It worried him that someone so close to his father and Lucky Strike was going with them.

"Why now?" Nita asked suspiciously. "What do you want?"

Tool glanced at Sadna, then nodded toward the beach. "The patrons down on the ship have half-men of their own. They will have questions about my presence. It will not be a convenience for anyone."

"We can make it alone," Nailer said.

"I'm sure," Tool answered. "But perhaps you will benefit from my wisdom." His sharp teeth showed briefly.

"Be glad he's willing to help," Sadna said. She turned to Tool and clasped his huge hand in both of hers. "I owe you now."

"It is nothing." Tool smiled and his sharp teeth showed again. "Killing in one place or killing in another; it makes no difference."

15

THE GROUND SHOOK as the train came up at them. They crouched in the ferns. The engine roared toward them and then flashed by. Nailer swallowed as machinery rushed past. Wind pummeled his face and tore at the leaves of the trees and ferns around him. The train seemed to suck him forward to where the huge wheels, each as high as his chest, blurred past. They beckoned him to throw himself under their passing weight, inviting him to be chopped into pieces and left bleeding as the train roared on. With rising fear, Nailer realized that it was one thing to speculate idly about jumping a train, another to watch freight cars hurtle past.

It was enough to make him reconsider his options. To review the possibility of stealing a skiff, of sailing the coast instead, or of walking the jungle and swamp route...but they had no supplies to make that run. And if they went by water, the clipper ship out in the bay would pursue them with ease. There was no other option. They needed to run and they needed to run now.

The train cars whipped past in a blur. From a distance, they seemed much slower. Now, close up, they were horribly fast. Was the train speeding up? When Reni had jumped the train, it had always seemed to be going slower, had seemed easier. Nailer knew that depending on how aggressive the engineer was, the train could go much faster than was actually jumpable. That was how Reni had finally gone under: misjudging the speed he could leap aboard. He'd also been drunk and stupid, but he'd been lulled by all his other successful jumps.

Nailer and Nita and Tool all stepped out from the vines and clambered up the raised rail bed to the tracks. The wind buffeted them as the train roared past. The noise of rushing cars was as bad as a city killer storm. Nailer glanced back at his companions. Nita's eyes were wide with fear. Tool watched impassively, perhaps even with contempt. This would be nothing to the half-man. Nailer found himself wishing that Tool were big enough to simply pick them up and carry them as he jumped aboard.

Quit fooling yourself. Hurry up and jump.

They were running out of time. The end of the train would be approaching. He needed to commit. It was like being in the oil room all over again, knowing that the only way to survive was to dive, and dive deep. But that time he'd known that there were no other choices. This time, he kept trying to find another way out. *Go*, he told himself. But his feet stayed rooted.

Reni had jumped the trains all the time. Had boasted about it. As Nailer's heart pounded in his chest, he tried to remember everything Reni had ever told him. He took Nita's shoulder and shouted in her ear, "You run ahead of the car, let it catch up and then grab the ladder and don't let go no matter what." He pointed at the wheels. "If you fall, you go under, so never let go, no matter how much it hurts." He said it again. "Don't let go!" He paused. "And get your legs up in a hurry."

She nodded again. He took a deep breath, trying to get his bravery up.

Suddenly Nita dashed ahead.

Nailer stared, surprised, as she ran beside the train. She seemed pathetically small beside the rushing wheels and the ladders that ran up the sides. One ladder whipped past her. Another. She wasn't even looking at the ladders of the train cars. She was just charging along beside the train, her black hair bouncing behind her in a ponytail.

One ladder, two, three, went by. At the fourth, she leaped. Her hands caught the crossbars and she was jerked forward. Her legs flew into the air, torn out from under her. Her feet came down, then flew into the air again as she hit the ground. She was like a rag doll being dragged. She was going to be sucked under the wheels. Nailer waited, thinking he would see her torn apart, but then she curled her legs under her and she was suddenly aboard, clambering up the side of the train car. She hooked her arm in the ladder and looked back. Already she was becoming distant, carried away by the speed of the train.

"The end of the train is coming," Tool observed.

Nailer nodded. Took another breath, and started running.

Almost immediately, he understood why Nita hadn't looked back. The ground was uneven beside the track, even though it looked smooth from a distance. The tracks where Reni had jumped the train had always been smoother than this. Nailer had to keep his eyes ahead if he wasn't going to fall.

Beside him, the speed and noise of the train were dizzying. Cars blurred past. He kept imagining himself tripping and falling under the wheels, torn apart by the train. He was running as fast as he could over the uneven ground, and still the ladders whipped past him.

How the hell had she done it? How had she…? He glanced behind, wanting to be able to see the cars coming up. The movement and noise were dizzying. He stumbled and almost fell into the train's rush. He caught himself and forced himself to look straight ahead. Picked up his pace. He counted time as ladders flicked past. *One, two.* And then a count of three for the center of a train car to pass, and then one, two again. He prayed to Pearly's Ganesha and the Fates. *One, two. Pause, one, two, three. One, two…*

The first ladder flashed past. Nailer grabbed for the

second. It caught his hand and slammed him away, spinning him. His legs tangled. He fell, rolling over gravel and weeds and came to a stop. Train cars whipped past as he lay in the dirt, bruised and stunned. Blood ran from his scraped knees and numbed hands. His shoulder was a bright blossom of pain.

Tool flashed by, hooked easily on a ladder. The half-man looked down at Nailer as he went past, yellow eyes watching, impassive to Nailer's failure.

Nailer scrambled to his feet. Nita was almost gone. He started running. The end of the train was coming up. His leg was bruised from the fall and he limped as he ran. His shoulder felt as if he'd torn it once again. Limping, he couldn't get as much speed. Ladders blurred past. Again he timed them. He glanced back. The end of the train was here.

Now or never.

Nailer put on a burst of speed and leaped as a ladder swept past. Instead of grabbing for a rung, he grabbed the side of the ladder with both hands. His shoulders exploded with pain as his arms were yanked forward and he was dragged with the train. His feet bounced over rocks—bright pain blossoms—and then he pulled himself into a ball, dangling low off the ladder.

The ground blurred beneath him. Wind ripped at his clothes, choked him with its heat and force. He scrabbled for a new handhold, found a rung, and pulled himself painfully away from the rush of rocks beneath. Another handhold, and then he was up and climbing with the wind tearing at him and the trees of the jungle blurring emerald as he shot past. His arms were shaking; his whole body tingled with adrenaline. His legs felt weak. But he climbed, clawing his way higher until he was at the top of the freight car and could see down the length of the train.

His feet were scraped and battered, his knee was oozing blood, his hands were raw, but he was safe and he was alive. Far ahead, Nita and Tool were watching. Nita waved. He waved back tiredly, then hooked his arm in the ladder and let his body shake. Eventually he'd have to make his way down the length of train and rejoin them, but for now he just wanted to rest, to be grateful that for the first time in days, clinging to a speeding train, he felt absurdly safe. He looked back the way he had come. The twin rails of the train tracks were being swallowed by the dense jungle. Every minute on this train took him farther from his past.

He had to smile. His whole body hurt, but he was alive and his father was in the distance and whatever lay ahead, it had to be better than what lay behind. For the first time in his life he was safe from his father.

The thought of safety reminded him of Pima and her mother, still there, still facing more days on the crews, facing whatever retribution his father might think to devise. It worried him. In the heat of the escape, he hadn't been able to concern himself with what the consequences might be for them; he had so desperately wanted to get away that he couldn't think of anything else, but now, suddenly, the two of them were on his mind, like spirit demons, plucking at guilt.

Looking back the way they'd come, he used his free hand and touched his forehead to the Fates and prayed they would be all right. That they would be able to hold Richard off, that he would believe the story that Tool had betrayed him for the sake of a reward, and that Pima's mother and Pima hadn't been the ones who had stolen a Lucky Strike from his hands. Nailer prayed for the people he had abandoned and then he turned his face forward again and let the wind rush past. He opened his mouth, gulping at the heat and speed and smells of the jungle.

Through the trees, a flash of ocean showed, blue and bright. The train was slipping toward the shoreline. In the far distance, he caught sight of the moored clipper ship, its sails glinting in sunlight, a white gull resting on a mirror sea. He grinned at the sight, at the thought of all those swanks who would be scrambling now, trying to find them in the jungle, all of them never realizing they had been fooled and that their quarry had outwitted them.

The view of the ship and ocean disappeared, hidden again by the emerald tangle of blurred trees and vines. Nailer turned and peered down the length of the train, looking ahead to where the towers of drowned Orleans would eventually rise.

16

THE PROBLEM WITH a clever escape was that it helped to have planned for it.

In their rush to slip away, they'd left with few supplies, and riding in the gaps between train cars meant it was impossible to scavenge for food. Within hours, Nailer was starving. He thought longingly of the dinner he'd had the night before.

He would have thought that by sitting still they would have hardly needed to eat. After all, it wasn't like working light crew. But his body was already whittled by a lack of food from his time of fever and now his belly pressed against his backbone. There was nothing to do about the problem, so he gritted his teeth and felt his belly grind on emptiness and promised himself he would scavenge a feast when they arrived in the drowned city.

The train, in addition to the access ladders to the roofs, had tiny service platforms between the cars, but these were hardly more than steel planks two feet wide, suitable for standing and working, but terrible for hours of riding. Early on, Tool made his way down the length of the train, hunting for open bays in the train cars, but he was unable to crack any of the sealed compartments and so they huddled in the train gaps with the ground blurring beneath them and the wind whipping all around. It was awful, and yet still better than the hot roofs of the train with no protection at all from the blaze of the sun.

Sleeping on the brink of the wheels was nearly impossible. They pinned themselves between the ladders, perched precariously above the blurred ground and slept in nodding shifts that broke off at abrupt moments when the train jerked forward or slammed to a slower speed. All of the train's braking and acceleration came in jerks and shuddering decelerations that threatened to throw them off their perches. After Nailer and Nita were nearly thrown down into the train gap, they rode with their arms threaded through the ladders. Another time, as the train slammed itself to a slower speed, Tool almost crushed them, his whole bulk smashing them against metal and leaving Nailer's head ringing.

But all of those discomforts were nothing against their lack of water. The few bottles they carried in their pack were quickly drunk and by the second day all of them were parched and hollow in the heat and humidity. There was nothing to do but watch the landscape rush past and hope that the train would reach its destination soon. Sometimes huge lakes spooled past. They debated jumping from the speeding train into the cool inviting water, but Tool shook his head and said that they would never catch a train again at this speed, and unless they wanted to spend days walking, they must suffer instead.

Nailer resented the idea, even though he didn't want to ever try to jump a train again and knew that the huge creature was correct. So while they killed time and watched the landscape roll past, they talked.

"Who are the people who are after you?" Nailer asked Nita. "Why are you so important?"

"It's Nathaniel Pyce. A business-marriage uncle." She hesitated, then said, "He and his people want me for leverage."

Nailer frowned, confused. Nita saw his lack of comprehension. "My father learned about some of his dealings. Pyce was misusing the family's corporate resources. Now Pyce wants to use me to keep my father from making trouble. I'm the best way to put pressure on him."

"Pressure?"

"Pyce wants my father to allow something he disagrees with. If Pyce controls me, my father has to acquiesce. Pyce stands to make billions, and not in dollars. Chinese red cash. Billions." Her dark eyes bored into him. "That's more money than your ship-breaking yards will make in their entire lifetime. It's enough to build a thousand clippers."

"And your dad's against that?"

"It's tar sands development and refining. A way to make burnable fuel, a crude oil replacement. The valuation has gone up, because of carbon production limits. Pyce has been refining tar sands in our northern holdings and secretly using Patel clippers to ship it over the pole to China."

"Sounds like a Lucky Strike to me," Nailer said. "Like falling into a pool of oil and already having a buyer set up. Shouldn't your dad just take a cut and let this Pyce run with it?"

Nita stared at him in shock. She opened her mouth. Closed it, then opened it again. Closed it, clearly flummoxed.

"It's black market fuel," Tool rumbled. "Banned by convention, if not in fact. The only thing that would be more profitable is shipping half-men, but that of course is legal. And this isn't at all. Is it, Lucky Girl?"

Nita nodded unwillingly. "Pyce is avoiding carbon taxation because of territory disputes in the Arctic, and then when it goes to China, it's easy to sell it untraceably. It's risky, and it's illegal, and my father found out about it. He was going to force Pyce out of the family, but Pyce moved against him first."

"Billions in Chinese red cash," Nailer said. "It's worth that much?"

She nodded.

"Your father's crazy, then. He should've done the business."

Nita looked at him with disgust. "Don't we already have enough drowned cities? Enough people dying from drought? My family is a clean company. Just because a market exists doesn't mean we have to serve it."

Nailer laughed. "You trying to tell me you blood buyers got some kind of clean conscience? Like making some petrol is different than buying our blood and rust out on the wrecks for your recycling?"

"It is!"

"It's all money in the end. And you're worth a lot more of it than I thought." He looked at her speculatively. "Good thing you didn't tell me this before I burned the boat with my dad." He shook his head. "I might have let him sell you after all. Your uncle Pyce would have paid a fortune."

Nita smiled uncertainly. "You're serious?"

Nailer wasn't sure how he was feeling. "It's a lot of damn money," he said. "The only reason you think you've got morals is because you don't need money the way regular people do." He forced down a feeling of despair over a choice that was made and couldn't be gone back on.

You want to be like Sloth? he asked himself. *Do anything just to make a little more cash?*

Sloth had been both a traitor and a fool, but Nailer couldn't help thinking the Fates had handed him the biggest Lucky Strike in the world and he'd thrown it away. "So how'd you end up in the storm, if you're so valuable?"

"My father sent me south, to keep me out of reach if there was violence. No one was supposed to know where I was." Her eyes got a faraway look. "We didn't know they were coming. We didn't suspect—" She corrected herself. "Captain Arensman said we needed to run. He knew. I don't know how. Maybe he was one of them and changed his mind. Maybe he had a feel for the Fates." She shook her head. "I don't know. I'll never know now. But I didn't believe him, and so I delayed. And our people died because I didn't believe I was at risk." Her face hardened. "We barely got out of port, and even then they were after us, chasing us all day and all night.

"When the storm came, we didn't have any choice. It was either try to run the storm, or surrender. Captain Arensman gave me the choice."

"You couldn't make a deal?" Nailer asked.

"Not with Pyce. That man doesn't negotiate when he's already won. So I told Arensman to head into the storm. I don't know why he agreed. The sea was already high." She made a motion with her hands. "Waves coming over the decks, almost impossible to walk, and no clear winds, just a storm howl, all around us, tearing us to pieces. I was sure I was going to die, but if we surrendered to Pyce it would have been the same."

She shrugged. "So we turned into the storm and the waves kept coming and our sails snapped and we lost our masts and the waves came in through the windows." She took a shuddering breath. "But Pyce's people turned back."

"You risked everything," Tool rumbled.

"I'm a chess piece. A pawn," she said. "I can be sacrificed,

195

but I cannot be captured. To be captured would be the end of the game." She stared out at the greenery. "I have to escape, or die, because if I'm captured they will have my father, and they will make him do terrible things."

"If your father wishes to sacrifice himself for you," Tool said, "perhaps he knows best."

"You wouldn't understand."

"I understand that you sacrificed an entire crew to a storm."

Nita stared at him, then looked away. "If there had been another choice, I would have taken it."

"You have loyal people, then."

"Not like you." She said it with surprising venom.

Tool blinked once, slowly, yellow eyes bright. "You wish that I was a good dog-man? That I had kept allegiance to Nailer's father, maybe?" He blinked again. "You wish that I was a good beast like the ones on your clipper ships?" He smiled slightly, showing sharp teeth. "Richard Lopez thought your clean blood and clear eyes and strong heart would fetch an excellent price from the Harvesters. You wish I had stayed loyal to that?"

Nita gave Tool a dirty look, but her knuckles were pale as she clenched her fists. "Don't try to scare me."

Tool's teeth showed bright and sharp. "If I wished to scare a spoiled rich protected creature, I would not have to try very hard."

Nailer interrupted. "Cut it out, you two." He touched

Tool's shoulder. "We're glad you came with us. We owe you."

"I didn't do it for your debt," Tool said. "I did it for Sadna." He looked at Nita. "That woman is worth ten times whatever your wealthy father is worth. A thousand times what you are, whatever your enemies may foolishly think."

"Don't tell me about worth," Nita said. "My father commands fleets."

"The wealthy measure everything with the weight of their money." Tool leaned close. "Sadna once risked herself and the rest of her crew to help me escape from an oil fire. She did not have to return, and she did not have to help lift an iron girder that I could not lift alone. Others urged her not to. It was foolhardy. And I, after all, was only half of a man." Tool regarded Nita steadily. "Your father commands fleets. And thousands of half-men, I am sure. But would he risk himself to save a single one?"

Nita scowled at him, but she didn't reply. Silence stretched between them. Eventually everyone settled down to sleep as well as they could in the creak and jolt of the train.

The great drowned city of New Orleans didn't come all at once, it came in portions: the sagging backs of shacks ripped open by banyan trees and cypress. Crumbling edges of concrete and brick undermined by sinkholes. Kudzu-swamped clusters of old abandoned buildings shadowed under the loom of swamp trees.

The train rose into the air, rail pilings lifting it over the swamps below. They passed over cool green pools full of algae and lily pads, the white flash of egrets and the whir of flies and mosquitoes. The entire elevated track system was reinforced against the city killer storms that rolled into the coast with such astonishing regularity, but it was the only evidence that any people successfully inhabited the jungle swamplands now.

They sped above the mossy broke-back structures of a dead city. A whole waterlogged world of optimism, torn down by the patient work of changing nature. Nailer wondered at the people who had inhabited those collapsing buildings. Wondered where they had gone. Their buildings were huge, larger than anything in his experience at the ship-breaking yards. The good ones were built with glass and concrete and they'd died just the same as the bad ones that seemed to have simply melted in on themselves, leaving rotting timbers and boards that were warped and molded and sagging.

"Is this it?" Nailer asked. "Is this the Orleans?"

Nita shook her head. "These were just towns outside the city. Support suburbs. They're everywhere. Stuff like this goes for miles. From when everyone had cars."

"Everyone?" Nailer tested the theory. It seemed unlikely. How could so many people be so rich? It was as absurd as everyone owning clipper ships. "How could they do that? There's no roads."

"They're there." She pointed. "Look."

198

And indeed, if Nailer scrutinized the jungle carefully, he could make out the boulevards that had been, before trees punctured their medians and encroached. Now, the roads were more like flat fern and moss-choked paths. You had to imagine none of the trees sprouting up in the center, but they were there.

"Where'd they get the petrol?" he asked.

"They got it from everywhere." Nita laughed. "From the far side of the world. From the bottom of the sea." She waved at the drowned ruins, and a flash of ocean. "They used to drill out there, too, in the Gulf. Cut up the islands. It's why the city killers are so bad. There used to be barrier islands, but they cut them up for their gas drilling."

"Yeah?" Nailer challenged. "How do you know?"

Nita laughed again. "If you went to school, you'd know it, too. Orleans city killers are famous. Every dummy knows about them." She stopped short. "I mean..."

Nailer wanted to hit her smug face.

Tool laughed, a low rumble of amusement.

Sometimes Nita seemed okay. Other times she was just swank. Smug and rich and soft. It was those moments that made Nailer think she could have learned a thing or two on Bright Sands Beach, that even Sloth with all her greed and willingness to betray him had been better than this rich swank who still looked pretty even after living amongst them all, as if she weren't touched by the grime and pain and struggle that the rest of them felt.

"I'm sorry," Nita said, but Nailer shrugged away her apology. It was clear what she thought of him.

They rode in silence. A village showed through the jungle, a clearing carved from the trees and shadows, a small fishing community perched amongst the bogs, dotted with slump shacks like the ones that Nailer's own people constructed, with pigs and vegetables in their yards. To him, it looked like home. He wondered what Nita saw.

At last the jungle parted, opening on a wide expanse where the trees were lower and the height of the train gave them a view. Even from a distance, the city was huge. A series of needles, piercing the sky.

"Orleans II," Tool said.

17

NAILER CRANED HIS NECK to see over the tops of the trees and take in the mangled metropolis. "There's got to be good scavenge there," he said.

Nita shook her head. "You'd have to knock down the towers. You'd need all kinds of explosives. It's not worth it."

"Depends how much copper and iron you can pull," Nailer said. "Put a light crew in the building, see what's what."

"You'd have to work in the middle of a lake."

"So? If you swanks left a lot behind, it would be worth it." He hated the way she acted like she knew everything. He stared out at the towers. "I'll bet all the good stuff's been stripped, though. Too good to leave lying there."

"Still"—Tool nodded at the many buildings spread out

and covered with greenery — "a lot of scavenge if someone organized."

Again Nita disagreed. "You'd have to fight with the locals for scavenge rights. Fight for every inch. If it weren't for treaties and the trading militias, even the transshipment zone would be contested." She made a face. "You can't bargain with people like that. They're savages."

"Savages like Nailer?" Tool goaded. Again his yellow eyes flickered with humor as Nita blushed and looked away, pushing her black hair behind her ear and pretending to watch the moving horizon.

Whatever Nita thought of the scavenge opportunities, there was a lot of abandoned material spread out before them, and if Nailer understood correctly, this was just Orleans II. There was also the original New Orleans, and then there was Mississippi Metropolitan — aka MissMet — what had been originally envisioned as New Orleans III, before even the most ardent supporters of the drowned city gave up on the spectacularly bad luck enjoyed by places called "Orleans."

Some engineers had claimed it was possible to raise hurricane-resistant towers above Pontchartrain Bay, but the merchants and traders had had enough of the river mouth and the storms, and so left the drowned city to docks and deep-sea loading platforms and slums, while they migrated their wealth and homes and children to land that lay more comfortably above sea level.

MissMet was far away upriver and higher in elevation

and armored against cyclones and hurricanes as none of the others had been, a city designed from the ground up to avoid the pitfalls of their earlier optimism, a place for swanks that Nailer had heard was paved in gold and where gleaming walls and guards and wire kept the rest of the chaff away.

At one time in the past, New Orleans had meant many things, had meant jazz and Creole and the pulse of life, had meant Mardi Gras and parties and abandon, had meant creeping luxurious green decay. Now it meant only one thing.

Loss.

More dead jungle ruins flashed past, an astonishing amount of wealth and materials left to rot and fall back to the green tangle of the trees and swamps.

"Why did they give up?" Nailer asked.

"Sometimes people learn," Tool said.

From that, Nailer took him to be saying that mostly people didn't. The wreckage of the twin dead cities was good evidence of just how slow the people of the Accelerated Age had been to accept their changing circumstances.

The train curved toward the hulking towers. The shambled outline of an ancient stadium showed beyond the spires of Orleans II, marking the beginning of the old city, the city proper for the drowned lands.

"Stupid," Nailer muttered. Tool leaned close to hear his voice over the wind, and Nailer shouted in his ear, "They were damn stupid."

Tool shrugged. "No one expected Category Six hurricanes. They didn't have city killers then. The climate changed. The weather shifted. They did not anticipate well."

Nailer wondered at that idea. That no one could have understood that they would be the target of monthly hurricanes pinballing up the Mississippi Alley, gunning for anything that didn't have the sense to batten down, float, or go underground.

The train flew over its pylons, curving toward the center of the trade nexus, speeding over brackish water, bright with leaked waste oil and scrap trash and the stink of chemicals. They shot past floating platforms and transshipment loaders. Massive containers were being loaded into clipper ships via cranes. Shallow-draft Mississippi river boats with their stubby sails were being loaded with luxuries from across the oceans.

The train rolled past scrap and recycling yards, men and women's backs sheened mirror bright with sweat as they stacked hand carts with purchased scrap and moved it to weighing platforms for sale. The train began to slow. It shunted onto a new series of tracks, dipping down to a barren zone of rail yards and slum shacks, before shunting again. Wheels squealed on steel and the train cars shuddered as the brakes were applied. The ripple of the slowdown thudded back through the cars to the tail of the train.

Tool touched their shoulders. "We get off now. Soon

we'll be in the rail yards and then people will ask why we are here and if we have the right."

Even though the train was going slowly, they all ended up falling and rolling when they hit the ground. Nailer stood, wiping dust from his eyes, and surveyed the area. In many ways, it was not much different from the ship-breaking yards. Scrap and junk, soot and oily grime and slumped shacks with people watching them, hollow-eyed.

Nita surveyed her surroundings. Nailer could tell she wasn't impressed, but even he was glad they had Tool with them, someone to protect them as they threaded between tightly packed shacks. A few men were lounging in the shade, tats and piercings showing unknown affiliations. They watched as the three interlopers moved through their turf. Nailer's neck prickled. He palmed his knife, wondering if there would be bloodshed. He could feel them evaluating. They were like his father. Idle, crystal sliding probably, dangerous. He smelled tea and sugar. Coffee boiling. Pots of red beans and dirty rice. His stomach rumbled. The sweet reek of bananas rotting. A child ahead of them urinated on a wall, watching them with solemn eyes as they slipped past.

At last they poured out onto a main street. It was full of junk and scrap dealers, men and women selling tools, sheets of metal, rolls of wire. A bicycle cart rattled by, full of scrap. Tin, Nailer thought, and then wondered if the driver had purchased it or was selling it, and where it might be going.

"Now where?" Nailer asked.

Nita frowned. "We need to get to the docks. I need to see if any of my father's ships are there."

"And if they are?" Tool asked.

"I need to know the captain's names. There are some I know I can trust still."

"You're sure of that?"

She hesitated. "There have to be a few."

Tool pointed. "The clippers should be in that direction."

She motioned Nailer and Tool to follow. Nailer glanced at Tool, but the massive man seemed unconcerned at her sudden authority.

They trudged down the thoroughfare. The smell of sea and rot and crushed humanity was strong, much stronger than in the ship-breaking yards. And the city was huge. They walked and walked, and still the streets and shacks and scrap bunkers went on. Men and women rode by on rickshaws and bicycles. Even an oil-burning car slipped through the broken streets, its engine whining and grinding. Eventually, the hot open slum gave way to cooler tree-covered lanes and large houses, with shacks around their edges and people going in and out. On them were signs that Nita read out to Nailer as they went by: MEYER TRADING. ORLEANS RIVER SUPPLY. YEE AND TAYLOR, SPICES. DEEP BLUE SHIPPING CORPORATION, LTD.

And then abruptly the street slipped into the water, dipping down. Boats and river taxis were moored, men sitting with their oared skiffs and tiny scrap sails, waiting to ferry anyone who needed to move into the Orleans beyond.

"Dead end," Nailer said.

"No." Nita shook her head. "I know this place. We're close. We have to go through the Orleans, to get to the deep-sea platforms. We'll need a water taxi."

"They look expensive."

"Didn't Pima's mother give you money?" Nita asked. "I'm sure it's more than enough."

Nailer hesitated, then pulled out the wad of red cash.

"Better to save it," Tool said. "You'll be hungry later."

Nailer stared at the brackish water. "I'm pretty thirsty now."

Nita scowled at him. "Then how are we supposed to get out to the clippers?"

"We could just walk," Nailer said. Some people were wading out into the water, which seemed only waist deep. They moved slowly through the green and oily murk.

Nita stared at the water with distaste. "You can't walk there. It's too deep."

"Spend your money on water," Tool said. "There will be a way for the laborers to get to the loading platforms. The poor will lead us."

Nita reluctantly agreed. They bought brownish water from a water seller, a man with yellow rotting teeth and a wide smile, who swore that his water was salt-free and well boiled, and after they had bought, he cheerfully directed them. He even offered to row them there, but he wanted too high a fee and so instead they went the long way, threading around drowned and rotting streets, down floating board-walks. The reek of fish and petroleum came in waves, making Nailer's eyes water and reminding him of ship-breaking yards.

Eventually they reached the shore. A series of buoys stretched out into the placid water.

Nita stared at the water with distaste. "We should have taken a boat."

Nailer grinned at her. "Afraid?" he asked.

She gave him a dirty look. "No." She stared at the water again. "But it's not clean. The chemicals are poisonous." She sniffed. "There's no telling what's in there."

"Yeah, well, that'll kill you tomorrow, not today." He waded out into the gunk and slime of the water. A thin, jewel-like oil sheen covered it. "It's better than around the ship yards. This is nothing at all in comparison to that. And it hasn't killed me yet." He grinned again, enjoying taunting her. "Come on. Let's go see if there's a clipper waiting for you."

Nita compressed her lips but followed. Nailer wanted to laugh at her. She was smart, but it was weird how damn prissy she was. He watched as she waded deeper into the water, enjoying the fact that the swank was about to drag herself around in the filth like a normal person for once. As soon as Lucky Girl was in, Tool waded after her, his huge form pressing a ripple in the lily pads and petroleum murk.

They all started forward, walking slowly. The water deepened, rising to their chests.

Ahead of them, someone had tied plastic buoys, marking a lane for people without boats. One of them was orange, another white. As Nailer passed one, he spied the faded image of an apple stamped on its surface along with letters. Another had an ancient automobile embedded on its face. The path of discarded containers led them out to where the last portions of housing foundations disappeared and where much of the wreckage was gone, and still the path went on.

They waded carefully through the waters, following a stream of struggling bodies that waded, swam, and splashed forward toward the far docks. At one point, Nita lost her footing and went under. Tool grabbed her and pulled her up and set her back on the careful path that everyone else followed.

She pushed long wet strands of hair off her face and stared to the distant ships and their docks. "Why don't they just use boats?"

"For these people?" Tool looked around at their fellow waders. "They are not worth it."

"Still, someone could make a boardwalk. It wouldn't even cost that much."

"Spending money on the poor is like throwing money into a fire. They'll just consume it and never thank you," Tool said.

"But it would probably save money, for people to have easy access."

"The water doesn't seem to stop them." And indeed, there was a steady stream of people ahead of them; a few of them had scavenged plastic bags wrapped around some possession that they wanted to keep dry, but mostly the stream of people seemed unconcerned that they were forced to swim through the brown waters and green algae. Nita waded on, grimly determined, Nailer thought, not to show how disgusted she was by her circumstance.

Every time Tool spoke, his words were like a whip, lashing her. Nailer wasn't sure why, but he liked to see her embarrassed. Part of him sensed that she thought of him as something like an animal, a useful creature like a dog, but not actually a person. Then again, he wasn't too sure that she was a person either. Swanks were different. They came from a different place, lived different lives, wrecked whole clipper ships just so one girl could survive.

"Why are you even here, Tool?" Nita asked suddenly. "You aren't supposed to be able to just walk away from your patron."

Tool glanced at her. "I go where I please."

"But you're a half-man."

"Half a man." Tool looked at her. "And yet twice the size of you, Lucky Girl."

"What are you talking about?" Nailer asked.

Nita glanced at Nailer. "He's supposed to have a patron.

We take them on their oaths. My family imports them from Nippon, after training. But not without a patron."

Tool's eyes swung to focus on her fully. Yellow dog eyes, predatory, examining a creature he could destroy in a moment if he chose. "I have no patron."

"That's impossible," Nita said.

"Why's that?" Nailer asked.

"We are known to be fantastically loyal," Tool said. "Lucky Girl is disappointed to discover that not all of us enjoy slavery."

"It can't happen," Nita insisted. "You're trained—"

Tool's huge shoulders rippled in a shrug. "They made a mistake with me." He smiled slightly, nodded to himself, enjoying a private joke. "I was smarter than they prefer."

"Oh?" Nita challenged.

Again the yellow eyes evaluated her. "Smart enough to know that I can choose who I serve and who I betray, which is more than can be said of the rest of my...people."

Nailer had never thought to wonder why Tool was amongst the ship breakers. He had just been there, much as the boat refugees had been. The Spinoza clan and the McCalleys and the Lals had all come to work, and so too had Tool. They were there for the work.

But it was true what Lucky Girl said. Half-men were used for bodyguards, for killing, for war. Those were the stories he had heard. He'd seen them with Lawson & Carlson's bankers. Seen them clustered around the blood buyers when they came to inspect the yards. But always with others. Swanks. People who could afford to buy creatures mixed from a genetic cocktail of humanity, tigers, and dogs. And they were expensive. The human eggs that jump-started their development were always in demand, and commanded a high price. The Life Cult often supported itself on the ovum of its devotees, and the Harvesters were always buying.

"Where's your master, then?" Nita asked. "You're supposed to die with your master. That's what ours always say. That they'll die when we do, that they will die for us."

"Some of us are astonishingly loyal," Tool observed.

"But your genes—"

"If genes are destiny, then Nailer should have sold you to your enemies and spent the bounty on red rippers and Black Ling whiskey."

"That's not what I meant."

"No? But you descend from Patels, and so you are all intelligent and civilized, yes? And Nailer, of course, is descended from a perfect killer and we know what that means about him."

"No. I didn't mean that at all."

"Then do not be so certain of what my kind can and cannot do." Tool's eyes bored into her. "We are faster, stronger, and whatever you may think, smarter than our patrons. Does it worry the swank girl to run across a creature like me, running free?"

Nita flinched. "We treat your kind well. My family—"

"Don't bother. My kind will serve you, regardless."

Tool looked away and kept wading. Nita fell silent. Nailer pushed on through the waters, thinking about the strange conflict between the two of them.

"Tool?" Nailer asked. "*Did* they train you? Did they make you have a patron?"

"A long time ago, they tried."

"Who?"

Tool shrugged. "They are dead now. It hardly matters." He nodded at the approaching docks. "Do you recognize any of the clippers?"

Nita looked out at the ships against their floating docks in the distance. "Not from this far."

They made their way closer, slogging through the water. The water's cool was a relief from the tropic heat, but Nailer was tiring from wading. It was a slow process.

The water deepened, and they finally came to floating docks, where they were able to pull themselves out of the water. Lucky Girl wrung the brackish water out of her clothes with distaste, but Nailer enjoyed the breeze on his wet skin. Out in the distance, the clippers were sailing. From this vantage, the whole world stretched before him. Clippers and freighters at their anchor slips. The blue hulls of England, the Red flag of China North. He had memorized many of the flags from the old wrecks the ship breakers worked, the hulls painted with nation and merchant tags. The mass of shipping here was a catalogue of the world.

A small patrol boat, burning biodiesel and kicking up fumes, moved between huge sailing vessels, carrying pilots out to ships that waited to be guided in to dock. All around them the docks bustled. Swanks came down out of ships and were put on water shuttles to make their transfer upriver or to the rail lines inland. A pair of half-men guarded a yacht of some swank, staring at Tool with an open challenge in their eyes and guttural growling of acknowledgment as he went past. All around them, coolie people swarmed—black, pink, brown, blond, redheaded, black-haired, tall and short, all of them with labor tattoos and levy ensigns—working cargo down into shallow-bottom rafts for transfer. More shallow bottoms moved out from the drowned wreckage of the city, sailing in a slow wallow to the big ships.

"We could have just hitched with the freight," Nailer muttered, nodding at rail containers wallowing their way toward the clipper ships. Some of the cargo barges were old broken sailing vessels, but others were larger, more massive. Built to burn coal and also to take advantage of wind. Huge finlike wind wings stuck up along their lengths, harnessing the breezes to help move the lumbering ships and their scrap loads of nickel, copper, iron, and steel.

The activity was intoxicating, busier even than the shipbreaking swarms of Bright Sands Beach. Nita craned her head over the crowds of people. Pointed. "Those ships over there," she said.

Ahead, a line of clippers lay anchored. A schooner, a catamaran freighter, and a yacht, all of them lying across a bridge at a separate dock. They were beautiful, the fastest things on the high seas, equipped with rocket cannon and small missile systems for pirates, armed and deadly and fast, and nothing about them like the rusting wreckage that Nailer had always known and worked to disassemble. Comparing the clippers to those old-world wrecks was like squinting into daylight after coming out of a rust hold.

As they got closer, Nita scanned the ships and said, "They're not mine." She slumped, obviously disappointed.

Nailer felt a stab of disappointment himself, but stifled it. If he was realistic, it was unlikely they'd find a friendly ship immediately. Still, the river port was full of traffic. Ships were arriving all the time. Even as they watched, one of the clippers was unfurling its sails, long rippling canvas streams swishing down into place on fast pulley systems. They snapped in the breeze as the ship cast off and slipped away from the dock.

"We'll come back tomorrow," Nailer said.

Lucky Girl nodded, but still she scanned the ships as if hoping one of them would magically turn into something else. Finally she nodded and they went back through the shallows and down along the dock bridges, making their way back into the Orleans as dusk fell.

That night, they bought rats on a stick from a boat seller, and watched the street river traffic. Small boats poled past, carrying food and laborers and shore-leave sailors. From somewhere in the distance came a mournful sound of brass instruments, a death dirge echoing over the water. A few children played in the black water. Nailer took the children to mean that their current place was as safe as any could be. The serious drunks and crystal sliders were somewhere else.

The noise of crickets and cicadas filled the dark air. Mosquitoes swarmed around them, biting. The insects were much worse than on the beaches. There, the sea breeze blew many away, but here, amongst the still air of the swamps they swarmed close and tore at them, a misery of biting insects. Nailer and Nita slapped at the bloodsuckers, while Tool watched amused. Nailer wondered if Tool's skin was exceptionally thick or if there was something about him that scared even mosquitoes away.

"How much money did Sadna give you?" Tool asked.

"A couple reds and a yellow back."

Nita asked, "That's all?" then bit back her words.

"That's two weeks' heavy crew," Nailer said. "What, you spend that in an afternoon shopping?"

Nita shook her head, but said nothing. Tool said, "Tomorrow you will need to work if you wish to keep eating."

"Where?" Nailer asked.

Tool gave him a yellow-eyed stare. "You're not stupid. Think for yourself."

Nailer considered. "The docks. If we work at the docks, we can make money and keep an eye out for her people."

Tool grunted and turned away. Nailer took it as agreement.

18

GETTING WORK WASN'T HARD. Getting work that paid as well as ship breaking was impossible. Only Tool had easy access to work, acting as muscle on valuable goods as they transshipped to the Mississippi and the rail yards. Without a clan system or union contact or a family, Nailer and Nita were left with the dreg work, running messages, hauling small items, begging. A man in an alley offered to buy their blood, but his hands and needles were filthy, and his eyes said he wanted to harvest more than their veins. They ran from him, and were relieved when he did not follow.

A week passed, and then two. They settled into poverty-ridden routine as they watched ship after ship arrive and then depart, making way for a new disappointment to come gliding in on white canvas wings.

Nailer had expected Nita's prissy distaste for the slums of the Orleans to continue, but she adapted quickly, with a fierce attention to whatever Tool and Nailer taught. She threw herself into work, contributed her share, and didn't complain about what she ate or where they slept. She was still swank, and still did weird swank things, but she also showed a determination to carry her weight that Nailer was forced to respect.

One early morning, with Nailer and Nita both elbow deep in blood as they gutted black eels for a grub shack, he admitted what he'd been thinking.

"You're okay, Lucky Girl."

Nita filleted another eel and dropped its carcass into the bucket between them. "Yeah?" She was only half listening as she worked.

"Yeah. You work good," Nailer said as he yanked a fresh eel from another bucket and handed it across to her. "If we were still at the ship-breaking yards, I'd vouch you onto light crew."

Nita took the eel and paused, surprised. The eel coiled around her wrist, thrashing.

Nailer stumbled on. "I mean, you're still a swank, but, you know, if you needed work, I'd stand for you."

She smiled then, a smile as bright as the blue ocean. Nailer felt his chest contract. Damn, he was crazy. He was actually starting to like this girl. He turned and fished out another eel for himself and slashed it open. "Anyway, I'm just saying you do good work." He didn't look up again. He felt his skin darkening with a blush.

"Thank you, Nailer," Nita said. Her voice was soft.

"Sure. It's nothing. Let's get these eels done and get out to the docks. I don't want to miss the first work calls."

Nita had given Nailer and Tool a bunch of names to memorize, writing them in the mud for Nailer so that he could memorize the pattern of their letters. She described the flag her company flew, so that they could look for the ships and between the three of them be sure of spotting any likely candidates.

None of her instructions turned out to matter.

Nailer was running a message to the Ladee Bar from the first officer of the *Gossamer*, a sleek trimaran with fixed wind-wing sails and an impressive Buckell cannon on its foredeck, when everything went wrong.

The message was a sealed envelope, waxed and marked with a thumbstrip as well, and Nailer had a chit for payment on delivery, if the captain was willing to thumb it. As he ran down the boardwalk to the deep swim he was already thinking about the annoyance of having to make the passage back to the Orleans with one hand above water. If he soaked the letter, he might not get a tip from the captain —

Richard Lopez appeared like a ghost.

Nailer froze. His father's pale bare head bobbed above the crowds of laborers, an apparition of evil with his red dragon tattoos running up his arms and curling about his neck. His pale blue eyes stared at everything that went past, taking in the docks. Nailer's mind screamed at him to run, but at the sudden sight of his father he was filled with terror and couldn't move.

Two half-men were with him. Their huge bodies pushed through the crowds, towering over everyone else. Their blunt doglike faces stared at the people with contempt, their noses twitching for a scent, their dappled dark skin and yellow eyes watching hungrily. After weeks in Tool's company, Nailer had forgotten how frightening a half-man could be, but now, as these great beasts moved through the crowd, his fear returned.

Move move move move MOVE!

Nailer ducked low, hiding himself in the crowd, and lunged for the boardwalk's edge. He dropped over the side, the letter for the captain at Ladee Bar forgotten. He sank into the waves and swam under the floating dock. There was just enough space for him to breathe if he craned his neck back and stuck his nose into the small gap between the water and the bottom of the boards.

Overhead, the planks creaked and thumped with foot traffic. Water and grime lapped around Nailer's cheeks and jaw as he peered up through the gaps in the planking. People moved past. Nailer held silent, watching for another glimpse of his father.

What was the man doing? How did he know to look for him here?

The trio appeared in Nailer's vision. All of them were well dressed. Even his father had new clothes, not a stain on them, no tears. Not beach clothes at all. Swank. The half-men had pistols in shoulder harnesses and whips coiled at their belts. They stopped above Nailer and surveyed the crowds of coolie laborers hauling freight.

Grimy waves sloshed over Nailer. The wake of a passing boat. The waves shoved him up against the planks beneath his father's shoes. His face scraped and he held his breath as he sank and then bobbed up against the boards again, trying not to make any sound. Splinters stung his lips and water ran up his nose. Nailer fought the urge to splutter and cough. If he gave himself away, he was dead. He ducked his head under water and blew his nose clean, then surfaced, forcing himself to be silent. He took a careful shuddering breath.

The three hunters still stood over him, surveying the cargo activity. Nailer wondered if they had just guessed that he would go to the Orleans or if they had somehow tortured Pima or Sadna for an answer. He forced the question from his mind. There was nothing he could do about that. He needed to solve his own problem first.

The half-men surveyed the dock workers with a calm detachment so much like Tool that they could have been brothers. The half-men watched the people and Nailer watched them, putting his hands up against the boards as more waves threatened to shove him into the wood. He kept hoping they would say something, but if they did, the rumble of the boards and the splash of the waters around him obscured it. He prayed that Lucky Girl had the sense to be on the lookout. Tool as well. It was just the barest luck that had allowed Nailer to recognize his father and duck away. He trembled at the realization of how close he had come.

Richard and the half-men moved on, still surveying the people. They had to be looking for Lucky Girl. Nailer trailed after them, eeling silently beneath the boardwalk. The trio walked quickly, and Nailer almost lost them twice amongst the thump of workers and crew on the floating docks. He was swimming so quickly that he almost revealed himself when his father climbed off the dock and into a skiff. His father's face flashed into view below dock level. Nailer sank into the water and kicked silently away, surfacing safely in the shadows.

When he came up his father was saying, "—see if any of the other crews had any success, then send word back to the ship."

The half-men nodded but didn't respond. They loosed the skiff's sail and it pulled away from the dock. Nailer watched them go, wondering if he would ever be rid of his father. No matter how far he ran, no matter how he tried to hide, always the man was there. Nailer started swimming beneath the boardwalk, easing his way to the buoys. He didn't know where Tool was, but Lucky Girl was supposed to be cleaning pots for a fishhouse down on the water's edge. If his father caught sight of her, it would be all over. Tool... Tool would have to take care of himself.

When he got to Nita, she was excited. She took her hand out of the murky brown water that she was washing dishes in and pointed out to a ship in the harbor. A new one that had just arrived.

"That one! *Dauntless*. It's one of the clippers I've been looking for."

Nailer glanced at the ship, chilled. "I don't think so. My dad's here. He's got goons with him. Half-men. I think he's linked up with your swank uncle, Pyce." He tugged her away from the cook shop. "We need to lie low. Disappear for a while." He searched the crowds for signs of his father. The man was nowhere to be seen, but that didn't mean he wasn't there, or that he didn't have others searching. The man was sly. Had a way of popping up.

"No!" Nita shook his hand off her arm. "I have to get onto that ship." She pointed. "That's my ticket out. All we have to do is get to it."

"I'm not sure that's the ship you want. My dad was just talking about a ship. It's a big coincidence to have your ship and my dad show up at the same time." He tugged her arm. "We need to lie low. My dad sounded like he had more people with him. They're going to spot us if we don't duck and cover."

"So you just want to let *Dauntless* sail away?" she asked, incredulous.

Nailer stared at her. "How come you aren't listening to me? My dad is here with half-men. Swank dressed, all of them. And he was talking about a ship." He nodded at the ship. "Probably that one."

"Not *Dauntless*. The captain is Sung Kim Kai. She's one of the best captains my father has. Absolutely loyal."

"Maybe not anymore. You don't know what's happened since you went running. Maybe someone else is commanding."

"No. It's not possible."

"Don't be stupid," Nailer said. "You know I'm right. My dad and the *Dauntless* showing up on the same day? It's the only thing that makes sense."

"It wasn't *Dauntless* that was chasing me before," she said stubbornly. "It was *Pole Star*. I trust Captain Sung."

Nailer hesitated. "We'll check," he said finally. "But we're not just going to walk out and get snagged like a couple of crawfish jumping into a pot. It's too big a coincidence to have my dad and your ship show up at the same time. It's probably a trap." He tugged at her. "Right now we have to get out of sight. None of this matters if they bag us while we're gabbing in broad daylight. I'll go out again tonight, check things out."

"What if the ship leaves before?" she pressed. "What then?"

"Then it leaves!" Nailer said heatedly. "Better not to get bagged than to rush things on a hope. Maybe you're eager to get yourself caught, but I'm not. I know what my dad will do if he catches me and I'm not risking it. There'll be other ships, but you won't get a second chance if we screw this up."

"There's worse things than hope, Nailer."

"Yeah. Getting caught by my dad would be at the top of my list. What's yours?"

Nita gave him a dirty look, but he could tell she'd gotten the point. She'd lost the feverish excitement that had first filled her. "Okay," she said. "Let's get out of here." She carried her basin of cracked pottery back into the fish shack, and came back a minute later.

"They won't pay me for today unless I stick until dinner."

"It doesn't matter." Nailer could barely contain his fear and frustration. "We need to get out of sight."

They hurried down the boardwalk and then slipped into brackish waters, wading until they reached one of the old mansions that filled the area. The bottom floor was entirely flooded, and the place was caving in on itself, but the upper floors held a slew of squats. Tool had convinced the gang who ran the place to let them crash in one of the rooms above. He had chosen it because one of the upper windows afforded a view down to the boardwalks, and also out to the ships. A decent squat, and with Tool as their protector, no one bothered them. Lucky Girl was glad enough to have a place to crash that she had barely complained about the snakes and roaches and pigeon nests that they shared space with.

Together, they climbed the creaking stairs, stepping over broken and mildewed missing steps and finding their way around the holes and gaps in the floors to their room. A rusty spring bed without a mattress lay at one side, but they didn't keep anything else in the room.

Nita went to the window and stared out at the ship. She looked like the little kids who squatted outside of Chen's, hoping for scrap bones. Starving. Desperate and starving for something that they weren't quite sure would come to them.

Nailer said, "If the ship's still here tonight, we'll go after it then, when not so many eyes can pick us out. Maybe we'll do some asking around. See if we can run a message out to your smart captain, see if she's real, then we decide what to do. But we'll test it first, right? You don't jump into a pond until you check for a python at the hole, and you sure as hell don't go out to that ship without a way to get off if things go wrong."

Nita nodded reluctantly. They watched as darkness settled on the boardwalks. Laborers streamed back to their squats and street stalls opened for dinner. Music came from the bars, zydeco and high-tide blues. Mosquitoes swarmed.

Nailer studied the crowds, glad they were in darkness. He had a prickling feeling that his father was still out there, watching for him; that the old man knew just where he was, and was circling in for a kill. He fought off the fear.

"Tool's late," Nita said.

"Yeah."

"You think your dad got him?"

Nailer shook his head, frustrated, trying to scan the crowds. "I don't know. I'm going to go look around."

"I'm coming, too."

"No." He shook his head vigorously. "You stay here."

"Like hell. I'm no more recognizable than you." She pulled her long hair over her face so that she was shielded by ratty lengths. The days in the swamps and water of the Orleans hadn't been kind to the silky strands. "Probably even less."

Nailer had to admit she had a point. She didn't look much like the swank he and Pima had found in the shipwreck. She was pretty, maybe one of the prettiest girls he'd ever seen, but definitely different than before. Now she blended.

"Okay, sure. Whatever."

They slipped out of the building and down into the water, making their way slowly toward the crowds. They found a place in the swamp land bordering the main boardwalk and crouched together, scanning the night traffic, looking for signs of Tool or of Nailer's father and the half-men he had appeared with.

Nailer shuddered at the thought of his father with goon muscle like the half-men at his beck and call. Tool was terrifying enough without a man like Richard Lopez in charge. Nailer cursed, feeling pinned down. He didn't like any of the options. Didn't relish testing the loyalty of Nita's Captain Sung out on the *Dauntless*. Didn't like sitting here, half exposed, trying to figure out why Tool was missing.

Nita was watching him. "Do you ever wish you just took the gold off my fingers when you had the chance?"

Nailer hesitated, then shook his head. "No." He grinned. "At least, not lately."

"Not even now? With your dad looking for you?"

Nailer shook his head again. "It's not worth thinking about. It's already done." He saw a hurt look cross her face and hurried to explain himself. "That's not what I meant. I'm not saying you're just some mistake I've got to live with. I mean, it's part of it." Again the hurt look. Damn, he was making a hash of this, and he didn't even know what he was trying to say. "I like you. I wouldn't trade you to my dad any more than I'd trade Pima. We're crew, right?" He showed her the palm of his hand where he'd slashed it for their blood oath. "I got your back."

"You've got my back." Nita smiled slightly. "And you'd vouch me onto light crew. You're full of compliments, aren't you?" Her dark eyes held him, intense, serious. "Thank you, Nailer. For everything. I know if you hadn't saved me..." She paused. "Pima didn't care. She just saw a swank." She reached out and touched his cheek. "Thank you."

There was something in her eyes Nailer hadn't seen before. It filled him with a tingling hunger. He realized that at this moment, if he was bold...

He leaned forward. Their lips touched. For the briefest moment, she leaned in to him, let her lips press more strongly against his. Then she drew back, flustered, and looked away. Nailer's heart beat wildly. He could hear his blood in his ears, thudding excitement. He tried to think of something to say, something smart, something to make her look at him again, to renew the connection he'd felt just a moment before. But the words didn't come.

Nita pointed. "Tool's coming," she said thickly. "Maybe he'll know something about the ship."

Nailer turned and caught sight of Tool in the crowd, headed in their direction. He felt a confused rush of relief and frustration at the interruption. And then something else caught his eye: across the crowds, two half-men hurrying to intercept Tool.

"It's them," Nailer said. "Those were the ones with my dad."

Nita sucked in her breath. "They see Tool."

"We have to warn him." Nailer tried to get up, but Nita grabbed him and yanked him down.

"You can't help him," she whispered fiercely.

He tried to shout to Tool, but she pressed her hand over his mouth. "No!" she whispered. "You can't! We'll all be caught then!"

Nailer looked into her fierce, solemn eyes and nodded slowly. As soon as she took her hand away, he sprang up and gave her a withering look. "You're a cold one, aren't you? Hide if you want. He's our crew."

Before she could stop him again, he was off and running, jumping through the vines and out onto the boardwalk. Tool saw him running and waving. "Look out!" Nailer shouted.

Tool turned and saw his hunters converging. Snarls echoed in the night and then the half-men were all moving. Fast. Blurringly fast. Faster than any natural human could ever move. Machetes appeared in the dog-men's hands. They dove for Tool, snarling. One of them flew back, thrown by Tool's strength, but the other swung his machete. Blood sprayed the air, an arc of black liquid gleaming in lantern glow. Nailer cast about for a weapon, something he could throw, a club, anything—

Nita grabbed him and dragged him back. "Nailer! You can't help him!" she said. "We have to run before they see us!"

Nailer looked back desperately, fighting her pull. "But—"

Crowds roiled where the half-men snarled and battled. Nailer heard wood beams cracking. The crowd obscured what was happening, but suddenly the rotten frontage of a building gave way and collapsed. Dust boiled up into the air. People screamed and stampeded from the wreckage. Nita yanked his arm. "Come on! This isn't a fight you can survive! They're too fast and too strong! You've never seen half-men fight. You can't help him!"

Nailer stared at where Tool had disappeared in dust and wreckage. More snarling rose, and then a scream, high and animal.

Hating himself, Nailer turned and ran, ducking and dodging with the crowd.

They huddled near the water's edge, watching the lights out in the deeps, watching for more of Pyce's creatures. People walked by, ignoring the two urchins on the shore, just another pair of the many that came and went like the junk in the tides.

"I'm sorry," Nita said. "I didn't want to leave him, either."

Nailer gave her a withering look. "He was helping us."

"There are some fights you can't win." She looked away. "Half-men don't fight like people. More like hurricanes. We would have been killed or caught, or just made it harder for Tool to fight on his own."

"And now he's dead."

She was silent, lips pressed together, staring out at the blackness and the reflections of torches and LED beacons on the waters. Oars rattled in oarlocks and the distant buzz of a pilot boat wafted across the water to them.

Finally, Nita said, "We have to try to get to the *Dauntless*. It's the only way."

Nailer didn't want to agree, but he didn't see any better option. Without Tool to give them protection in this city, they were minnows waiting to be eaten. They couldn't even keep their squat if he wasn't around to provide muscle. But the sudden arrival of the ship along with his father and the half-men filled him with unease. They were too closely linked. The ship had come and his father had appeared like a wraith on the boardwalks and it was only dumb luck that allowed Nailer to avoid the man.

And now the *Dauntless* sat out there in the waves, beckoning like bait on a line.

Throughout the Orleans, Lucky Girl's enemies would be searching harder now, sure that they were on the scent. The finding of Tool would bring more people down, waves of searchers. It would inspire his father for certain. Surviving in the drowned streets of the Orleans would be impossible. They couldn't work in the open, couldn't let their faces be shown without drawing attention.

Nita said, "We're going to that ship out there, and Captain Sung will help us get to my father."

Nailer shrugged. "It's your funeral."

"Yours too."

Nailer stared at the distant docks and the bustle of nighttime Orleans. The dead city, still half alive, like a zombie corpse reanimated, because people needed the trade, and the mouth of the Mississippi still poured down through the center of the continent with its great barges full of food and whatever manufactured objects came from the northern cities. All sorts of places upriver, probably, lots of places to hide. All sorts. And them just a couple bits of driftwood. They could float...

"We could go up the river," he suggested.

"Not until I know about the *Dauntless*." Nita stabbed her finger toward the distant shape of the ship. "That's where I'm going. With or without you."

Nailer searched the crowds, then sighed. "Fine. But I'll do it by myself." He held up a hand, forestalling protest. "If your captain's there, I'll find her. If I find her, then we bring you out."

"But they don't know you."

"You're the one everyone wants. They're not hunting for me, except to get to you. There's a chance I can at least look things over. But you'll be recognized in a second. These aren't my people, they're yours."

"What about your dad?"

Nailer made a sound of exasperation. "If you're worried he's on the boat, then why go out there at all? Since you won't listen to me and stay away, I'll go take a look. I know how to sneak up on them, and it's a hell of a lot easier if I go alone." He grimaced. "Stay out of sight. I'll meet you at the squat and let you know."

Without waiting for a response, he jogged down the planking and waded into the black water. He made his way out toward the floating docks, swimming slow and off the main marked path through the water. At least this way he could approach unnoticed.

Cool water lapped around him, the darkness almost total. He kept swimming, making his way toward the beautiful ship. He had dreamed about ships like this, about being on their decks, about sailing on them, and now he was on the verge of sneaking aboard one.

When he thought about it, the only thing that had ever seemed truly beautiful to him were these ships with their carbon-fiber hulls and fast sails and hydrofoils that cut the ocean like knives as they crossed the great oceans or made their way over the pole. He wondered how cold it was in the North. He had seen photos of ships rimed with ice as they went through the polar night on their way to the far side of the world. The distances were immense and yet they sailed so fast and so sleek, undeterred.

It took fifteen minutes of swimming and his arms ached by the time he reached the *Dauntless*. He slipped beneath the docks, bobbing in the salt water, and listened. Conversation: men and women joking, talking about shore leave. Another complaining about resupply rates and local con men. He listened as he bobbed in the depths.

A pair of half-men waited at the gangway, keeping guard and another pair were on the ship fore and aft. He shivered. He'd heard they could see in the dark, and Tool had never seemed uncomfortable in dim light. Now, all of a sudden, the fear that they would pick him out in the blackness filled him with an almost paralyzing terror. They would see him. They would hand him to his father and he would die. His father would cut him open.

Nailer drew deeper under the dock, listening to the tramp of feet. A few conversations mentioned a captain, but no name to go with it...only "the captain" wanting to be under way. "The captain" having a schedule.

Nailer waited, hoping for some mention of the saintly Captain Sung. The waves jostled him. He was starting to get cold from a lack of exercise. Even this warm tropic water was starting to suck the heat from him. The floating dock and its anchor moved and swayed. Footsteps thumped overhead. The whine of a motor launch, someone burning biodiesel to reach the ship. Faces gleaming in the darkness. Men and women with scars and hard looks. Someone hurried down to greet the craft.

"Captain."

The man didn't respond, just climbed out. He looked back. "We need to be under way."

"Yes, sir."

Nailer waited, heart thudding. It wasn't Captain Sung. This was a man, not a woman. And there was nothing of the Chinese about him. Lucky Girl had been wrong. Things had changed. Nailer forced down his disappointment. They'd have to find another way.

The captain was standing almost directly above Nailer. He spit into the water no more than a foot away.

"Pyce's people are all over the docks," he said.

"I didn't see a ship."

The captain spit again. "Must have anchored off site and shuttled in."

"What are they doing here?"

"No good, I'm guessing."

Nailer closed his eyes. *The enemy of my enemy is my friend*, he thought. The captain and his lieutenant were climbing the gangplank. "We'll leave with this tide," the captain said. "I want to be under way before we have to speak with them."

"What about the rest of the crew?"

"Send back for them. But hurry. I want to be gone before dawn."

The lieutenant saluted and turned for the launch. Nailer took a deep breath. It was a risk, but he didn't have any other choices. He swam out from under the dock and called up.

"Captain!"

The captain and his lieutenant both startled. They drew their pistols. "Who's there?"

"Don't shoot!" Nailer called. "I'm down here."

"What the devil are you doing down in the water?"

Nailer swam close to the planking and grinned. "Hiding."

"Get up here." The captain still was wary. "Let's see your face."

Nailer scrambled out of the water, praying that he hadn't made a mistake. He squatted, panting on the deck.

"Dock rat," the lieutenant said with distaste.

"Swank." Nailer made a face at him, then turned his attention to the captain. "I have a message for you."

The captain didn't approach and he didn't put down his pistol. "Tell me, then."

Nailer glanced at the lieutenant. "It's only for you."

The captain frowned. "If you've got something to say, say it." He called behind him. "Knot! Vine! Toss this rat back in the water." The two half-men rushed forward. Nailer was stunned at how fast they were. They were on him, grabbing his arms before he even had a chance to consider fleeing.

"Wait!" Nailer cried. He struggled against the iron grip of the half-men. "I have a message for you. From Nita Chaudhury!"

A sudden intake of breath. The captain and his lieutenant exchanged glances.

"What's that?" the lieutenant asked. "What did you say?" He stormed over to where Nailer was held. "What's that you say?"

Nailer hesitated. Could he be trusted? Could any of them? There were too many things he didn't know. He had to gamble. Either he'd gotten lucky or he'd walked into a trap. "Nita Chaudhury. She's here."

The captain came up close, his face hard. "Don't lie to me, boy." He took Nailer's face in his hand. "Who sent you? Who's behind you with lies like this?"

"No one!"

"Bullshit." He nodded at one of the half-men. "Whip him raw, Knot. Get me some answers. I want to know who sent him."

"Nita sent me!" Nailer screamed. "She did, you rotten bastard! I told her we should run, but she said you could be trusted!"

The captain stopped. "Miss Nita is dead more than a month. Drowned and dead. The clan mourns."

"No." Nailer shook his head. "She's here. Hiding. Back in the Orleans. She's trying to get home. But Pyce is hunting her. She thought she could trust you."

The lieutenant smirked. "Christ almighty. Look what the Fates dragged in."

The captain stared at Nailer. "You baiting me?" he asked. "Is that it? You're baiting me the way they did Kim?"

"I don't know Kim."

237

The captain grabbed him, pulled him close. "I'll strangle you with your guts before I go down like she did." He turned away. "Whip him. Find out who sent him. If the girl's out there, we'll go hunting."

The lieutenant nodded and turned. As he did, the captain raised his gun and shot the man in the back. The gunfire echoed in the darkness, running flat across the water. The lieutenant crumpled to the planks. Smoke curled from the barrel of the captain's pistol, slowly disbursing.

Nailer stared at the dead man. The captain turned back to the half-men. "Let the boy go."

Nailer found his voice. "Why did you do that?"

"He was my minder," the captain said simply. To the half-men he said, "Weigh him down and then go with the boy. We're leaving with the tide."

"And the rest of the crew?"

The captain grimaced. "Find Wu and Trimble and Cat and Midshipman Reynolds." He stared out at the water. "And do it damn quietly. No one else, you understand?" He turned to look at Nailer. "You'd better not be lying to me, boy. I don't fancy a life of piracy, so you'd better damn well be right."

"I'm not lying."

The half-men Knot and Vine guided him into the launch. They were huge and daunting. The boat moved slowly away from the dock, aiming for the deep streets of the Orleans.

"Where are we going?" Nailer asked. "She's close to shore. We don't need to go so deep into the drowned city."

"First our men, then her," Knot said.

Vine nodded. "She will need protection. It is better not to drag her into the open until we are ready to run."

"Run from what?"

Vine grinned, showing sharp teeth. "The rest of our loyal crew."

19

KNOT AND VINE were fast and efficient, moving from bar to nailshed to bar, seeking silently and collecting their fellows. They said little to Nailer as they worked the Orleans. The rest of the crew were regular people, not half-men at all. Wu: tall and blond and missing fingers. Trimble: thickly muscled, with forearms like hams and a tattoo of a mermaid on one bicep. Cat, with his green eyes and steady stare. Reynolds, with a long black braid running down her back, short and stocky and with a pistol in her belt.

Reynolds was the first located and she took command. At each venue, all she said was "Nita" and the drunken crew sobered or dropped their whores and came away until they were a fast-moving knot of muscle and bare steel cutting through the drowned city's revelry of sailors and traders.

It was astonishing to watch how efficiently they moved. An entire team mobilized instantly at the invocation of Lucky Girl's name. Astonishing to see the value these people placed on her. Until recently, Nailer had mostly thought of her just as a rich girl who bought the muscle she needed, but here was something else, this clustered tribe of weaponry and purpose. Total loyalty. More intense even than crew loyalty in the ship-breaking yards.

Reynolds pointed them to scouting locations. "Anyone seen Kaliki and Michene?"

Heads shook. She smiled tightly. "Good. Keep your eyes out for anyone you've seen on another of the company ships. We know Pyce's lackeys are around and they're hunting, too." She turned to Nailer. "Where is she?"

Nailer pointed out the drowned mansion that overlooked the Orleans waters. "Up there. In one of those rooms. Where the trees are growing out of the roof."

Reynolds nodded at Vine and Knot. "Go get her." She waved at Wu. "Bring the skiff around."

Nailer said, "I'd better go, too. We saw some other half-men before. Pyce's. They were hunting for her. She'll think you're with Pyce."

Reynolds hesitated.

Cat shrugged. "Captain Candless believes him, right?"

"Go," she said.

Nailer ran to catch up with Knot and Vine. "She's up here," he said breathlessly. He slipped ahead of them, leading.

They sloshed into the collapsing house, water splashing

around them. Rotten stairs creaked as they made their way up to the squat. The house was strangely silent. No one was in it at all. None of the other slum dwellers, none of the other scavengers and dock laborers. It should have been full of the snoring bodies of coolie laborers, all exhausted and unconscious from their day shift work. Instead, there was silence. Their own room was empty except for the rusted bed and its springs.

Nailer came down the stairs to the flooded main floor, shaking his head, followed by the half-men. "I don't get it. She's—"

A shadow in the waters moved, sending ripples. Knot and Vine growled.

"Lucky Girl?" Nailer called softly. "Nita?"

The shadow resolved into a thickly muscled form, slumped against a rotting wall, water up around its waist as it sat, breathing heavily in the darkness. One hard yellow eye opened, flaring like a lantern in the darkness.

"Your father has her now," the shadow rumbled.

"Tool!" Nailer rushed forward.

Blood smeared the half-man's muzzle and more black blood ran sticky down his chest, slashes from machete cuts. His cheek was laid open with claw marks and one eye was completely closed with a swelling bruise, but it was Tool nonetheless.

"And you didn't fight for her?" Captain Candless stared at Tool, incredulous. "Even when your patron wished her protected?" They were all on the *Dauntless*, a huddle of demoralized sailors standing around Nailer and Tool, as Tool explained what had happened.

"The boy is not my patron," Tool rumbled. He daubed at the blood still oozing from the cut above his half-closed eye.

The captain scowled and stalked over to *Dauntless*'s rail. Dawn was just breaking the sky into pale gray, illuminating the floating docks and the distant mist-shrouded structures of drowned Orleans. "They said they were taking her to a ship? You're sure?"

"I am." Tool turned his gaze to Nailer. "Your father was disappointed that you weren't with Lucky Girl. He wanted to keep the ship waiting while he hunted for you longer. The man has plans for you, Nailer."

"And you just sat and listened while all this went on?" Midshipman Reynolds demanded.

Tool blinked once, slowly. "Richard Lopez had many half-men, well armed. I do not lunge into battles that cannot be won."

Knot and Vine curled their lips at Tool's answer and growled guttural contempt. Tool didn't flinch, just looked at the pair. "The girl is your patron, not mine. If you enjoy dying for the sake of your owners, that is your business."

Nailer felt a thrill of dread at the half-man's words. There was a challenge there, and these other half-men, Knot and Vine, sensed it. Their growling rose. They started forward.

The captain waved them off. "Knot! Vine! Go below. I'll handle this."

243

Their growls cut short. Their stares were still hard, but they turned away and went down through one of the clipper's gangways, disappearing belowdecks. The captain turned back to Tool. "Did they say the name of their ship?"

Tool shook his huge head.

Midshipman Reynolds pinched her lip, thoughtful. "There's a couple ships that might be down here. We've got *Seven Sisters* on the north-south passenger run. The *Ray* running charter. *Mother Ganga* carrying iron scrap down to Cancun." She shrugged. "No one else scheduled down here until harvest season when the grain comes down the Mississippi."

"The *Ray*, then," the captain said. "It will be the *Ray*. Mr. Marn was quick enough to declare confidence in Pyce when Nita's father was forced aside. It must be the *Ray*."

Nailer frowned. The list of ships bothered him. "Are there any other ships on your list?"

"None that would be carrying half-men as crew."

Nailer chewed his lip, trying to remember. "There was a ship, another one, or a different name at least, that chased Lucky Girl into the storm. It was a big ship. Built for the north...*North Run*, maybe?"

Reynolds and the captain looked at him, puzzled.

Nailer scowled, frustrated. He couldn't quite remember the name. *North Run*? *North Pole Run*? "*Northern Run*?" he tried. "*North Pole*?"

"*Pole Star*?" the captain prompted, suddenly interested.

Nailer nodded uncertainly. "Maybe."

Reynolds and the captain exchanged glances. "An ugly name," Reynolds muttered.

The captain looked hard at Nailer. "Are you sure? *Pole Star*?"

Nailer shook his head. "I just remember that it was a ship for crossing the pole."

The captain grimaced. "Let's hope you're not right."

"Does it change anything?"

He shook his head. "Nothing that concerns you." He glanced at Reynolds. "Even if it is *Pole Star*, they shouldn't know that we're their enemy yet. None of you did anything to identify yourselves onshore."

"Except you," Reynolds observed dryly.

"Our late lieutenant is hardly going to complain." The captain paused, thinking again. "We can take them. With a bit of trickery and their trust, it can be done. A bit of trickery, a touch from the Fates—"

"—and a blood offering," someone muttered.

The captain grinned. "Anyone on the *Ray* or *Pole Star* we can trust?"

The others shook their heads. "They've been shuffling crews," Reynolds said. "I think Leo and Fritz might have ended up on the *Ray*."

"And you trust them?"

Reynolds smiled, showing black teeth from chewing betel nut. "Almost as much as I trust you."

"Anyone else?"

"Li Yan?"

Cat shook his head. "No. If she's there, she's gone over."

Nailer watched, not comprehending. The captain glanced at him. "Ah, boy, you're in an ugly fight, you are. A bit of a contested leadership right now in the shipping clan."

"Rook," Trimble said suddenly. "Rook would stay loyal."

"Is he on *Pole Star*?"

"Yes."

"That's it, then?" When no one else spoke, the captain nodded. "Well, then. We're hunting for Pyce's traitorous lackeys and we're going to take their ship and we're going to free Miss Nita, and take back our company from the usurper." He nodded at the crew. "Get us under way. Reynolds, you're promoted now that poor Henry took the plunge."

Reynolds grinned. "I was doing his work anyway."

"Wouldn't have gotten rid of him if I didn't know it."

The crew scattered to their jobs, running to release the lines on the ship and raise the anchors.

Tool heaved himself upright. "Hold the ship," he said. "I will not be joining you."

Nailer turned, surprised. "You're leaving?"

"I do not crave death on the seas." The half-man's sharp teeth showed briefly, a feral smile. "If you're wise, you will join me, Nailer. Walk away from this."

The captain watched, curious. "Who is your patron, then?" he asked. "Not the boy, not Miss Nita. Who, then?"

Tool regarded him steadily. "I have none."

The captain laughed, incredulous. "Impossible."

"Believe what you wish." The half-man turned and shambled for the dock.

Nailer ran after him. "Wait! Why can't you come with us?"

Tool paused. He scanned the crew, then turned his fierce one-eyed gaze on Nailer. "I told Sadna I would protect you. But I will not protect you from foolishness. If you choose to risk yourself on the sea, it is nothing to do with me. You have a new crew, I think. My debt to Sadna is repaid."

"But what about Lucky Girl?"

Tool looked at Nailer. "She is just one person. These people think she is infinitely valuable. But she is just one more who will die, if not now, then later." He nodded at the bustle of the ship. "Come with me, or stay and risk yourself with these ones. It's your choice. But you should know that they are fanatics. They will die for their Miss Nita. If you go with them, be sure you are willing to do the same."

Nailer hesitated. With Tool, he could be safe. They could go anywhere.

Nita's face intruded on his thoughts, her smug look when she teased him about not eating with a fork and knife and spoon. Contrasted with that, her frantic urging that he get medicine for his shoulder when he was still nothing but a ship breaker to her. And then, finally, the look in her eyes when they hid beside the boardwalk. Her hand on his cheek...

"I'm going," he said firmly.

Tool studied him. "So. You bite like a mastiff and never let go. Just like your father, then." Nailer started to retort, but Tool waved him silent. "Don't argue the obvious. Lopez never let anything stand in his way, either." Tool's teeth showed briefly. "Be certain that you aren't biting something bigger than you, Nailer. I have seen hunting hounds corner a great Komodo dragon, and they died as a pack because they didn't have the sense to retreat. Your father is more than a dragon. If he catches you, he will slaughter you. And this merchant vessel is no warship, no matter what its captain foolishly believes."

Nailer started to answer, tried to say something full of bravado, but something in Tool's eyes stopped him. "I understand. I'll be careful."

Tool nodded sharply and turned away, but then he paused. He crouched down, his great head leaning close. His remaining eye regarded Nailer, and his breath was laced with the stench of combat and blood.

"Listen to me, boy. Scientists created me from the genes of dogs and tigers and men and hyenas, but people always believe I am only their dog." Tool's eyes flicked to the captain, and his sharp teeth gleamed in a brief smile. "When the fighting comes, don't deny your slaughter nature. You are no more Richard Lopez than I am an obedient hound. Blood is not destiny, no matter what others may believe."

Tool straightened again and turned away. "Good luck, boy. And good hunting."

The captain watched the half-man limp down the gang-plank. "A strange creature, that one."

Nailer didn't answer. The anchors were rising. The gang-plank reeled inward and sealed itself into a compartment in the side of the clipper. Already Tool was disappearing down the dock. Nailer felt suddenly alone. He wanted to call after Tool. To run after him...He looked around at the bustling crew, all of them working at jobs he didn't understand, all of them crew, all of them knowing one another and familiar with one another's work. He felt terribly out of place.

Pale sails unfurled, rippling in the breezes. The ship's boom swept across the deck and crewmen ducked under its swing. The sails filled with air and the ship heeled slightly under their pressure. It began to move, urged forward by the increasing breezes of the dawn.

The captain motioned at Nailer. "Come below, boy. I want a look at you."

Nailer wanted to stay on deck, to watch the activity, to see if he could still spy Tool on the docks, but he let the captain guide him down the narrow steps to the cramped interior of the ship.

The captain opened a door to his own cabin. A small bunk filled most of the space. A window peered out the stern. In the increasing light, the ship's wake curled white behind them, a spreading vee in the still gray water of morning. The captain nodded to Nailer that he should fold down a bench. He released a seat of his own, nearly filling the room.

"Space is at a premium," he said. "We're for cargo. Not a lot of comfort."

Nailer nodded, even though he didn't know what the captain was talking about. The ship was divine. Everything was clean and ordered. No one seemed to sleep in a room with more than three other people. The hammocks were all strung tidily. Nothing was out of place. It wasn't like the ship that Lucky Girl had come off, but it was damn close.

"Tell me, Nailer, where did you come from, originally?"

"Bright Sands Beach."

"Never heard of it."

"It's up the coast," Nailer said. "A hundred miles, maybe."

"There's nothing up there…" The captain frowned. "You're a ship breaker?" When Nailer nodded, the captain made a face. "I should have guessed from your ribs and work tattoos." He studied Nailer's marked skin. "Ugly work, that."

"It pays, though."

"How old are you? Fourteen? Fifteen? You look so starved, I can't tell."

Nailer shrugged. "Pima was sixteen, I think. And she was older than me…" He shrugged.

"You don't know?"

Nailer shrugged again. "Doesn't really matter. Either you're small enough for light crew, or you're big enough for heavy crew, and either way, if you're too stupid or lazy or untrustworthy, then you're neither, because no one will vouch for you. No. I don't know how old I am. But I made it onto light crew, and I made quota every day. That's what matters where I come from. Not your stupid age."

"Don't be testy. I'm just curious about you." The captain seemed about to say something more on the topic, but instead turned to the subject of Richard Lopez.

"The half-man said your father was hunting you?"

"Yeah." Nailer described the beach and his father, the way things ran on the wrecks. Described how his father dealt with people who opposed him.

"Why didn't you just go along?" the captain asked. "It would have been easier for you. More profitable, certainly. Pyce has no hesitation about buying loyalty. You would have been rich and safe if you'd just sold Miss Nita."

Nailer shrugged.

The captain's face turned hard. "I want an answer," he said. "You're going against your own blood. Maybe you've got second thoughts. Maybe you'd like to work out a truce with your father."

Nailer laughed. "My dad doesn't give anyone a chance for second thoughts. He cuts you first. He talks about family sticking together, but what he really means is that I give him money so he can slide crystal, and make sure he's okay on his binges, and he hits me when he wants." Nailer made a face. "Lucky Girl's more of a family than he is."

As soon as he said it, he knew it was true. Despite the

short time he'd known her, Nailer was sure of Nita. He could count the people on one hand who were like that, and Pima and Sadna were the ones who topped that list. And surprisingly, Lucky Girl was there, too. She was family. An overwhelming sense of loss threatened to swallow him.

"So now you want revenge," the captain said.

"No. I just—" Nailer shook his head. "It's not about my dad. It's Lucky Girl. She's good, right? She's worth a hundred of some of my old crew. A thousand of my dad." His voice cracked. Nailer took a breath, trying to master himself, then looked up at the captain. "I wouldn't leave a dead dog with my dad, let alone Lucky Girl. I have to get her back."

The captain studied Nailer thoughtfully. Silence stretched between them.

"You poor bastard," the captain murmured finally.

"Me?" Nailer was confused. "Why?"

The captain smiled tightly. "You understand that Miss Nita belongs to one of the most powerful trading clans in the North?"

"So?"

"Eh. Never mind." The captain sighed. "I'm sure Miss Nita would be pleased to know she inspires such loyalty from a ship breaker."

Nailer felt his face turn hot with embarrassment. The captain made him sound like a starving mongrel, tagging at Lucky Girl's heels, hoping for scraps. He wanted to say something, to change the captain's impression of him. To make the man take him seriously. The captain saw a ship breaker, tattooed with work stamps and scarred with hard labor. A kid with his ribs showing through. That was all. A bit of beach trash.

Nailer stared at him. "Lucky Girl used to look at me the same way you're looking at me. And now she doesn't. That's why I'm going with you. No other reason. Got it?"

The captain had the grace to look embarrassed. He glanced away and changed the subject. "Lucky Girl. Again with the nickname," the captain said. "Why that?"

"She's got the Fates with her. She came through a city killer and everyone else on that ship was dead. Doesn't get much luckier than that."

"And your people value luck," the captain said.

"My people. Yeah, ship breakers like the lucky eye. Not much else to hang on to when you're on the wrecks."

"Skill? Hard work?"

Nailer laughed. "They're nice. But they only get you so far. Look at you. You got yourself a swank ship and a swank life."

"I've worked very hard for what I have."

"Still born swank," Nailer pointed out. "Pima's mom works a thousand times harder than you and she's never going to have a life as nice as what you got on this boat." He shrugged. "If that ain't being born with the lucky eye, I don't know what is."

The captain started to answer, then stopped and nodded shortly. "I suppose even our bad luck looks good to you."

"Unless you're dead," Nailer said. "That's about it, though."

"Yes, well, I don't plan on being dead quite yet."

"No one does."

The captain grinned. "I've got myself a regular oracle here." He stood. "I'll have to ask you to throw bones for me sometime. In the meantime, I can at least foretell that I'm willing to keep you aboard." He looked Nailer up and down. "We'll need to get you cleaned up and find some clothes and a decent meal for you." He urged Nailer out the door and into the squeezeway beyond. "And then we'll see about getting you trained with a pistol."

"Yeah?" Nailer tried to hide his interest.

"Your half-man Tool was correct in one thing. If we're going to bring Miss Nita back to us, there will be a fight. Pyce's people won't let her go easily."

"You think you can take them?"

"Of course. Pyce took us once unawares, but we won't make the mistake of underestimating him again." He clapped Nailer's shoulder. "With a little luck, we'll have Miss Nita back and safe in no time."

The ship was starting to dip into deep water, the waves churning under it as it made its way out of the safety of the bay. Nailer swayed unsteadily in the passageway, trying to keep his footing. The captain watched him. "You'll get your sea legs soon, don't worry. And when we're up on the hydrofoils, it's almost like standing on dry land."

Nailer wasn't so sure of that. The deck came up under

his feet and sent him stumbling into a wall. The captain watched amused, then strode down the corridor, untroubled by the surge and roll of the deck.

Nailer staggered after. "Captain?"

The man turned.

"Your guy Pyce might be bad, but don't underestimate my dad, either. He might look just like me, all skinny and cut up, but he's deadly. He'll kill you like a cockroach if you don't watch him."

The captain nodded. "I wouldn't worry too much. If Pyce's people haven't killed me yet, your father won't either." He turned and led Nailer up onto the deck.

Wind ruffled Nailer's face as they came up into the dawn. The sun's light increased, a golden wave reaching across the ocean. *Dauntless* buried herself in the glittering waves, slicing for deeper waters.

Hunting.

20

WHITE SPRAY EXPLODED over *Dauntless*'s prow and showered Nailer in cool shimmering drops. He whooped and leaned far over the rail as the ship plunged into the next wave trough, then surged skyward again.

What had always looked so smooth and sleek on the horizon was a rough adventure when experienced from the prow of the *Dauntless*. Waves flew toward him, huge surges that exploded in spray as the low-density hull slashed through. All across the decks, crewmen called and labored under the hot sun, orienting sails, drilling for fire attacks, clearing deck materials as they readied for the fight that they hoped would come.

Dauntless was patrolling the blue waters just a few miles off the Orleans, hoping for a glimpse of their potential quarry. Everyone hoped it would be the *Ray* holding Nita. *Dauntless* was more than a match for that soft target, but the other ship, *Pole Star*, everyone feared. Even the captain was worried about that one. Candless was too good a leader to admit that he was frightened, but Nailer could tell from the way his face turned stony at the mention of the cross-global schooner that it represented an unequal fight.

"She's fast, and she's got teeth," Reynolds said when Nailer asked about the ship. "She's got an armored hull, she's got missile and torpedo systems that can blow us right out of the water, and we'd hardly have a chance to pray to God before we died."

She explained that *Pole Star* was a trading vessel but also a warship, accustomed to fighting Siberian and Inuit pirates as it made the icy Pole Run to Nippon. The pirates were bitter enemies of the trading fleets and perfectly willing to kill or sink an entire cargo as revenge for the drowning of their own ancestral lands. There were no polar bears now, and seals were few and far between, but with the opening of the northern passage a new fat animal had appeared in the polar regions: the northern traders, making the short hop to Europe and Russia, or over to Nippon and the wide Pacific via the top of the melted pole. And with the disappearance of the ice, the Siberians and the Inuit became sea people. They pursued their new prey the way they had once hunted seals and bears in the frozen north, and they hunted with an implacable appetite.

Pole Star was a vessel that relished these encounters, baited them even.

Still, despite Nailer's warnings, Reynolds said they would most likely encounter the *Ray*. "*Pole Star* is on the far side of the world," she said.

"But Lucky Girl——"

"Miss Nita could have been mistaken. In a storm, under pursuit, anyone could make a mistake."

"Lucky Girl's not stupid."

Reynolds gave him a hard look. "I didn't call her stupid. I said she could have made a mistake. *Pole Star*'s shipping schedule puts her just out of Tokyo, and that's assuming the winds have been favorable. No closer."

The work on the decks continued. An astonishing amount of the ship ran on automation. They could raise and lower the sails on winches electronically with power from solar batteries. The sails themselves were not canvas at all, but solar sheets, designed to feed electricity into the system and add to the power available already from roof skin solar cells. But even with the electronics and automation, still Captain Candless drilled everyone on how to reef a sail if everything was dead and how to work the hand pumps if the ship was sinking and the power failed. He swore that all the technology in the world wouldn't save a sailor if he didn't use his head and know his ship.

The crew of the *Dauntless* knew their ship.

Sailors clambered up the masts, checking winch hooks and loop points for rust or repair. Near Nailer, Cat and another crewman were loading the huge Buckell cannon that was set near the prow, fitting the parasail into its barrel and checking the monofilament tether line—gossamer thin and steel strong—that sat in a shining reel beside the gun.

If anyone cared about the loss of crewmen ashore when they sailed, no one said anything. The captain muttered that a few of the crew still on board would probably have preferred another master, but that hardly mattered now. They were on the waves and if they had a grumble they kept it to themselves. Candless's core of loyal followers kept everyone in line and so *Dauntless* surged through the waves of the Gulf, patrolling and waiting for its target.

On the first night, Nailer had slept in a soft bunk and woke with his back aching from it, unused to sinking into a mattress instead of lying on sand or palm ticking or hard planks, but by the second day he felt so spoiled that he wondered how he would sleep when he went back to the beach.

The thought troubled him: *when* he went back?

Was he going back?

If he went back, his father or his father's crew would be waiting for him, people who would look for payback. But no one on the ship was indicating that he would be able to stay on *Dauntless*, either. He was in limbo.

A splash of water shook him from his reverie. The ship plunged through another wave crest, dousing him and shaking him from his perch. He skidded across the deck until his life line caught him short with a jolt. He was hooked to the rail to keep himself from washing overboard, but still the huge blue-green waves that surged over the bow and poured off the sloped deck were astonishingly powerful. Another wave rushed over them. Nailer shook seawater out of his eyes.

Reynolds laughed as she saw him climbing to his feet again. "You should see what it's like when we're really going fast."

"I thought we were."

"No." She shook her head. "Someday, if we use the high sails, you'll see. Then we don't sail, we fly." Her eyes took on a faraway look. "We truly fly."

"Why not now?"

She shook her head. "The winds have to be right. You can't fire the Buckell cannon unless you understand the high winds. We send up kites first to test, to make sure, and then if the water's right and the high winds are right." She pointed at the cannon. "Then we fire that bad baby and she jumps out of the water like she's been shot."

"And you fly."

"That's right."

Nailer hesitated, then said, "I'd like to see it."

Reynolds gave him a speculative look. "Maybe you will. If we have to run, maybe we'll all be skating the ocean."

Nailer hesitated. "No. After we save Lucky Girl, I mean. I want to come with you. Wherever you go. I want to go, too."

"Careful what you wish for. We'd work you."

"Is that all?" Nailer made a face. "I'm not afraid of work."

"All I see you doing is standing on a deck and riding waves."

Nailer locked eyes with her. "I'll do anything you want, if you take me on. You just say it. I'm not afraid of any work."

Reynolds grinned. "Guess we'll have to send you up the mast and see."

Nailer didn't blink. "I'll go."

The captain came up behind her. "What's all the conversation?"

Reynolds smiled. "Nailer here wants a job."

The captain looked thoughtful. "A lot of people want to work on the clippers. There are whole clans dedicated to it. Families who buy the right to get on as deckhands and hope to move up. My own family has worked clippers for three generations. That's a lot of competition."

"I can do it," Nailer insisted.

"Hmm," was all the captain said. "Perhaps this is a conversation better saved for after we've located our Miss Nita."

Nailer wasn't sure if Candless was trying to put him off or if he was just saying no in a polite way. Nailer wanted to press the issue, but didn't know how without angering the captain. "You really think you can find Lucky Girl and get her back?" he asked instead.

"Well, I've got some tricks," Candless said. "If the captain of the *Ray* is still Mr. Marn, then we'll be over their gunwales before they know what's hit them." He smiled, then sobered. "But if it's Ms. Chavez, then we're in for a rare fight. She's no fool and her crew is hard and all our decks will be bloody."

"It won't be *Pole Star*," Reynolds insisted.

"Do they both use half-men?" Nailer asked.

"Some," the captain answered. "But *Pole Star* has almost half its crew staffed with augments."

"Augments?"

"Your half-men. We call them augmented because they're people-plus."

"Like Tool."

"A strange creature, that one. I've never heard of a salvage company that would bond that sort of muscle."

"He wasn't with Lawson & Carlson. He was on his own."

The captain shook his head. "Impossible. Augments aren't like us. They have a single master. When they lose that master, they die."

"You kill them?"

"Goodness no." He laughed. "They pine. They are very loyal. They cannot live without their masters. It comes from a line of canine genetics."

"Tool didn't have a master."

The captain nodded, but Nailer could tell he didn't believe. Nailer dropped the subject. It wasn't worth making the captain think he was crazy.

But it did make him wonder about Tool. Everyone who was familiar with half-men and their genetics said that Tool was an impossible creature. That no independent half-men existed. And yet Tool had walked away from many masters. He had worked for Lucky Strike and Richard Lopez, had worked for Sadna, had worked to protect him and Lucky Girl, and then had simply walked away when it no longer suited him. Nailer wondered what Tool was doing now.

Nailer's thoughts were broken by Captain Candless drawing a gun. "I almost forgot," the captain said as he handed it to Nailer. "I promised you this before. Something for when we find our ship. You're going to need to practice with it. Cat will be drilling the crew, and you will drill with them. Boarding actions and the like."

Nailer held the lightweight thing in his hand, so different from the sorts of pistols he had seen others use. "It's so light."

The captain laughed. "You can swim with it even. It won't drag you down. The ammunition is a penetrator. It doesn't use weight to enter the body—well, not as much—it uses spin from the barrel. You've got thirty shots." He offered Nailer a fighting knife as well. "You know how to cut someone?" He indicated the soft parts. "Don't worry about a killing blow and don't go for the head. It will extend you. Go low and hit them in the belly, the knees, behind the legs. If they're down..."

"Cut their throat."

"Good boy! Bloodthirsty little bastard, aren't you?"

Nailer shrugged, remembering Blue Eyes's blood hot on his hands. "My father is pretty good with a knife," he said. He forced the memory away. "When do you think we'll fight?"

"We'll patrol here. We should get a visual on anyone within fifteen miles. We've got the scopes to get a good look at them, and then we can decide if we want to chase or play friendly." He shrugged. "We don't know what they're up to. Maybe they're going to stay for a little while, lie low down south while they wait out the boardroom tactics up north, but I doubt it. They're going to run north and try to make contact with Pyce."

The captain turned and headed for the conning deck. As he departed, he nodded at Nailer's pistol. "Practice with it, Nailer. Make sure you can hit what you aim at."

Nailer nerved himself up and called after the man. "Captain!"

When Candless turned, Nailer said, "If you trust me with a gun, maybe you could trust me with some work, too." He waved at the busy ship. "There must be something you can use me for."

Reynolds shook her head. "You're like a tick on a dog. Just won't stop trying to latch on."

"I just want to help."

The captain studied him thoughtfully, then nodded at Reynolds. "Fair enough. Get him unclipped and make him useful."

Reynolds gave Nailer an appraising look. "Nicely done, boy." Then she smiled. "I think I've got just the job for you."

She led him down into the hold of the clipper, to where the hydraulic systems of the ship lay exposed. It was gloomy. Maintenance panels were pulled up out of the deck and stacked in bins. Huge gears lay exposed under the floor, wicked teeth intertwined, gleaming with oily coatings. Small LED indicators glowed beside control decks. The air reeked with grease and metal. Nailer felt vaguely sick. It reminded him of being back on light crew.

A huge form crawled out from within the gearing system, hoisted itself out. It stared at the two of them with bestial yellow eyes. Knot.

Reynolds said, "Nailer says he wants to be useful."

Knot examined him, his doglike muzzle sniffing the air with questions. "So." He nodded shortly. "He's small enough. I have a use for him."

When Reynolds was gone, he gave Nailer an oiling can and spray applicator that Nailer strapped to his back, and then Knot put Nailer to work lubricating the gearing systems that extended the hydrofoils. Knot indicated where the massive gears, some of them with wheels more than a meter in diameter, sat in the flooring.

"Make sure each gear is degreased, then reoiled. Be thorough. We don't want rust getting into the systems. But don't take long, either. The captain knows we're servicing the system and we've already set the overrides." Knot indicated a row of levers and LED indicators beside the gears. "Technically, no one can extend the hydrofoils as long as we have them locked down, but"—he shrugged—"accidents happen. I've seen crewmen lose an arm because someone forgot to recheck the lockdowns, so even if you think no one's going to run out the foils, don't dawdle."

Nailer studied the wicked-looking gear systems. The teeth glinted dully, looking like they wanted to chew him up. "That bad, huh?"

"The hydrofoils extend very quickly. You would have no chance to react or pull away. They start spinning and they suck anything in, even from a short distance away. Thousands of pounds of pressure running through them. You'd be nothing but ground meat."

"Nice."

"You asked for work." Knot looked at him steadily. "This is the work I have."

Nailer got the message. He crawled down into the maintenance compartment, threading through the gears. Knot watched him for a moment, then said, "You should also lubricate the break valve joints for the monofilament feed."

Nailer craned his neck around. "Which are those?"

The half-man gave him an irritated look. "The ones that are labeled as such." He waved at peeling greasy tags that were stuck to various components of the system.

Nailer stared at the unintelligible words. He looked from the labels to the half-man, then back at the labels. "Sure. Okay."

The half-man made a face of contempt. "You can't read?"

"I can make my mark. I know numbers. Stuff like that."

Knot blew out an exasperated breath. "Your ship-breaking company has a great deal to answer for." He shook his head. "You will need to be taught, then."

"What's the big deal?" Nailer asked. "Just show me which things you want oiled. I'll remember. If I can remember the quota count, I can remember this."

Knot made a face of disgust. "You will be useless to me if you cannot read." He waved a hand at a series of levers. "How will you know which of these disengages the gears from the foil and which will allow you to test the lubricants? How will you know which fires the drive system and which reengages the foils?" Knot slapped a lever and tapped a button inside the service hole. He reached down and yanked Nailer out of the guts of the gears. "Stand back!"

A red light burned bright and Knot yanked another lever. The gears screamed alive, blurring wheels. An oily breeze blew over them as teeth bit against one another and spun up to their maximum speed. The entire maintenance compartment had become a vortex of whirling gears that seemed to want to suck Nailer in. If he'd been down in there, he would have been nothing but a fine spray. Nailer's skin crawled as he fully understood the work Reynolds had given him.

"How will you know what to do?" Knot shouted over the gear scream. "How will you know how to stop it?" He slapped another button and braked the system. The blurring gears slowed, came to a smooth stop, returning the room to silence.

"I need someone who will not make a mistake and tear their own arm off because they pushed the wrong button," he rumbled. "I will inform Reynolds of your deficiency."

"Wait!" Nailer hesitated. "Can't you just teach me? If you don't tell Reynolds, I'll learn whatever you want. Don't cut me off your crew before I have a chance to start."

Knot's yellow dog eyes regarded Nailer. "You wish me to keep a secret from my patron?"

"No." Nailer's voice caught as he realized how uncertain the ground was between himself and the half-man. "I'm just saying I can learn anything you throw at me. Just give me a chance. Please."

Knot cocked his head and smiled. "We'll see if your words match your performance, then."

"So you won't tell her?"

Knot laughed, a low rumble. "Oh no. We don't keep secrets on this ship. But perhaps Lieutenant Reynolds will give you a grace period...assuming you stay motivated."

"I'm motivated. Trust me."

Knot's teeth showed in the dimness, bright and sharp. "It's always a pleasure to see the young take an interest in learning."

21

THEY CAUGHT THE LUCKY EYE on their eighth day of sailing. The *Ray*, out in the deeps, was skating for the Florida cut and the open Atlantic beyond. The news ran through the ship like an electric wire. Soon everyone was up on deck. Captain Candless allowed himself a smile at their good fortune.

"The *Ray*," he said. "Not *Pole Star* at all."

Nailer could tell he was relieved. Nailer strained to see the speck on the horizon where Lucky Girl was running, but it was impossible. The captain saw him straining, grinned, and took him up to the con where a scope and photograph system shot distance pictures of the horizon and then magnified them. Blurs on the horizon became ships, became bow and stern and the smears of faces. All from fifteen miles away. Nailer stared at the images, awed.

"We'll close on them and get some more shots," the captain said. "We'll want to know who's on deck." He nodded to his own decks. "And we'll want to keep our own clear now as well." He paused. "You'll be staying below until we're ready to engage. If Miss Nita gives you away or if your father catches sight of you, they'll be ready for us. We don't want that." The captain looked out at the horizon again, thoughtful. "No. We certainly don't want that."

"Can you catch them?" Nailer asked. They seemed impossibly far away.

Reynolds, who was at the ship's wheel, grinned. "We're a fast ship and they're a luxury wallower."

"So we can?"

"Oh yes. We'll catch them and we'll board them. And we'll take ourselves a right prize." She and the captain exchanged confident smiles.

"I won't be sorry to see Mr. Marn reap a bitter harvest," the captain said. He waved at Nailer. "Come. It will be a while before we close the gap. As long as you're below-decks, you might as well make use of the time. Back to your letters, then."

Nailer forced himself not to sigh.

Knot had taken on the project of teaching Nailer to read, and it hadn't taken long for Nailer to begin resenting the tedium of book learning. But Knot didn't care. The massive creature simply pressed and tested and forced Nailer to memorize and then to write.

In reality, the work wasn't as hard as Nailer had always

believed, especially with the yellow-eyed glare of a half-man looking over his shoulder, but it wasn't exactly interesting in itself. Mostly it was just a question of work and time, and with the ship pitching around and the hydrofoil gears all cleaned and lubricated, all Knot would let him do was study. For the last couple nights, Nailer had lain in his bunk, his head filled with words and letters, dreaming of spellings that Knot had tricked him with.

The half-man liked trickery. Letters were fine, but words were hard. Lots of words didn't spell like they sounded. But still, in the end, it was a memorization trick, like counting turnings in the ducts and keeping the quota count. And Knot wasn't half as mean as old Bapi if you screwed up the counts.

Nailer let himself be ushered belowdecks, and Knot was found and soon they were working their way through a book of Knot's, all about an old guy fishing on a boat. But it was hard for Nailer to concentrate, knowing that Lucky Girl and a fight loomed on the horizon.

At last he closed the book and looked up at the half-man. "Have you always had a master?" he asked.

Knot looked at him steadily. "I work for Captain Candless."

"Yeah, but if you wanted, could you work for someone else?"

Knot shrugged. "I do not wish it."

"Could you?" Nailer pressed.

Knot's eyes hardened. His nostrils flared and his teeth

271

showed slightly behind curling lips. "I do not wish it," the half-man growled.

Nailer flinched. Knot suddenly looked like a mastiff backed into a corner, ready to bite. All of that muscle, previously so calm and steady, was suddenly bunched and bristle-backed. Nailer wanted to press again, but the half-man had become too frightening. He shut up.

The half-man stared at Nailer a moment longer. "I do not wish it," he said again, and then looked away.

Nailer suddenly felt weirdly ashamed that he had prodded the huge creature. "We were reading," he said hesitantly. The half-man nodded slowly.

"Yes. Please continue."

For a while, Nailer read, with Knot correcting him. At last the half-man said, "I think you have done enough for now. I have other preparations I must attend to."

"Are you ready to fight?"

Knot smiled and his sharp teeth showed. "It is my nature to fight." He paused. "But this time it is also a pleasure."

"Because of Lucky Girl?" He corrected himself. "Because of Miss Nita?"

"Yes."

"Is she your mistress?" he asked, hesitantly. "The one you swore loyalty to?"

Knot regarded him. "Not exactly. Captain Candless serves her. I serve the captain. But we swear dual oaths to the clan."

"But her clan is split now. Pyce has half-men working for him, too."

"Yes. It is a difficult time."

Nailer wanted to ask more about the nature of Knot's loyalty, but he was afraid of irritating the creature. The last time it had felt as though he were on the verge of goading a tiger to attack. There were sensitivities that he didn't understand. "You wouldn't ever work for Pyce?"

Sharp teeth showed. A low growl issued. "He is nothing. He turned against us."

"But Captain Candless was working for him, too. Up until just a couple days ago—"

Knot stood abruptly. "As long as Miss Nita survives, we do not serve Pyce. We thought she was dead. Now we know better. That is all. We will serve her until she dies or her clan grants true control to Pyce and his inheritors. Her father will do anything for her. We cannot do less."

"He cares that much?"

"She is his daughter. Family."

"Right. *Family.*" Nailer forced down a stab of jealousy. "The only thing family ever got me was a slap upside the head."

"Some families are different."

Nailer didn't have much to say to that. Knot went to see to his duties, leaving Nailer to lie back in his bunk, waiting as *Dauntless* closed on its prey.

Family. It was just a word. Nailer could spell it now.

Could see its letters all strung together. But it was a symbol, too. And people thought they knew what it meant. People used it everywhere. Ship breakers. His father, *Dauntless*'s crew. Tool. It was one of those things everyone had an opinion about—that it was what you had when you didn't have anything else, that family was always there, that blood was thicker than water, whatever.

But when Nailer thought about it, most of those words and ideas just seemed like good excuses for people to behave badly and think they could get away with it. Family wasn't any more reliable than marriages or friendships or blood-sworn crew, and maybe less. His own father really would gut him if he ever got hold of him again; it didn't matter if they shared blood or not. Nita had an uncle hunting for her.

But Nailer was pretty sure that Sadna would fight for him tooth and nail, and maybe even give up her life to save him. Sadna cared. Pima cared.

The blood bond was nothing. It was the people that mattered. If they covered your back, and you covered theirs, then maybe that was worth calling family. Everything else was just so much smoke and lies.

22

THE *RAY* WAS a sleek yacht with a small crew. *Dauntless* stalked her with Captain Candless making small talk over the ship radios and making friendly observations on the state of the weather during hurricane season.

As they drew closer, the captain's confidence increased. The ship was lightly crewed, and he was not frightened by what he saw. It took the yacht a long time to guess what Candless was planning and start to flee in earnest.

When the *Ray* finally shook out its sails and began to flee before the wind, the captain laughed, delighted. "Ah! Mr. Marn isn't quite as stupid as we supposed," he said. "Now we'll have a nice little chase."

He shouted at his crew to prepare for speed. More sails unfurled and *Dauntless* surged after its quarry. *Dauntless* was a larger ship and much faster and the captain laughed at the *Ray*'s attempt at flight. "Like a tiger chasing a kitten," he crowed.

Still, the other captain, Mr. Marn, was clever. He veered, he dodged, he forced them to overshoot once, and the men on his deck fired their pistols across the gap. But it was only a matter of time before *Dauntless* overtook them and grappled.

"Heel over or I'll sink you and leave you swimming!" Candless roared, and the other ship gave up the fight.

Before they even were fully reefed, Candless's crew was leaping across the gap, hunting, pistols in hand. They swarmed across the deck and poured below. After a few bated-breath minutes, the rest of the *Ray*'s crew came up on deck with their hands on their heads. Half-men guards and cooks and stewards and finally, Captain Marn. They glared across at the *Dauntless*.

"Where's Miss Nita?" Candless shouted.

Marn grinned and shouted back, "If you can't find her, you've got no business with her, you mutinous bastard!"

"Mutinous?" Candless muttered. "I'm not the one who lapped red cash out of Pyce's hand." He turned to his lieutenant. "Reynolds, take the ship." He made his way down the steps with Nailer following. The jump from one ship to the other was nerve-racking, but Nailer was determined not to show any fear. He leaped and landed badly on the moving deck, but at least he was aboard.

Captain Candless surveyed the deck. "Go see if you can sniff out Miss Nita, boy. She's got to be somewhere."

276

Nailer slipped down into the bowels of the ship, making his way from state room to state room, but every place he looked revealed no sign of Lucky Girl. Nothing. She wasn't in any of the astonishingly large staterooms. She wasn't anywhere. Others were searching this ship as well, Knot and Vine and Cat, and all of them were increasingly nervous as they went through the rooms.

"What about secret places?" Nailer asked.

"Wouldn't she make a racket?" Cat wondered.

"Not if she's drugged or tied."

Cat made a face of distaste. They continued their search. Finally they came back on deck.

"Nothing," Cat reported. "We've got nothing anywhere."

The captain cursed and turned on Marn. "Where is she?" He poked his finger in Marn's chest. "If you free her, I won't drop you over the side. Which is better than you deserve. You've gone against all your clan oaths, and you should be hung."

"From where I sit, there's only one person against his clan oaths and it's you, you piratical bastard."

Captain Candless scowled and turned to shout at his crew. "Take it apart! Take the whole damn ship apart. Take it apart piece by piece! I want Miss Nita found and then I want this ship sunk." He glared at his opposite. "You had a chance to do the right thing. More than enough chances."

Suddenly Captain Marn grinned. "We always suspected you of not being loyal. You couldn't have been. Not after what happened to Ms. Sung. We always knew. But you

277

were more careful than most of them. Biding your time. Keeping your head low. Some people thought you deserved the benefit of the doubt."

Candless smiled tightly. "Mighty grateful for that." He tipped his hat. "I'll think about your kindness while I'm watching your boat sink under you."

"Don't bother with thanks," Marn laughed. "Now that we know where you stand, we'll hunt you to the ends of the earth."

"Not once the board convenes. You'll be gone and I'll be back at sailing."

Captain Marn grinned and shook his head. "I'm amazed at you. You used to be such a clever bastard."

Candless's eyes narrowed. "What's that supposed to mean?"

Marn shrugged. "Just that you're not as sly as you used to be. You used to have a sixth sense. I was sure you'd smell a trap and never fall into it, and then you came all the way in, just like they expected."

"Like who expected?" Captain Candless stared at Marn. A look of fear flitted across Candless's face, an anxious thought; then the captain roared, "Reynolds!"

"Captain?"

"What's our horizon?"

"Clear, sir."

"Check again."

A pause, then Reynolds called down, "I've got a sail."

"Identify!"

Another pause and then she was shouting over the side. "It's *Pole Star*, sir! It's *Pole Star* for certain!"

Captain Marn and his crew grinned as the news went through Candless's crew. "If you surrender now," Marn said, "we'll treat your crew as combatants rather than mutineers." He said it loud, so that everyone could hear. "You can go free if you surrender now! Or you can die like dogs with your captain. Your decision!"

Captain Candless stared at the decks full of his crew around him, his face white. His first attempt at an order came as a croak. He tried again, and this time his voice was there, loud and angry, "Back to the ship! Ready sails!"

Already his crew was streaming back, but not all of them. Cat and three others stood by the rail watching. Cat gave a sad wave to them, and then he was allowing himself to be disarmed by the crew of the *Ray*.

Candless wasn't done yet. "Vine! Knot! Destroy their nav."

Dauntless's gun swung around. Marn started to protest, but Candless just pointed his pistol in the man's face. "I'd sink you, but your crew doesn't deserve to drown just because you're a lying dog."

The gun fired and the con exploded in flames. Vine and Knot ran to the sails with torches and suddenly silk and ropes were burning. Flames rose high. Mutters of anger ran through the *Ray*'s crew. The flames leaped into the sky.

The rest of Candless's people leaped aboard and *Dauntless* heeled away from the burning ship.

"Full sails!"

Nailer looked to where the ship was closing on the horizon. Even without *Dauntless*'s scope, it looked large.

"*Pole Star*'s a fighter," Candless said. "All we can do is hope they want the ship as a prize, or they'll blow us up where we sail and we all die."

Nailer watched the ships. "Why would they let us live?"

"We don't have their armaments. It makes them confident." Candless glanced back at the *Ray*, where the crew was pumping seawater onto their burning sails. He smiled without humor. "So now we're the kittens being hunted." He turned and shouted orders.

"What are you going to do?" Nailer asked.

"We're going to run for the coast, and then see if we can make them make a mistake. They've got the jump on us, but it'll be a long chase." He looked out at the ocean. "We'll just have to see if we can maybe make some trickery."

"What kind?"

Candless was smiling, but to Nailer it looked forced. "I won't know until I see it."

He hurried up to his con, and Nailer, without any specific task, followed. The captain and Reynolds spread out maps, looking at the depths of the ocean.

"Our draft is shallower than *Pole Star*," Candless muttered. "We have to find some place we can sneak into and hide."

"We could try going up the Mississippi," Reynolds suggested.

"They'll radio down reinforcements for sure. I don't want to be trapped into fighting on that river."

Nailer stared at the maps, trying to make sense of them. The captain pointed to lines on the map. "These are our depths. Anywhere deeper than six meters, we're okay. Shallower..."—he shrugged—"we run aground." He pointed to a spot on one of the charts, deep in the Gulf's blue water lines. "We're about...here." He pointed to a distant bit of shore. "That's your old beach." He returned to his discussion with Reynolds.

Nailer stared at the map, at the letters that made up Bright Sands Beach, and was surprised that he could actually make out words. He ran his finger along the depths and indicators, reading the numbers. The island where he and Pima had found Nita's wrecked ship showed as a point of land, still connected to the mainland. "Are these maps old?" he asked.

"Why?"

"The depths aren't right. This should be an island, at least at high tide it is."

Reynolds and the captain exchanged amused glances. "Actually, you're right. The real numbers are all deeper than when the maps were made, but the ratios are the same, even with the rising sea levels. So everything will be deeper than what you see on the map."

Nailer absorbed this, studying how the island used to be

connected before the sea rose and isolated it, comparing his memories of Bright Sands Beach mapped against this paper version from long ago. He frowned.

"Your map's still wrong." Nailer pointed to the waters off the edge of the island, where the Teeth lay. "This whole area, it's wrong. It's not more than a couple meters' clearance, even at high tide."

"Oh?" Candless studied the map, then looked at Nailer, speculative. "How do you know?"

"Ships get hung up there all the time." Nailer's finger traced the area of the Teeth. "There's a bunch of buildings down there. We call them the Teeth; they chew the hell out of anything that comes into them." He pointed. "You have to come in around this way if you don't want to get sunk."

"Is it possible?" Reynolds asked doubtfully. "Someone missed a whole city?"

"Maybe." Candless looked thoughtful. "People were abandoning all sorts of real estate when these maps were being made. Rising waters and famine were taking a toll. If the city was abandoned, it might have been deleted from the overlays. It didn't matter to these people. They didn't know we'd be sailing over it in another hundred years."

"They missed a lot," Nailer said. "There's a whole city down there. All kinds of buildings and iron poking up. The depth isn't anything like that."

"How deep?"

"At high tide?" Nailer shrugged. "Maybe a meter or

two?" He shrugged. "You can see bits of the tall ones when the water's low. They stick up."

Reynolds still looked skeptical, but Candless said, "It's not a major shipping area. It would be easy to make a mistake." He jerked his head toward Nailer. "And none of his kind would complain. Even if they did, who would listen? Half that coast has been given up as drowned wilderness. Just malaria and convicts now."

"Chavez has the same maps," Reynolds observed.

"That's right." Candless smiled, suddenly feral. "Company issue."

"You'd have to time it." Reynolds was thoughtful. "Tricky bit of sailing."

"I'll take tricky sailing over an impossible fight any day."

Candless motioned Nailer close. "Now, tell me, boy, just how does this city of yours lie? And where are all the sharp and pointy bits?"

23

AFTER NAILER EXPLAINED the layout of the Teeth, Reynolds turned against the idea.

"This is risky. You don't know if the boy is right about the depths. And trying to come in with the tide at night?" She shook her head.

"You have a better idea?" Candless asked mildly.

She didn't, but she wasn't willing to say so. They were back in the con, under the peep and whine of radar systems after Captain Candless had ordered *Dauntless* onto a course for Bright Sands Beach. The captain had judged the winds acceptable to use the high sails and the boom of the Buckell cannon had shaken the ship.

The cannon's missile, trailing its gossamer tow line, arced high into the sky and then its parasail unfurled, red and gold, bright in the sky with Patel Global's colors. *Dauntless* shuddered and leaped onto her hydrofoils, rising above the waves. The ship's main sails rippled and furled, and suddenly Nailer felt wind on his face. He hadn't notice it before, but now, suddenly the wind was strong.

"The wind's slower down here than up there," the captain explained. "Before, we were going with the wind, so you didn't feel the breeze so much. Now we're with those winds up there."

The ocean rushed beneath their hull. When Nailer looked down into the glitter refraction of the waves it seemed that all the light and shimmer of the water had merged, a blur of motion too fast to understand.

"Fifty-two knots," the captain said with satisfaction.

Behind them, *Pole Star* fired its own high sails. The boom resounded across the water.

"If we're lucky," Candless said, as they watched the missile rise, "she'll tangle and we'll get the jump on them. Damn ticklish to catch a wind. Once you're up, it's fine, but damn ticklish to start."

But *Pole Star*'s sails caught. Through the long glass of *Dauntless*'s nav system they watched as the ship heaved itself up onto its own hydrofoils, its feral bulk skimming above the water.

"Why don't they just shoot down our sails?" Nailer asked.

"They may. Once they're within a mile, they can torch the parasail with a chemical round."

"But they won't light us up the same way? Sink us?"

The captain exchanged glances with Reynolds. "Chavez is greedy. If she can take us as a prize, she'll call us pirate. If she wrecks us, tangles us, and sinks us, she doesn't get the money."

The two ships sliced across the ocean. Sometimes it seemed as if *Dauntless* had gained a little ground, but when Nailer looked again, always the pale ship on the horizon had grown. He shivered at the sight of the other clipper, hunting them like a shark.

The captain pointed again at the map. "If Nailer's right, we can slip these Teeth here, and it will even look as if we're intending to hide."

"If he's right," Reynolds emphasized.

"I am," Nailer insisted. "I know that water."

"Ever sailed it?"

Nailer hesitated. He wanted to tell them that he had. That he knew the waves. That he knew he was right.

"No," he admitted. "But I know the Teeth. I've seen them at low tide." He pointed at the numbers on the map. "If your charts are right about the old depths, at high tide, you can run straight across. Right here." He pointed to the edge of the island. "Between the island and the Teeth, there's a gap."

"It's an invitation for a sinking," Reynolds said. "High tide won't be until dark, so you won't have much for landmarks, and GPS margin of error might not tell us we're wrong until we're dead on some old I-beam."

"I know where it is," Nailer said sullenly. "I know the gap."

"Yeah?" she asked. "In the dark? With only moonlight? With one chance to get it right?"

"Let the boy alone," the captain said.

Nailer glared at her. "You've got a better idea? You're dead either way, right? What are you going to do? Surrender? Let them call you a pirate and string you up?" Nailer scowled. "You swanks are damn soft. You're afraid to gamble even when you're already dead."

The ship lurched underneath them. Everyone reached to catch their balance. Candless and Reynolds exchanged a look. All afternoon the seas had been thickening, and now, as they came out on deck, the water was running high and rough. The hydrofoils kept the *Dauntless* above much of the chop, but as the waves grew higher, the prow of the ship was starting to bury itself in foam. Candless studied the high-altitude parasails where they flew against gathering clouds.

"We're not going to be able to stay up on the foils much longer. Not with the ocean running like this."

The ship surged through another wave, rocking. Water rushed over the decks as the ship plowed out of a trough. The deck tilted abruptly as one of the foils lost its grip in the foam. Nailer grabbed a railing for support. The ship righted itself and lunged forward again, dragged by the parasail high overhead. The storm clouds darkened and roiled like a seething cauldron of snakes. Lightning flickered in their bellies.

"Is this a city killer?" he asked.

The captain shook his head. "No. But still a complication. Makes everything more ticklish."

"We can dodge them in the storm," Reynolds suggested.

"They'll have their radar on us, pinging us the whole way," Candless said. "The only way we escape is if we leave them wrecked."

"You could get Miss Nita killed if she's aboard."

Candless scowled at Reynolds. "You think I don't know it?" He looked away. "It's an ugly business. We'll put a crew of boarders on, try to pull her off in the confusion."

"You don't know it will work."

"Thank you, Reynolds. I appreciate your input. But I'll be damned if I'm going to let us all die because we're too squeamish to take the one advantage we've got."

Dauntless hurtled through the storm. When the winds became too uncertain, the captain ordered the high sail reefed. It came down, its monofilament wire ripping and squealing as the cannon reels dragged the flapping parasail toward the deck. A shriek rose over the lash of the storm. The reel jammed. Knot and Vine and Trimble hurried for the cannon. The parasail whipped sideways in the wind and *Dauntless* heeled with the sudden shifting drag.

From the con, through the rain, Nailer could see the crew fighting with the reel. Beside him, Captain Candless held the ship's wheel. He shook his head. "Tell them to cut it," he said.

Nailer looked at him uncertainly.

"Go, boy! Now! Cut it loose."

Nailer dashed down to the deck. He barely remembered to hook himself to an anchor before he went out into the wind's lash. A wave washed over the prow of the deck, knocking him off his feet. He skidded into the main mast with a numbing impact. He struggled to his feet and stumbled across the pitching deck.

"Cut it!" he shouted over the storm's roar.

'Knot glanced at him, then up at the captain. A blade came out and with a fierce slash, the monofilament line parted. The wire whipped up and away, writhing like a snake. The parasail disappeared into cloud belly darkness.

Watching it go, Nailer wondered if the ship had lost an advantage that they would miss later. Knot gave him a sad little smile. "Can't be helped, boy." And then he was running to join the rest of the crew as they unfurled the main sails in the storm.

Nailer watched in awe as the crew fought to do their work. Rain slashed them. The seas rose and tried to drown them with huge surging waves, but still they grimly wrestled the ship to their will. And *Dauntless* responded. She surged through the stormy sea, lunging into wave troughs and then climbing their slopes before plowing down into the next deep liquid ravine. All around, waves rose high and monstrous. Nailer clung to the rail, clipped to his safety lines and out of the way of the feverish work as the crew fought their ship forward.

Night fell heavy on them. Except for the occasional blast of lightning, it was black. Somewhere behind them, *Pole Star* pursued, but Nailer couldn't see it and had no idea where it was. It was nice to pretend that its sleek outline wasn't back there, hunting, but it was a fantasy.

Eventually Captain Candless gave the word and they started shunting toward the coast, running closer to where they would attempt their trickery. Despite night blindness, the *Pole Star* would follow, sniffing at them with its radar arrays. And indeed, when Nailer finally ducked out of the elements to drink a hot cup of coffee, *Dauntless*'s main radar showed the bloody blip of the fighting ship closing still.

Nailer sucked in his breath. "They're close."

The captain nodded, his face grim. "Closer than we'd like. Go aft and look."

Nailer ran to a ladder and climbed up through the ship's aft hatch. Rain beat down on him. Salt foam rushed around his ankles as the ship tore through another wave and climbed sickeningly.

Nailer stared back into the slash of rain.

Lightning ripped the darkness and thunder exploded. The *Pole Star* appeared, closer than he would have guessed, rising over a wave crest and crashing down again. It disappeared again into the darkness.

When Nailer returned to the con, the captain said, "They kept their high sails up longer than we did. They've got a more stable ship."

"What are they going to do?"

The captain stared at the radar blip of their pursuer. "They're going to threaten us and then they're going to board us."

"In the storm?"

"They've fought in worse seas. The Arctic is the worst fighting on the planet. They aren't afraid of a little rain and waves."

The captain leaned close to Nailer. "Just between us, boy, you're sure about those teeth?"

Nailer made himself nod, but the captain didn't let him go. "This is a gamble. The kind I don't like. The kind that killed Miss Nita's last ship, you understand?" He jerked his head toward the decks, indicating his crew. "Maybe you think your own life's cheap, but you're risking everyone else here, too."

Nailer looked away. "In clear weather..." He trailed off. Finally he looked up at the captain. "I don't know. In the dark? In a storm?" He shook his head. "I've been out on the bay, and been through the gap, but I don't know if it will work or not. Not like this."

The captain nodded. He stared back again into the darkness where their pursuer lurked. "Fair enough. Not the answer I wanted. But honest. We'll trust the Fates, then."

"You're still going to try?" Nailer asked.

"Sometimes it's better to die trying."

"What about everyone else?"

Candless was solemn. "They knew the risks of coming with me when we left the Orleans. There were always safer options than crewing with an old loyalist like me." He pointed to the nav screens and the infrared feeds of the shoreline, glowing green before them, flaring with lightning flashes. "Now be my eyes, boy. Help us find safe harbor."

Nailer watched the screens. The shadows of shoreline showed, lit by more lightning flashes. A cannon boomed behind them. A missile streaked overhead.

"She's afraid we're going to make a run into the jungles," Candless observed.

Nailer looked back. "Are they going to sink us?"

"*Pole Star* is not your problem!" The captain grabbed Nailer's shoulder and pointed him forward. "Your problem is out there! Show me where we need to be!"

Nailer bent to the screens, scanned the black shoreline ahead. The island glowed on screen. He frowned. No. That was wrong. It was some other hill. Everything was different in the dark and rain. The ship heaved through the waves.

"I don't see it," he said. He tried to peer though the rain-spattered glass. Saw nothing but blackness.

"Look harder, then!" The captain's fingers dug into his shoulder.

Nailer stared at the darkness. It was impossible. The land in the scopes' view was all a blur of vegetation and selfsame coast. He stared into the rain again, looking through the

292

forward windscreens. Another slash of lightning. Another. And then a ripping crack of thunder. He saw the island and gasped. They were too far off.

"Back there!" He pointed. "We're past it!"

The captain cursed. He hurled the wheel over, calling orders to the crew. The sails cracked and flapped ineffectually. The ship rocked violently as a wave took it from an unexpected angle. The shadow of a crewman plunged from the mast, then jerked to a halt, dangling precariously from a harness. The sail's boom swept across the deck. *Dauntless* came around. Suddenly the great bulk of the *Pole Star* loomed over them, bearing down. *Dauntless* was wallowing in the waves, her sails flapping uncertainly. Down on the deck, Nailer could hear Reynolds shouting, "Make fast! Make fast!" as she prepared the crew to run aground. "Hands on the pumps!"

Pole Star was on top of them. Nailer could see half-men on the gunwales, twirling grappling hooks, eager to leap aboard. *Dauntless*'s sails flapped and then suddenly filled with wind. *Dauntless* surged forward again, gaining speed. *Pole Star* threw herself up beside them, seeking to grapple, but *Dauntless* lunged past, carried by the surf.

"Right!" Nailer yelled. "Go right!" He could see the island. The teeth were already beneath them. The big ones would be. They were going to run aground.

"*Starboard* is what we call it," Candless said dryly as he spun the wheel. The man seemed strangely relaxed suddenly. *Dauntless* surged forward, shoved by the waves toward the rocky outcrop of the island, and then they were sucking through the shallows and past the island and the Teeth.

The ship settled into the bay's relative calm.

"Storm anchors!" Captain Candless shouted as the crew furled the ship's sails. *Dauntless* wallowed, then shuddered and swung about as prow anchors bit. Waves rushed against her sudden immobility. She turned with the waves, her nose pointing out into the surf, and then the aft anchors dropped and the ship stilled.

Nailer clambered down from the conning deck and out into the slash of the rain.

"Launch in two!" Reynolds shouted. "Prepare to board!"

Lightning flashed. The great bulk of the *Pole Star* was coming for them. Nailer clutched the rail as the monster roared in. "Fates," he whispered, and touched his forehead. He hadn't realized he was religious until just now, but suddenly he found himself praying.

Reynolds came up beside him, watching the fighting ship plow down on them. "We'll see if you're right, boy."

Nailer's throat was dry. *Pole Star* surged forward, seemingly planning to simply crush them under its weight. As it poured through the surf, Nailer was suddenly seized with a new terror: In the high seas of the storm, the Teeth would all be much deeper under water. *Pole Star* could slip across after all. Despair engulfed him. He hadn't thought about the storm surge. No wonder *Dauntless* had come across unscathed even when they were in the wrong position.

Pole Star was reefing its own sails and slowing, guiding itself with the minimum acceleration so that it could come up beside them and board. Nailer watched with sick despair. He'd been wrong. He thought he'd been so damn smart, and now they were going to be boarded, all because he hadn't thought of all the details.

"Captain!" Nailer shouted. "They're not—"

Pole Star stopped moving forward. It hung in the waves, stilled, even as water rushed around it. A wave crashed against it. Another. A bustle of activity on the decks was suddenly visible. An ant mound of people suddenly kicked to life. The ship swung slowly sideways, then stopped. A huge wave smashed into it. Another. The ship turned completely broadside and then it snagged again, caught on another spire from the deep. A huge wave smashed into its hull and the entire ship heeled.

Reynolds laughed and clapped Nailer on the shoulder. "They've got their hands full now!" she shouted over the storm roar. "Let's finish this!"

They ran for the launches, Nailer piling in behind Reynolds. The little raft swung above roiling seas, dangling from a pair of drop clips. Knot and Vine and Candless and a half-dozen other crewmen were all in with him. Down the length of the ship, two other launches dangled over the side, full of *Dauntless*'s crew. The high whine of biodiesel engines firing live carried over the storm's rush. Prop blades blurred as motors revved. Their own launch's motor fired alive, vibrating.

The boats ahead of them cut free. They dropped like rocks into the waves, engines screaming. They hit water and shot forward, arrowing for the sinking *Pole Star*.

"Clear!" Reynolds shouted. Drop hooks snapped open. Their launch plunged. Nailer's stomach flew into his mouth. Free fall. They slammed into the ocean. Nailer jackknifed forward and slammed into Vine's broad back. Pain blossomed. He'd bitten his lip. Their raft surged forward, and he grabbed for balance as they accelerated.

"Weapons check!" Candless shouted. Nailer reached for the pistol strapped to his waist. He could feel his heart pounding. Trimble grinned beside him.

"Nothing better than a storm boarding, right, boy?"

Nailer nodded sickly. Their tiny boat hurtled through foam and breakers under Reynolds's sure hand. They shot up beside the tilting *Pole Star,* coming at her from the stern. Enemy crew were out on the deck. Nailer thought he saw the captain clinging to a rail, trying to send her people out to stabilize the wreck. He felt a stab of victory. One moment she must have been so confident, and now she was frantic. He laughed in the rain, feeling water gushing down his face. He'd done that.

Their launch slammed up against *Pole Star*'s hull. Knot hurled a rope ladder grapple up over the rail, then rushed up the side with Vine close behind. They surged over the rail with their guns and machetes, followed by the rest of the crew.

Reynolds slapped Nailer's back. "Move it, boy!"

Nailer grabbed the ladder and clambered up. He came

over the side in time to see Captain Candless grappling with the other captain. He twisted his body and the woman plunged over the rail. She landed in the sea, splashing for survival. Candless pointed his sea pistol at the remaining crew.

"Stand down and surrender!" he shouted over the roar of the storm and even if his voice wasn't clear, the gun was. Nailer looked down into the surging surf and wondered what had happened to the other captain. She was simply gone, sucked under in the Teeth.

They'd taken the *Pole Star*.

Nailer turned to smile at Reynolds when a wave of half-men boiled up from the hold, guns firing. Candless went down in a spray of blood. Reynolds threw Nailer aside and her gun cracked beside him. Nailer lifted his own pistol, shooting through the rain, sure that he was missing and yet squeezing the trigger anyway. A huge wave hit the ship. *Pole Star*'s deck tilted sideways. Combatants went sliding into the sea.

Nailer grabbed for the rail as he went over the edge. His gun plunged into the water. He dangled half off the deck. Storm surf surged up around his legs, grasping and eager to take him under. Nailer dragged himself out of the vortex and clung to the rail. The great clipper, so seemingly impregnable, had become impossibly small. It was sinking.

Reynolds was shooting at someone in the darkness, but Nailer couldn't see who. She caught sight of him. "Get Miss Nita!" she shouted as bullets ricocheted around her.

One of *Pole Star*'s half-men rose up from the water beside them. Unkillable, they seemed. Reynolds turned her pistol on the creature and shot him in the chest. He sank back. Nailer couldn't see any of *Dauntless*'s half-men at all. Maybe Knot and Vine and their kin were already dead.

Reynolds's pistol cracked again. She glared at Nailer. "Go!"

Nailer drew his fighting knife and fumbled his now-useless ammunition over to Reynolds. He scrambled for the nearest hatch, praying that he wasn't about to run into another lot of half-men, and dove through.

The storm's fury muted. Nailer wiped his face frantically, clearing his vision, blinking in the sudden stillness. Emergency LED lights lit the corridor, running on current from the ship's batteries. Nailer couldn't help inanely calculating scavenge value of the lighting systems as he made his way down the corridor. He passed brass fittings and steel doors, noting easily stripped service lines. The corridor tilted, rocked by the storm waves outside. Nailer staggered.

Focus, you idiot. Find Lucky Girl and get out.

Nothing moved in the dim red glow of the corridors. Somewhere above, guns were still firing, but the interior was strangely silent. Nailer made his way deeper into the ship, listening to the creak and rush of water outside, his stealthy footsteps and the rasp of his own loud breathing. He paused, trying to get his breath back. He listened for signs of movement ahead.

Nothing.

He crept farther down the corridor, his knife held ready beside him. He couldn't be alone down here. Lucky Girl had to be around, and where she was, there would be others, too.

Once again, Nailer wondered at his capacity for suicidal stupidity. Betraying his father had been colossally stupid, but hunting around in a sinking ship topped it. If he'd been smart he would have let the whole thing go when Lucky Girl disappeared in the Orleans. He could have found other work. He could have walked away without a problem. Gone up the Mississippi. Anything. But instead he'd been swept up in the loyalty that her people displayed: Candless and Reynolds and Knot and Vine...and if he was honest, his own silly fantasies about the beautiful swank girl had played a part, too.

Nice going, hero.

He shook his head. Here he was, back at Bright Sands Beach, where he'd started, worse off than ever, and about to get his head shot off by a half-man because he thought some swank girl —

Movement ahead. Noises. Nailer pressed against the corridor wall. Muffled shouts echoed to him. He peered down the corridor. A ladder led down. He slipped closer and stuck his head close to the hole, listening.

"Get me another seal! No! There! Not there! Here! Here!" More shouts. Crew trying to contain the damage. Trying to block the rushing sea as it poured into the ship.

Nailer peered through the hole. Down below, the corridor

was filling with water. Men and women splashed through the water, knee-deep in its embrace. More water sprayed from the walls, and still the crew labored. Nailer wished he had a gun. He could have shot them all…He stifled the thought. It was insane to pick a fight with people who didn't care about him one way or the other.

One of the crewmen turned. His eyes widened. "Hey!"

Nailer jerked his head back up the hole and ran.

"Boarders!" The cry went up. "Boarders!"

But Nailer was far down the hall. Boots clanged on the ladder as he ducked into a cabin and closed the door. He was in a crew cabin, bunks and gear strewn wildly by the heaving of the ship. Boots pounded past.

Nailer took a deep breath and slipped back out. The tilt of the ship was making it difficult to move around. The corridors were all canted so that the door in the wall was slowly turning into a door in the floor. He actually had to lift the door in order to slide out of the room, and then he slid to the far side of the corridor before getting his footing. The ship was trying to turn turtle. He scrambled for the ladder, praying that he wasn't about to run into more crew.

Climbing down was an odd experience of scrambling nearly sideways. The entire ship was almost on its side. Water poured around him. He ran past where the crew had sealed off a part of the cargo hold, headed deeper into the belly of the torn ship, searching desperately through cabins and storerooms. He found no one. Everyone had to be abovedecks or busy fighting to control the flooding. He was alone. Finally he gave up on stealth and simply shouted.

"Lucky Girl! Where the hell are you? Nita!"

No response.

She had to be higher up; that was the only answer. He'd somehow missed her.

Or else she'd been drugged.

Or she'd been taken off already.

Or she'd never been here at all.

He grimaced. She could have been left back in the Orleans. Or killed. He slogged through water, trying to find his way out. The water was in all the decks now. The wall had become the floor, and he was having a hard time keeping his orientation as the ship went onto its side. The ship jerked. The world turned again. Water sprayed. He yanked open a door and was rewarded with a flood of water that sent him sprawling and sliding down the corridor before he came up gasping and managed to get to his feet. He fled the rising waters.

"Lucky Girl!"

Still nothing. Water was everywhere. LEDs were shorting out, sending portions of the ship into blackness. The ship was sinking. He had to get out. Judging from the empty corridors and rooms, even the crew had run. He wondered what had happened with the fight. Who had won?

He scrambled through corridors made topsy-turvy by the ship's cant. The smell of oiled machinery was strong in his nostrils, reeking. It was like being back on one of the ship-breaking wrecks. Like being trapped in the oil room.

He pushed open another door and crawled through. He was lost all right. Inside, the hydrofoil gearings for the *Pole Star* sat in red dimness, clicking gears and whirring automation mechanicals for the sails and hydrofoils and parasail reels. Warning signs said: SPEED MECHANICALS IN USE! WATCH HANDS AND LOOSE CLOTHING. Nailer was amused that he could actually make out the meanings now. He was going to drown, but hey, he could read.

On one wall, flashers and safety overrides blinked to indicate that there were electric malfunctions and topside failures, probably from having the conning deck go under. The mechanicals were almost exactly the same as the ones he'd had to lubricate under Knot's supervision on *Dauntless*. Bigger, but the layout was awfully similar. As the ship had gone onto its side, the service panels that had been in place on the floor had come loose and fallen free, revealing the huge gears and interlocking hydraulic systems. It looked like ships in the Patel Global fleet were almost the same. Nita wouldn't be here. He turned to keep searching. The ship groaned and shifted under him again. Nailer wondered if he was going to end up like Jackson Boy after all. Dead in a different bit of scavenge, but dead just the same.

"Nita! Where the hell are you?"

He broke into a new corridor. The ship was trying to turn upside down, kept from capsizing only by the strength of its masts where they tangled in the Teeth. If the ship turned turtle, he'd have to swim out. He wondered if he'd be able to make it up through the waves and wreckage.

"Well, I'll be damned." A familiar voice interrupted his thoughts. "Hello there, Lucky Boy."

Nailer turned, his skin crawling.

His father stood in the soaking corridor with Nita slung over his shoulder, gagged and bound at her wrists and ankles. Water ran slick on his face and a machete gleamed in his hand.

Nailer stepped back, horrified. His father smiled. Even in the dimness of the red LEDs Nailer could tell the man was sliding high. He had the bright, wide eyes and the feral grin of an addict deep in his drugs.

"Goddamn," Richard Lopez said. "I didn't think I'd run into you here." He dumped Nita unceremoniously on the ground and swung his machete in an experimental arc. "Didn't think I'd ever see you again."

Nailer tried to shrug, tried not to show his fear. "Yeah. Me either."

His father laughed. The sound echoed in the cramped space. The dragons stood out stark on his bare arms, curling up around his Adam's apple like spikes. His ribs showed over the ripple of his fighter's muscles.

"You gonna just stand there?" his father asked. "Or you gonna help me?"

Nailer hesitated, confused. "Help you? You want me to help with the girl?"

His father grinned. "Just kidding. I should have let you

303

die when we found the scavenge. Should have known you'd be an ungrateful little bastard."

"Just let her go," Nailer said. "You don't need her."

"Nope." His father shook his head. "I don't need her. But I'm not going out empty-handed, and she looks like the best scavenge here."

"They'll catch you."

"Who?" His father laughed. "No one gives a damn anymore. Every man for himself and all that." He shrugged. "Anyway, they don't really care if she's alive or dead. If I sell her for spare parts to the Harvesters, it's all the same to them." He glanced at her. "She might have been a swank once. But she's scavenge now."

Nailer followed his father's gaze. Nita was conscious, he was surprised to see. She was fighting against her bonds, trying to get free.

Nailer's father kicked her hard. "Sit still," he said.

Nita grunted in pain, then sobbed as her breath returned. Richard turned to Nailer. He twitched his machete. "What're you thinking, boy? Thinking you're gonna cut down your old man with your little knife? Get back at me for all your whippings?"

He twitched the machete again, letting the blade bob before Nailer. "Come on, then." He beckoned Nailer forward. "Hand-to-hand, boy. Just like the ring." He bared his damaged teeth. "I'm going to spread your guts on the *floor!*"

He lunged. Nailer hurled himself aside. The machete slashed past his face. His father laughed. "Good job, boy!

You're damn quick!" He slashed again and Nailer's belly burned where the blade cut a shallow line. "Almost as quick as me!"

Nailer staggered back. The cut wasn't deep—he'd gotten worse on light crew—but it filled him with fear to see how fast his father was. He was as deadly as a half-man. Richard Lopez closed on him, making short jabs with his machete. Nailer gave ground. He feinted with his own shorter knife, trying to slash inside the machete, but his father anticipated him and this time the machete caught Nailer across the cheek.

"Still a little slow, boy."

Nailer backed off, fighting fear. He swiped away the blood that ran freely from his face. The man was horrifyingly fast. Amped on amphetamines, he was superhuman. Nailer remembered the time his father had beaten three opponents in the ring at the same time, on a dare. He'd been overmatched, but he'd left the others crushed and unconscious and stood over them all, bloody teeth gleaming with triumph. The man was born to fight.

His father slashed again. Nailer jumped back.

Concentrate, Nailer told himself.

His father exploded into motion. Nailer barely slid inside the machete's cut. His father's body slammed into him. Nailer's hand, slick with blood, lost his knife. It went flying. He and his father went over in a tumble. Richard grabbed at him, but Nailer wriggled free and scrambled down the corridor. His father laughed.

"You can't run away that easy!"

Nailer searched frantically for his knife but couldn't see it in the dimness. His father stalked him. Nailer turned and ran. Behind him, his father laughed and gave chase as Nailer dashed for the mechanicals room. Under the glow of emergency lighting, Nailer cast about, looking for some tool he could use as a weapon. His father burst into the room behind him.

"My my, you're a slippery one."

Nailer backed away. The damn *Pole Star* crew kept a tight ship, not even a wrench or a screwdriver lying around. Nailer grabbed a loose service panel and hurled it, but his father dodged easily.

"That the best you can do?" he asked.

Nailer grabbed another loose maintenance panel, then looked up at where it had fallen from. An entire wall of gears and hydraulic systems loomed beside him, the floor of the ship that had now become a wall. If he could climb up, he might be able to get out of reach inside a maintenance hole.

Nailer ran to the wall of exposed gears and pulled himself up. With the ship turned sideways, there were enough open panels that he could climb up along them. He peered into the slots between, almost sobbing with desperation. None of the gaps were big enough for him to hide from his father's machete reach. He climbed higher.

"Where you think you're going, boy?"

Nailer didn't answer. He got ahold of another huge gear

and hauled himself higher. He slapped at a service panel's lock and tore it away. He threw it down at his father, missing again. Below him, Richard Lopez was watching, bemused.

"You think I can't just climb up and pull you down?" He shook his head. "I used to think you were smart, boy."

Nailer pulled himself higher. His father said, "Why don't you just come down and die like a man? It would be so much easier for both of us."

Nailer shook his head. "Come get me, if you want me."

He loosened another panel. If his father could be convinced to start climbing, he could maybe drop the damn thing right on his father's head.

"All right, boy. I tried to be nice." His father took hold of a gear and reached up for another handhold in the next service panel. With the machete, his climbing was hampered, but he was horrifyingly fast, even so.

Nailer dropped the panel. For a moment, he thought it would catch his father perfectly, but then the entire ship heaved with another wave and the panel missed. Richard Lopez grinned up at Nailer, unfazed. "Guess you're not such a Lucky Boy after all." Then, quick as a spider, he clambered up after Nailer.

Nailer scrambled higher, but there was nowhere else to go. He clung to a huge gear, staring down at his dad. He was trapped. Richard Lopez smiled and swung his machete. Nailer yanked his feet out of reach. The machete clanged against steel.

A blinking LED caught Nailer's eye. He stared, and felt

a surge of hope. He was right beside a control deck, with its familiar label: FOIL OVERRIDE. KEEP HANDS AND LOOSE CLOTHING CLEAR.

Nailer slapped frantically at the release lever and hit the engagement override button. Just like Knot had done what seemed like ages ago. He looked down at his father. "Let me go, Dad. Just let me and Nita go."

"Not this time, boy." Richard Lopez grabbed Nailer's ankle.

Nailer said a prayer to the Fates, grabbed the engagement lever, and jumped free. His weight yanked the lever down and then he was falling.

The scream of machinery filled the room.

24

NAILER HIT THE FLOOR. His ankle blossomed with pain. The scream of machinery cut off abruptly. Nailer looked up. His father dangled above him, half his body sucked into the hydrofoil's gear system. The man was trying to reach into the machinery where an arm and leg had been consumed. Blood showed on his teeth.

"Damn," he said. He seemed puzzled, more than anything else. He tried to free himself again. Nailer's skin crawled. The man should have been dead, the way he'd been sucked into the gears, but still he fought for life. Fueled by amphetamines and sliding high, his father still didn't understand his predicament. For a terrible moment, Nailer was filled with dread that his father could not die. That he would pry himself free and come after him once again.

Richard stared down at him. "Come here, boy."

Nailer shook his head and backed away. His father's free hand went to the gears again. "What the hell did you do?" He stared at the gears, then stared at the blood dripping from within the mechanicals. In the LED dimness it was almost black. "I'm not done yet," his father said. He looked down at Nailer. "I'm nowhere near done yet."

But already his voice was weak. Nailer stared up at the man who had terrorized him for so much of his life. All of a sudden Richard Lopez was different, not the swaggering, dangerous man he had been, but something else. Miserable. Vulnerable.

"Come on, Lucky Boy," his father croaked. "We're family. Help me out." He tried to reach down to Nailer. Tried to smile. Licked bloody lips. "Please," he said. And then, more softly, "I'm sorry."

Nailer's body shook with revulsion. He gave his father one last look then turned away, limping for where Lucky Girl lay bound.

He ran into her at the door, and almost screamed before he recognized her. She hefted his fighting knife. "Thanks for the knife," she said. "Where's—" She gasped.

Nailer pulled her out of the room, nearly dragging her. "Come on." He hurried her down the corridor, half expecting his father to call after him again, but no more sounds followed them.

"Where are we going?" she panted.

"We need to get out." He dragged her to a ladder that

led to the upper decks. Suddenly the ship shuddered and rolled. The main mast had finally given way. They were completely upside down. Trying to get to the upper decks meant climbing down into the sea. "We've turned turtle," he muttered. "We can't go down." He peered down into the hole. It was already half full of water. The next deck down would be completely submerged.

"Can we swim out?" she asked.

"Not in the dark. Not without knowing where to go." The water was rising. "We're going under," he said. Despair filled him.

Nita stared at the water. "Then we go up, right?" She shook him. "Right? We go up!" She yanked his arm. "Come on! We need to find a way into the bottom of the ship."

"What are you looking for?" he asked.

"The ship's sinking, right? Water's getting in from somewhere. Maybe there's a hole in the hull."

Nailer nodded, suddenly understanding. He stopped her and tugged her in a different direction. "This way. We need to get into the holds. They're this way!"

"How do you know which way to go?"

"I'm a ship breaker." Nailer laughed. "Spend enough time tearing apart old ships, and you get to understand them." They dashed into another corridor, then clambered up a ladder. They ran along the ceiling of another corridor, the floor running over their heads. "There!" He smiled as he saw the ladder that led to where the crew had been working on sealing the hold.

"Get ready," he said as he put the fighting knife to the seals.

"For what?"

"A lot of water."

Nita grabbed a brass fitting with one hand and his belt with the other. She nodded to him. "Ready."

Nailer slashed the membrane that the crew had laid down in their vain effort to save the ship. The rubbery stuff parted. Water roared down over them. They slammed against the wall. Nailer clutched for Nita as the water tore at him. A moment later, the rush slowed to a trickle. It wasn't as much as Nailer had feared. He guessed that a lot of it had already drained down into the ship from other points. He clambered through the hatch. "This way."

"How did you find me?" Nita asked as she tagged behind. "When they caught me in the Orleans I thought I was done for."

"Captain Candless—" Nailer broke off, thinking of the shots fired in the darkness, the spray of blood as the captain went down. "He had an idea of how to hunt for you."

"And you came along?"

Nailer grinned. "Pretty stupid, huh?"

She laughed. "I'll say."

They threaded through wrecked cargo rooms, climbing over jumbled trash to reach the doors that were now upside down and above them. At last they dropped into the hold. Lightning cracked, illuminating a hole in the hull overhead. A ragged tear in the carbon fiber. Farther down, another

312

hole showed, a testament to the success of Nailer's plan. Seawater cascaded through the holes as a wave crashed across the hull, soaking strewn cargo boxes and jumbled equipment. Nailer squinted up at the torn hull. Lightning flashed. It wasn't much of a hole. More of a crack. And it was high, too damn high.

Nita yanked his arm. "The cargo crates," she said. "We'll stack them."

She grabbed a crate and dragged it below the hole. Nailer saw what she meant and rushed to help. They worked feverishly. Some crates were too heavy to move alone and others too heavy for both of them to lift. Nailer's ankle burned with pain as he tried to move and stack the junk into a semblance of a tower. More water poured down over them. Nailer was gasping with effort and pain. Nita crawled up the pile of crates, reaching down as he handed up more boxes.

Another wave rushed into the hold. A big one, that nearly knocked Nita from her perch.

"We're going under!" Nailer shouted over the storm roar.

Nita stared at the hole above her. "I think we're high enough."

"Then jump!"

"What about you?"

"You have to go first. My ankle might not make it. When you get up, gimme a hand."

Nita nodded and crouched, teetering at the top of the

pile. She leaped. A wave crashed down on her, but her hands caught the edge and held, and then she was clambering up and out of the hold. Nailer scrambled up after her. The crates were all uneven from the movement of the ship. His ankle was a bright blossom of pain. It was almost paralyzing. There was no way he'd make the jump.

Nita's face appeared in the opening above. She extended her hand. "Hurry!"

He got his feet under him and crouched. *Ignore the pain*, he told himself. *Just make the jump.* He took a deep breath and sprang upward. His ankle exploded. His fingers caught the hull's ragged edge. Slipped. Nita grabbed his wrist. "Hold on!" A wave crashed over, pouring down over them. He clung to the hull's edge, coughing and spitting water. Another wave poured down.

Nita's grip was slipping. "I can't pull you up!" she shouted.

Get up! he told himself. *If you keep hanging here, you'll fall and break your neck. You didn't come this far just to drown in the dark.*

But he was so tired.

"Crew up, Nailer!" Lucky Girl shouted. "You think I'm going to pull your ass up here like a damn swank?"

Nailer almost laughed. He clawed at the edge of the ship, and slowly hauled himself through the hole. Nita grabbed him under his arm, yanked at his shirt, dragging him higher. He scrabbled for a grip on the slippery hull. Another wave surged over them, but he was braced this time, and when it passed, he clawed his way out with Nita dragging him. At last he swung his legs out of the hold, and clung, gasping, to the hull.

Rain poured down over them. Nita lay beside him, her black hair hanging like thick wet snakes around her face. Lightning cracked bright and hard, blinding after the darkness of the ship. More rain sheeted down. A hundred meters away, *Dauntless* lay anchored, churning in the storm.

"That's where we're going," Nailer said.

"What? No water taxi?"

Despite himself, Nailer grinned. "You swanks always want it easy."

"Yeah." Her expression turned solemn as she stared at the *Dauntless*. "Sink or swim, right?"

"Pretty much."

She squinted into the rain. "I've swum farther," she said. "We can do this."

She tore off her shoes and waited until the next wave surged over them, then dove with it, letting its force carry her forward. She bobbed like a fish. Nailer said a prayer to the Fates, thinking of the disappeared captain of the *Pole Star*, and followed her in.

The sea swallowed him in churn and roar. Every time he kicked, his ankle exploded with pain. He paddled frantically for what he thought was the surface. Waves tried to suck him down. He flailed, struggling to find air. Clawed at foam and came up gasping. Another wave sucked him down. He tumbled. He fought again to free himself from the hungry depths and came up coughing and sputtering. Sucked air. Kicked and gasped with pain.

"Float it!" Nita shouted. "Let the current pull you!" She was riding the waves beside him. One curled over her and she dipped under and came up again, swimming strongly. "Don't fight it!" she shouted. And then she was up beside him, supporting him. Helping him swim.

He was surprised to see that she was smiling, and then they were swirling forward and the waves were all around and he could see there was a rhythm to them. They were past the Teeth and out of the vortex and now, suddenly, the current was on their side, pushing them forward, taking them exactly where they wanted to go.

Dauntless loomed over them.

Life rings sailed over the side, splashing into the swirl and froth. Nailer wondered briefly who controlled the ship and then realized that he didn't really care. He and Lucky Girl paddled for the life rings, stretching for salvation.

25

"Killing always costs."

It was Pima's mother, sitting beside him, both of them staring out at the sea. Nailer had told her what had happened on *Pole Star*, and was surprised to find himself crying, and then he had simply stopped. Now he seemed to feel nothing at all, just a strange hollow space under his ribs that refused to go away.

"He was bad news," she said. "I don't say that about many people, but Richard Lopez left a lot of hurt behind him."

"Yeah," Nailer agreed. But still, it didn't feel right. His dad had been crazy and destructive and if he was honest, downright evil. But now that he was dead, Nailer couldn't help remembering other times as well, times when the man hadn't been high, when he'd laughed at jokes, when they'd roasted a pig on the beach, good times. Safe times, his father smiling and telling stories about people who had made big scores. Lucky Strikes every one of them.

"He wasn't all bad," he murmured.

"No." Sadna shook her head. "But he wasn't good. Not at the end. And not for a long time before."

"Yeah, I know that. He would have killed me if I hadn't killed him."

"But that's not helping you, is it?"

"No."

She laughed sadly. "That's good. I'm glad."

Nailer looked at her, puzzled.

"Richard never felt a thing when he hurt people. Just didn't give a damn. It's good that you feel something. Trust me. Even if it hurts, it's good."

"I don't know." Nailer stared at the sea. "Maybe you're wrong. I—" He hesitated. "I was glad when I killed him. Really glad. I remember seeing all those levers and knowing just what I had to do. And I did it." He looked up at Sadna. "As soon as I heard the machines kick on, I knew I'd won. I felt like a Lucky Strike. It was better than anything. Better than getting out of the oil room. Better than finding Lucky Girl's wreck. I was alive and he wasn't, and I felt strong. Really strong."

"And now?"

"I don't know…" Nailer shrugged. "Blue Eyes. Now

him." He looked at Sadna. "Tool said I was just like my dad when I pigstuck Blue Eyes—"

"You're not—"

"Maybe I am, right? I don't feel a thing. Not a damn thing. I was glad when I did it. And now I don't feel anything at all. I'm empty. Just empty."

"And that scares you."

"You said my dad didn't feel anything when he hurt people."

Sadna reached over and took Nailer's chin, turned his gaze so he couldn't look away. "Listen, Nailer. You're not your dad. If you were your dad, you'd be down on the beach, drinking with your friends, looking for a girl to keep you company tonight, and feeling pleased with yourself. You wouldn't be up here worrying about why you don't feel worse."

"Yeah. I guess."

"I know. Believe me, if you don't believe yourself. Getting over something like this takes time. It won't be better today. Not tomorrow, either. Maybe in a year, though, it won't be like this. Maybe in a year you'll have mostly forgotten. But it will still be there. You've got blood on your hands." She shrugged. "It always costs. It never goes away." She nodded toward where Lucky Strike had started a Fates shrine in the trees. "Go make an offering to the Fates. Be glad you were lucky and fast and smart. And then go do something right in the world."

"That's it? That's all?" Nailer laughed. "Go do something good?"

"You want someone to beat you? Have Lucky Strike take an eye for an eye, maybe?"

"I don't know." Nailer shrugged. "At the end..." He hesitated, then let out a shuddering breath. "At the end, I think he was different. Like he came back to the way he was before. I think he could see me..." Nailer trailed off, then said, "He wasn't all bad." He shook his head. He kept circling back to that. He hated repeating it, didn't know why he bothered.

Why can't I just be glad he's dead?

"It will get better." Sadna gripped his shoulder. "Trust me."

"Yeah. Thanks." He took a deep breath, watching the blue surf beyond. They were silent for a while.

Pima came and squatted down beside them. "You two about ready?"

Sadna nodded. "I've got a few people to talk to." She clapped Nailer on the back. "Keep an eye on him, right?" She stood and made her way down to the beach.

Pima settled in beside him. Not saying anything, just waiting. Patient.

Together they watched the activity out in the bay. *Dauntless* was almost finished loading supplies. They'd be heading north, heading for Lucky Girl's people. They'd made contact with her clan and the news of Nita's survival and

Pyce's betrayal was already causing shifts in power. People loyal to Nita and her father were fighting to regain control of the company. Voting blocs were shifting, Nita said. Whatever that meant. She seemed pleased, so Nailer supposed it was a good thing.

"It's a damn strange world out there," Nailer said.

"Yeah," Pima agreed. "You about ready to go see what's in it?"

Nailer hesitated, then nodded. "Guess so."

They stood and started down to the beach. Skiffs were ferrying loads of fresh water out to the *Dauntless* under Lucky Strike's supervision. The man had been quick to make a bargain with the winners of the marine fight, and now, once again, Lucky Strike was looking pretty damn lucky. Nita said that he'd even made a deal for salvage rights on the sunken *Pole Star*, if he could figure out a way to raise her.

Dauntless gleamed in the sunlight. Nailer could see Captain Candless standing on the deck. White bandages muffled much of his chest and neck. Reynolds claimed that the only reason he was alive was that he was too stupid to know when he was dead. The captain's voice carried across the water as he shouted orders and supervised final repairs and preparations.

A breeze kicked up, carrying a whiff of the ship-breaking business with it. Farther down the beach, the old-world wrecks still lay black on the sand like mangled bodies, still leaking oil and chemicals, still swarming with workers. But he wasn't one of them. And not Pima. And not Sadna, either. He wasn't able to save everybody, but he could at least save family.

Pima followed his gaze. "You think Lucky Girl's for real? About twisting Lawson & Carlson? Making them do something about this place?"

"Who knows? If she gets control of her company, Patel Global's a big buyer." He nodded toward the *Dauntless,* where Nita had just emerged on deck. Her white skirts swirled around her, bright in the tropic sun. "Anyone with that much money must be able to do something, right?"

"She's damn swank, that's for sure."

"Yeah."

Nita gleamed with gold and silver, gifts of goodwill that Lucky Strike had miraculously located in order to curry favor with the *Dauntless*. Nita bent and said something to Captain Candless, then turned toward shore. Her black hair unfurled, a tangled banner streaming in the ocean breeze.

Nailer waved, smiling. Nita waved back.

Pima glanced over at him. "You can't be serious."

Nailer shrugged, trying not to blush. Pima laughed. "A swank like her?"

"You've got to admit she's pretty."

"Pretty rich, maybe."

"Pretty good at gutting eels, too."

Pima laughed and jabbed him in the ribs with an elbow.

"What makes you think some lower-deck grease monkey has a chance with a girl like that?"

"Beats me." Nailer glanced at Pima sidelong, then grinned. "Maybe I think I'll just get lucky."

"Oh yeah?" Pima grabbed him. "You think so?"

She tried to shove him into the sand, but Nailer ducked out of her grasp. He ran down the beach, laughing, and Pima chased after him.

Out on the bay, *Dauntless* continued its loading, surrounded by sunshine and waves. Beyond it, the blue sea stretched to the horizon, beckoning.

ACKNOWLEDGMENTS

EVEN THOUGH MY NAME is on *Ship Breaker*'s cover, I owe a number of people for their help and inspiration. The crew at Blue Heaven Writer's Workshop: Greg van Eekhout, Sarah Prineas, Jenn Reese, Cat Valente, Sandra MacDonald, Deb Coates, Paul Melko, and Daryl Gregory all provided valuable insights, particularly my first readers Sarah Castle—who knows far too much about drowning in oil—and Tobias Buckell, who provided much technical inspiration. An additional and very special tip of the hat to Charles Coleman (C.C.) Finlay for creating Blue Heaven, and inviting me to be a part of his writing community. I doubt *Ship Breaker* would have come to exist without it. I also owe a huge debt of thanks to my wife, Anjula, who continues to support this writing madness, even when I have doubts. And finally, I have to thank my father, Tod Bacigalupi. He introduced me to the wonders of science fiction when I was a boy, and it has made all the difference.

Any mistakes, omissions, or failures in the book are mine alone.